PLAY ME BACKWARDS

PLAY ME

BACKWARDS

ADAM SELZER

SIMON & SCHUSTER BFYR
NEW YORK LONDON TORONTO SYDNEY NEW DELHI

SIMON & SCHUSTER BFYR
An imprint of Simon & Schuster Children's Publishing Division
1230 Avenue of the Americas, New York, New York 10020

Also available in a SIMON & SCHUSTER BFYR hardcover edition
Book design by Chloë Foglia
The text for this book is set in Berling LT Std.
Manufactured in the United States of America
First SIMON & SCHUSTER BFYR paperback edition August 2015
2 4 6 8 10 9 7 5 3 1
The Library of Congress has cataloged the hardcover edition as follows:
Selzer, Adam.
Play me backwards / Adam Selzer.
pages cm
Summary: A promising and popular student in middle school, Leon Harris has become a committed "slacker" but with graduation approaching and his middle school girlfriend possibly returning to town, Leon's best friend Stan, who claims to be Satan, helps him get back on the right track—for a price.
ISBN 978-1-4814-0102-9 (hc)
[1. Self-actualization (Psychology)—Fiction. 2. Dating (Social customs)—Fiction. 3. Conduct of life—Fiction. 4. Devil—Fiction. 5. Soul—Fiction. 6. Iowa—Fiction.] I. Title.
PZ7.S4652Pl 2014
[Fic]—dc23
2013041619
ISBN 978-1-4814-0103-6 (pbk)
ISBN 978-1-4814-0104-3 (eBook)

To Tanner, my partner in Slushee-related crime.
The band we started in eighth grade may not have been
the first or last to be called Scapegoat, but we shall,
in time, both outpace and outlive them all.

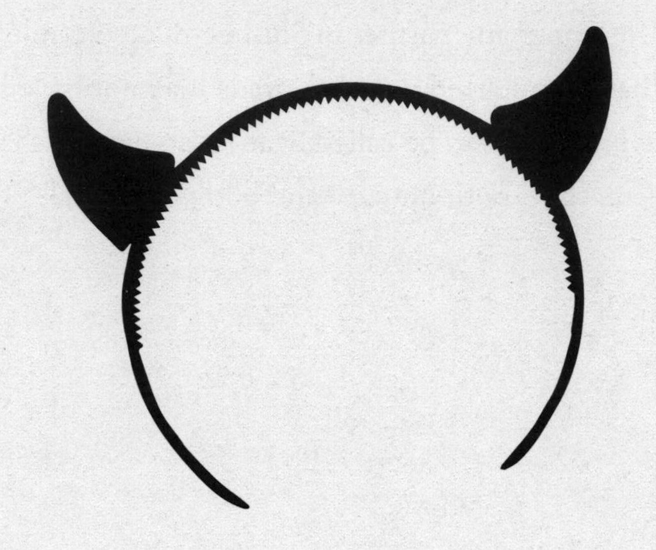

ACKNOWLEDGMENTS

Thanks to all the people who expressed support for this weird little project of mine over the years, including Alexandra L., Heathy Petty, Jennifer Laughran, A. S. King, Daniel Kraus, E. K. Anderson, and all those people on the Twitter chats who thought I was just kidding, but played along anyway.

A million thanks to my awesome agent, Adrienne Rosado, who convinced me that the project could be more than a little thing that I did for fun, and to Dani Young, a dream-come-true of an editor, and everyone else at Simon & Schuster, including Justin Chanda, and all the people I haven't even met yet.

To Ronni, for putting up with me rambling about this project all this time for the last few years. To Stephanie Elliot, who helped shape Leon and his pals in their earlier adventures. Not to mention S. J. Adams, Wild Bill Griffith, and the whole of the Smart Aleck Staff.

And don't let it be forgot: that once there was a spot, for one brief shining moment, that was known as the Maggie Moo's in Clocktower Square. Thanks to Tanner for taking me there one afternoon, to Brian Kirkman, who was "working" there that day, and to Chad Fitzgerald for confirming a few rumors.

1. MEAT

There are times when Satan really gets on my nerves. Like, he's been saying for years that he wants to buy my soul, but every time he gets enough cash saved he decides to get his car windows tinted or something instead. He can be a real dick like that.

And on Valentine's Day, a day when I was going to really need him and his evil powers, he was late for his shift at the ice cream place where the two of us worked. I had to hold off the morning rush, such as it was, alone. He finally strolled in an hour after he was scheduled, hands in his pockets and whistling a riff from a Misfits song, like he didn't have a care in the world.

"You're late," I said.

He stopped in his tracks and walked over to me.

"Let's do the list," he said. "World Wars I and II. The Black Death. That earthquake in South America last month. *The Phantom Menace*. Algebra. The decision to make Alpha-Bits a *healthy* cereal, instead of a sugary one. All me. And you're mad at me for being late to work at an ice cream place that has three customers a day?"

"Yes," I said.

"Priorities, man," he said. "Big picture."

And he disappeared into the back room.

Dick.

I suppose most geniuses can be dicks when they feel like it. Thomas Edison once electrocuted an elephant just to prove a point.

I first met the dark lord when I was nine. My mother is a Realtor, and now and then she'd take me along on house calls when she met with people who were thinking of listing their house. My job was to play with any kids who happened to be present in order keep them out of her way. It was a living, but not an easy one. The boys often wanted me to play sports that I wasn't any good at. Girls occasionally wanted to give me makeovers. Really little kids would make me play horsey or watch *Dora the Explorer*. Real estate is a tough business.

When we showed up at this one house, there was a pointy-faced kid with glasses standing in the doorway behind his mother, eyeing me like you'd eye a piece of furniture you weren't quite sure fit in your basement.

"Hi," said Mom. "You must be Stan."

He nodded and Mom put her hand on my shoulder.

"This is Leon," she said. "He's about your age. Go play."

The kid led me into his room, and we started playing video games on a boxy old TV that got the colors wrong. His room smelled weird. Other people's rooms always do, but this one didn't smell like anything I'd ever smelled before. Years later Dustin Eddlebeck and I tried to figure out what Stan's place smelled like and ended up on "grilled cheese, old people, and freshly spray-painted ass."

"You don't have to call me Stan," he said. "My name is actually Satan. My parents just leave out the first *A* so I can go to St. Pius."

Man, I thought, *I sure meet the weirdos on this job*.

Stan/Satan didn't try to beat me up or anything, and he didn't hit the reset button on the video game every five seconds just to mess with me, like some asshole kids did, but while we played, he told me that he used to be God's favorite angel until he grew too proud and got kicked out of Heaven and became the devil. Obviously he was lying, but he wasn't chuckling or using an "evil" voice or anything. He talked about going to Hell to reign over demons as casually as other kids talked about going to Omaha to visit their aunts.

He was just telling me how he was planning to have a tornado wreck a small town that spring when some kid with a bowl cut stuck his face into the window.

"Hey, Stan."

Stan gave him a tiny nod. "Hello, Josh."

"You wanna come over?"

Stan shrugged, thought for a second, then said, "Do you have any meat at your house?"

"Got some ham in the fridge, I think," said Josh.

"How much?" asked Stan.

"About three pounds."

Stan pursed his lips, like he was considering the offer, then he shook his head and said, "Nah."

Josh didn't argue; he just nodded and took off, like it was generally known and accepted in the neighborhood that if you wanted to hang out with Stan, you needed to have an ample supply of meat at your house.

Later on I tried to make sense of the whole exchange. How could three pounds of ham not be enough? Would Stan have gone if there had been a fourth pound? Or if it was honey-roasted turkey? And what about Josh? What kind of kid even knew how many pounds of ham were in his fridge to start with? I couldn't have possibly told you what was in my own refrigerator. I only kept track of what kinds of cereal we had in stock.

Now that I know that Stan is a genius, one possessed of dark powers that have saved my ass from certain doom on occasions too numerous to mention, I realize that he might not have been planning to *eat* the meat at all. He might have had some fantastic project in mind that required at least five pounds of fresh ham. I've asked him about it, but he says he doesn't remember that day at all, and that he never even knew a kid named Josh. I'm pretty sure he's lying, but you never can tell with Stan.

He was a year ahead of me in school, and he went to St. Pius Elementary and Dowling High, the local Catholic schools (yes, I know), so I didn't see him again until my sophomore year of high school, when he and I both ended up working at Penguin Foot Creamery, one of those awful ice cream shops where the employees have to sing songs and ring bells and shit every time someone orders a large sundae. This was where I learned that he may have been a weirdo, but he was the kind of weirdo who could be destined to lead nations.

He was still going around saying he was the devil, but he didn't seem particularly evil or mean or anything. In fact he had a pretty sunny disposition for a guy who claimed to be the prince of darkness. And his skills at messing with customers made the job a lot more tolerable.

In one of his most inspired moments he got the idea that instead of up-selling drinks or T-shirts to go with people's ice cream, like we were supposed to, we could make extra money by up-selling stuff that we stole out of the manager's office. When somebody ordered a dish of ice cream and mix-ins, we'd say, "Would you like a stapler with that?" Or, "You know what would go great with that sundae? Some envelopes!" If anyone said yes, we'd grab whatever we'd just sold them out of the office and charge them an extra buck or two. We almost sold the printer once.

Half the people just thought it was part of the store's shtick, but we still got in a ton of trouble when Jane, the manager, realized she wasn't just *losing* her staplers all the time. She was ready to fire us on the spot, but Stan talked her out of it with a brilliant defense that would have done any lawyer proud. In his genius brain, he was always three moves ahead of everyone else.

Then, one afternoon, a bearded guy in a pink shirt and red pants came in to give out brochures about how you'll end up in Hell with cartoon devils poking your butt with pitchforks if you don't start praying to cartoon God. Stan took one look at the picture of Jesus on the cover and said, "Oh, I remember that guy. He came into my place one time. Said he'd just been crucified."

The man in the pink shirt looked confused.

"Your place?" he asked.

"Yeah," said Stan. "I was like, 'Welcome to Hell, my name is Satan, hand me that pitchfork' and all that, but he was all, 'Look, is there any way I can be out of here on the third day?' 'Cause I got a thing on Sunday.'"

I played along, as usual.

"What did you tell him, Mr. Satan, sir?" I asked.

"Well," said Stan, "I told him he'd be there *forever*, so there was no way he could be out that soon, but then he was like, 'Do you know who my dad is?' And well . . . you've got the brochures, man. You know."

The man stared at us some more, like he was too shocked at our insolence to say anything. Maybe he was new to this whole "evangelizing" thing, and thought everyone who saw the cover of the pamphlet would instantly become filled with love or something. His salt-and-pepper beard began to twitch.

"Oh, sorry," said Stan. "Please allow me to introduce myself. I'm the angel formerly known as Lucifer. Lord of the Flies, Father of Lies, et cetera. You can just call me Satan, though." He bowed, then pointed at me and said, "This is Leon, one of my minions."

"Pleased to meet ya," I said.

"I'll probably be putting Leon in charge of you when you get to Hell," said Stan, "so I'd tip well if I were you."

"I'm not going to Hell," the guy said.

Stan smiled and wiped down a spot on the counter.

"That ain't what God told me," he said.

That's when the guy got mad.

Now, normally when we messed with customers, they actually seemed like they could take a joke, if they realized we were messing with them at all (which was fairly rare; most of the customers were a little slow on the uptake). But this guy decided to raise a bit of Hell of his own. He threw such a fit that there was practically smoke coming out of his ears. There are probably still tiny bits of spittle and pink shirt lint in every sundae they serve at that place.

Even Stan couldn't save our jobs after that one.

But getting fired turned out to be the best thing that ever happened to us, because he got us both jobs at the Ice Cave, the B-list ice cream parlor in the old part of town, nestled away in the old Venture Street triangle near Sip Coffee and Earthways, the new age store.

The Ice Cave was nothing like Penguin Foot Creamery. For one thing, there weren't many customers to deal with. And George, the owner, wouldn't have dreamed of making us sing songs about ice cream while we worked. He'd owned the place forever, and it had never been a moneymaker on its own—honestly, I was pretty sure it was just a front that he used to launder meth money or something. He only ever stopped in to see if there was some beer in the walk-in cooler, and if he found us sitting on the couch in the back instead of mopping something, he didn't write us up. He didn't worry much about inventory, and didn't have a problem with employees wearing name tags that said SATAN and MINION, or with us helping ourselves to all the mix-in candy we could eat. After he graduated, Stan got himself promoted to manager, which meant that Satan was officially my master during my senior year of high school.

To call what we did at the Ice Cave "work" at all would be a stretch. The back room, which contained a couch, some folding chairs, and a little desk with a computer, served as the office, the storage area, and the break room. We spent most of our time at work holed up back there, listening to old-school metal and helping ourselves to the Reese's Pieces and gummy bears that were stored in big plastic barrels along the wall. Over time it became a sort of a haven for the dredges of teenage suburbia—the headbangers, the minor criminals, the stoners, and assorted lost souls and hangers-on. Some days—a lot of days—we'd get more people coming into the store just to hang around in the back than we'd get coming in for ice cream.

I felt like I had found my calling. It was the kind of job you'd think you had to sell your soul to get, and I imagined myself growing old in that back room. I mean, I could go to college, but what for? To get some crappier job that I didn't like as much? When you get a job you like, you should lock it down.

Now, that Stan is a genius cannot be restated too many times. Stories of his unholy powers are numerous and legendary. Like, for instance, there's the story of the time Dustin Eddlebeck drank enough vanilla syrup to kill a wampa.

On that day Stan, Dustin, and I were hanging around in the back room, just killing time during a slow day. There hadn't been a customer in about an hour, which was not unusual. Stan was eating Cheez Whiz right out of the spray can. At some point, Dustin noticed that the big vanilla syrup containers listed "alcohol" among the ingredients.

"Bet we could get drunk off that stuff," he said.

"I doubt it," I said. "You'd probably have to drink a ton of it."

"It's worth a shot," said Dustin. "Let me open one."

We could have easily acquired some regular booze—there was probably even some hidden in the cooler someplace. But I guess Dustin was bored and in the mood to experiment that day.

Stan got some paper cups, and we all had a swig of the thick vanilla gunk. It tasted about like maple syrup, only sweeter, and with a hint of something that tasted like engine oil. It was thicker than most maple syrup too. You literally had to choke it down.

Stan and I quit after one chug, but Dustin kept going. Over the course of the afternoon and most of the evening, in between several trips to the bathroom, he drank about half a gallon.

Let me just repeat that: The man drank *half a gallon* of vanilla syrup.

He said he was drunk, and I believe him, but I think he was too sick to enjoy it. After he drank his last shot, he wandered around looking dizzy for a minute, then collapsed on the couch in the fetal position.

"Kill me," he groaned. "Either turn down the music or kill me."

"Headache?" Stan asked.

"I feel like The Slime that Ate Cleveland is on my frontal lobe."

"Don't worry," said the dark lord. "I know how to handle this."

And he went up to the front and came back with a glass of something that he forced Dustin to drink. Dustin downed the whole glass without taking a breath, then shivered for a second before hopping up onto his feet and shouting, "Holy shit!"

"How do you feel?" Stan asked.

"Like I could pull the ears off a gundark," said Dustin. "Damn."

"What did you put in that?" I asked.

"Trade secret," said Stan. "I got the recipe from Sinatra when he came into my place."

"He went to Hell?" I asked.

"Oh, I got just about the whole Rat Pack," said Stan. "All of them except for Sammy Davis Jr. But I let him come hang out sometimes. The parties are better at my place."

Stan always makes it sound like people in hell have a pretty good time when they aren't being stabbed in the ass with pitchforks. It seems believable enough, because in addition to his mastery of hangover cures and retail managers, Stan is a bit of wizard when it comes to planning parties. He is probably the only person alive who can make a heavy metal vomit party seem authentically Christmasy.

Dustin shook his head, like he couldn't believe what had just happened, and looked over at Stan with all due reverence. "Should I, like, sacrifice a goat to you or something now?"

"Nah," said Stan. "It's cool."

"I'll be damned," said Dustin.

"Just be careful when you come to Hell," said Stan. "That last step's a doozy."

So, yeah. The guy is a genius. I don't know how I ever managed to get through life without him. Obviously, I knew *intellectually* that Stan was not really a supernatural entity, but sometimes it was hard not to believe it. Any cop at a Mothers Against Drunk Driving assembly will tell you that the only thing that can actually sober you up is time. The concoctions Stan whipped up defied all known laws of biology.

But he *did* get on my nerves from time to time, which brings us to the day he showed up late for work on Valentine's Day. A day when I really needed some help.

It wasn't that I couldn't handle what passed for a rush at the Ice Cave alone, or that I actually needed supervision from a manager, but I didn't want to be by myself if any couples came in. I couldn't deal with being around couples that day.

Also, there was a pounding in my head that I was pretty sure meant that I was hungover and needed one of his miracle cures.

The day before, February 13, had been the "unofficial" Valentine's Day at school. I had sort of hoped that having Valentine's Day fall on a Saturday would mean I'd be spared watching all the couples at school having balloons and flowers and shit sent to each other, but I guess I was just being an idiot. Girls weren't about to give up the chance to have someone deliver them a giant thing of flowers in class just because the real Valentine's Day wasn't until the next day—people just did all that crap on the thirteenth instead. Between classes you'd see girls walking around with teddy bears bigger than they were, and couples were making out everywhere you turned. Every couple was trying to outdo each other for the gold medal in PDA. I was generally happy with my life as a perpetually single retail bum, and just about content to resign myself to that sort of status for life, but watching all the happy couples rubbing it in my face just made me feel lonely as hell.

Whoever made the laws about underage drinking clearly never had to get through a high school Valentine's Day. I'd rarely had more than a sip or two even in the back room of the Cave, where drinking stuff stronger than vanilla syrup was not exactly unheard of, but on Valentine's Day eve, alone in my room, I'd broken my own drinking record by a decent margin. And now, at work, I was feeling the results.

Stan emerged from the back room wearing his apron.

"Sorry I was late," he said. "I didn't think there'd be anything you couldn't handle alone."

"There wasn't," I said. "But can you mix me up a glass of that hangover concoction of yours?"

He smiled. "Rough night last night?"

"You could say that."

"Coming up," he said.

And he got to work mixing stuff from the soda machine, the cabinets, and some mysterious Tupperware containers from his backpack.

Meanwhile, I looked down at my phone to reread the e-mail I'd gotten the night before. Far more than the Valentine's couples it was the e-mail that had pushed me over the edge and into my dad's liquor cabinet.

From: anna.brandenburg236@gmail.com

To: leon.harris50322@gmail.com

Subj: Iowa

Hey, Leon! My parents were talking about coming back to Iowa the other night; maybe even moving. Not definitely, but maybe. It'd be good to see you (and the rest of the "gifted pool" hooligans) again, so I'll keep you posted. Happy Valentine's Day.

Anna B.

Anna B. Like I'd ever think it was some *other* Anna. It was the most I'd heard from her in almost three years.

And it scared the green shit out of me.

2. AMBITION

It might seem clever to say that my life started to go to hell when I started hanging out with Satan, but it really started three Valentine's Days before, when Anna Brandenburg kissed me for the last time before she moved to England with her parents. She took my heart with her. She probably left it in that pouch behind the seat in front of her on the airplane, squished between the airsick bag and a copy of *Sky Mall*.

Now, three years later, it was probably out in a landfill someplace. Or one of those garbage vortexes in the ocean.

On the couch in the back room of the Ice Cave, I gulped down the concoction Stan had prepared for me. It tasted like corn flakes, coffee, and some sort of chemical, and made me feel, for just a split second, like someone was flushing my body down a toilet of fire. But a moment after swallowing the first sip, I felt as good as new. Unbelievable.

"Hail Satan," I said.

Stan sort of nodded, like "yeah, yeah," then went into psychiatrist mode on a folding chair as I lay down on the couch.

"So," he said, "you only actually went out with this girl for, like, two months, right?"

"It was about a year," I said. "We were friends since fourth grade and I had a crush on her all through middle school."

"Were you thinking of her the first time you whacked it?"

"Probably," I said, though the real answer was *definitely*.

I sipped up the last of the drink and stared up at the ceiling.

Back in middle school I was in the "gifted pool," which is what they called the "smart class." When a kid on TV gets put in one of those, it's always a bunch of dorks who tuck their shirts into their underwear and speak in palindromes and shit, but at my school it was a bunch of commies, perverts, and beatniks who just happened to read from the adult section at the library. I was no slouch in those days. In the time I saved by not doing homework, I was watching foreign films, listening to jazz, and getting involved in protest movements and shit. And I liked that stuff. I really did. But it probably never would have occurred to me to do any of it if it hadn't been for Anna Brandenburg.

Anna came from a whole different world than I did. Her parents, whom she called by their first names, were both professors. She played the cello better than Stan played video games (which is saying something), and knew the difference between avant-garde and neofuturist art when she was in seventh grade. She sat in on college courses sometimes, including the art class where you draw naked people from live models.

My parents were just a couple of basic suburban dorks. Like me.

Even when Anna and I were going out, I never stopped feeling like she was out of my league. And that was three years, about fifty pounds, and billions of brain cells ago.

Stan lit up a cigarette as I grabbed another handful of Reese's Pieces from the only barrel I could reach without getting off the couch.

"How far did you get with her?" he asked.

"Not very."

"Was she in that pool thing with you and Dustin?"

I nodded. "We were the terrors of middle school."

And we were. The teachers feared our names.

Now most of my teachers probably didn't even *know* my name. It was the tail end of my senior year, and I hadn't taken the SAT or applied to a single college. I was telling my parents I was going to work for a year or so to save money, then get all the required courses out of the way at junior college or something, but I was really just planning to keep on working at the Ice Cave and hanging out in Stan's basement. I wasn't even sure I'd be graduating at all; I had to serve a whole lot of hours of detention time that I'd earned skipping gym before I'd qualify.

But I was generally satisfied with my life as a complete slacker. And why wouldn't I be? You show me a man who wants more out of life than an easy job that provides unlimited candy, and I'll show you a greedy bastard.

But when I got that e-mail, and it suddenly occurred to me that Anna might come back and see me like *this*, I suddenly felt disgusted with myself.

The drinks only made me feel worse.

Now, in the back room, I had this rotten feeling in my stomach.

When I tried to visualize it, I imagined a little cartoon monster inside of me, eating away at my innards.

I took another sip from the cup Stan had given me. It was empty now, but I wanted to look busy and distracted.

"When's she coming back?" asked Stan.

"She might not be."

"So don't worry about it. Have some more Reese's Pieces."

"She isn't even going to recognize me anymore if she does," I said. "Five minutes with me and she'll be on the first plane back to London."

Stan exhaled, reached for his can of Cheez Whiz, and sprayed some directly into his mouth.

The bell rang, meaning customers had come in the front door, and I got up from the couch to go deal with them.

It turned out to be Paige Becwar, one of the girls who circulated around the football team, and Joey Brickman. They were holding hands.

A couple. Fuck.

"Hey, man," I said to Joey.

"Whaddup?" he said.

Joey Brickman was the coolest kid in the world when I was in kindergarten, but he had sort of peaked by first grade. Now he was just another guy on the football team who thought that saying "whaddup" and wearing a sideways baseball cap made him look cool.

"What'll it be, guys?" I asked.

"I just want a banana split," said Paige.

"I'll give you a banana in your split," said Joey.

Paige laughed and socked him in the arm.

"Pretty witty," I said.

Sometimes I look at my class, the people I've known since kindergarten, and reflect on the fact that we all grew up to be dumbasses. Some school system we've got around here.

I made them a banana split, then watched them sit in a booth and eat it like a couple on a date in some TV show from the 1950s. I couldn't help but wonder if I would have been doing stuff like that with Anna for Valentine's Day if she'd never moved. Most of my "dates" now, if you could call them that, consisted of going to a couch in Stan's parents' basement with a girl I didn't really like, and who probably didn't really like me, to make out. I never did the whole formal "dinner and a movie" thing with anyone.

I probably wouldn't have with Anna, either. I imagined us out doing more interesting things. Art gallery openings. Amnesty International meetings. Trips to Chicago to go to jazz clubs. Knocking on doors for some presidential candidate during caucus season. Stuff like that.

When Joey and Paige left, I retreated to the back room, where Stan had lit a fresh cigarette. The first one was still smoldering in the ashtray, sending a plume of smoke into the air and obscuring his face.

"So let me get this all straight," he said. "Your ninth-grade girlfriend is coming back to the States, and you're afraid she won't like you anymore now that you aren't listening to opera."

I wondered how he even knew that her family went to the opera. I hadn't mentioned that.

"Pretty much," I said. "I mean, she's spent three years being all British and shit, and I've pretty much built my life around scratching my balls back here."

"Well, let me ask you something," said Stan. "What are we listening to right now?"

He pointed his cigarette over at the little stereo.

"Mayhem, right?" I asked. "True Norwegian black metal."

And I made the devil sign, as one does whenever one utters the phrase "true Norwegian black metal." Most of the metal bands who sang about worshipping Satan in the 1980s weren't really Satanists any more than Michael Jackson was really a zombie, but some of the bands in Norway actually went around burning churches, killing each other, and eating bits of one another's brains in stews, like they didn't realize they were just supposed to *pretend* they did shit like that to sell records.

"And what language is it in?" asked Stan.

I shrugged. "Norwegian, I assume."

"Right. It's *not in English*. And can you possibly tell me that the first chair violinist of the Oslo Philharmonic plays violin better than this guy plays guitar?"

"I wouldn't know," I said.

"I would," said Stan. "Guys in black metal bands start playing scales six hours a day at the age of seven. They can play circles around some orchestra putz. How is listening to a bunch of virtuoso psychopaths singing about worshipping me in Norwegian any different from listening to sad clowns singing about stabbing people in Italian?"

I thought about this. "I guess it's not much less intellectual in, like, a pure sense," I said.

"Nope," said Stan. "People used to think operas were evil too, back in the day. Half of them are about weirdos who sell their souls to me and burn people alive out of spite. And the guys in bands don't get laid any more than the composers did."

"Maybe," I said. "But I'll bet the composers got a higher class of groupies."

"What, you think they got, like, *courtesans* because the King of Prussia signed their paychecks?"

I shrugged. "The King of Prussia never commissioned a black metal album."

"Well, of course not," Stan said. "There hasn't been a fucking King of Prussia since World War I, and that ended a good fifty years before the first Black Sabbath album came out. But you're missing the point. You're not as far from being a snotty wenis as you think you are just because you're a total bum with no direction in life."

The bell on the front door rang again.

"Your turn," I said.

Stan stepped out to deal with the customers in the "front of the house" while I sat in the back and stared up at the ceiling, wondering what in the hell I should do.

I remembered the day I went over to Anna's house to watch *Un Chien Andalou*, the movie Salvadore Dalí made. It's got a scene with an eyeball getting cut open. Stan was right. The fact that that was in a movie by a famous artist didn't make it more intellectual than a vintage Megadeth video or whatever.

But, shit. She was probably off getting ready to study at some prestigious university and thinking of going into Parliament. Or making six figures as a photographer already or something. There was no way to sugarcoat the fact that I was about two steps away from having a beer belly, a receding hairline, and a car propped up on cinder blocks in the vacant lot down the road from some rickety apartment complex.

Anna and I had never *officially* broken up, exactly—I guess you don't have to when you're in ninth grade and one of you moves overseas. It's just, like, implied. Outside of a few long e-mails the first couple of months, we'd barely spoken since she moved. For the first year or so she was pretty steadily posting GIFs from movies and stuff on various social media sites, and now and then one of them would be romantic and I'd freak out wondering if she was thinking of me or had found someone else or what. But then she pretty much stopped posting things, or showing up online much at all, and for the last year she'd just been like a ghost. There was no trace of her, nothing to tell me what she was up to.

It wasn't like I had taken a vow of celibacy or expected her to wait for me or anything. I made out and fooled around with plenty of girls at Stan's parties and in the back at the Ice Cave. I even slept with two them. But every time I made out with a girl, I couldn't help but imagine I was making out with Anna. I always felt like I was cheating on her. I was only over her if I didn't have to see her or think about her.

I sniffed at the glass, trying to guess what Stan could possibly have put in that concoction. I thought I detected a hint of parsley.

The walk-in freezer hummed.

It went *hmmmmmmmmmmmmmmm*.

When Stan returned to the back room a minute later, he picked his cigarette up and relit it.

"Leon," he said, "you've been a fine minion, and I want to help you. I think I can help you feel so much better that you'll end up wanting to let me have your soul for free as a thank-you gift."

"We'll see," I said.

"Keep an eye on the front for a while, okay? I'll be back in a few."

I went up to the front and sat on the counter, and Stan went out to his car and drove away. I hoped he wasn't using all this as an excuse to ditch me at work or something, but that wasn't really his style. And there wasn't any work to leave me with, exactly; there was nothing for me to do around the store but defrost the front-of-the-house freezer with a screwdriver and try to keep my mind off Anna by wondering how the hell an ice cream place came to smell like the inside of a pizza box. Which it did.

Twenty minutes later Stan came back with an armload of CDs.

"Where did you go?" I asked.

"Library." He walked up and dropped the CDs on the counter.

"What the hell is all this?" I asked.

"It's the *Moby-Dick* audiobook," he said. "Unabridged on nineteen CDs. Start listening to it."

I stared at the pile of jewel cases. "You think listening to a classic novel is going to make me seem all intellectual or something?"

"It won't make you any dumber," said Stan. "But that's not the point. Drive around tonight and listen to it. "

I took the stack of CDs to my locker in the back and wondered what in the fresh, green hell Stan was thinking.

"You'll thank me later," he said when I came back out. "You'll see. Thus begins the Resurrection of Leon."

The walk-in cooler kept on humming, and I arranged three gummy worms from the mix-in tubs into an *A* for Anna.

Sometimes, you just have to trust that the dark lord knows what he's doing.

3. FISH

All through the rest of my shift, as the sun set over Venture Street and a round of fresh, wet, gloopy snow began to fall, I wondered what Stan's angle was in giving me an audiobook about hunting for a whale. Maybe he figured that with so many CDs, the answer to all my problems had to be in there *someplace*. Or maybe he thought it would keep me occupied for a really long time so he wouldn't have to hear me whining about Anna.

Or maybe he thought listening to a book about a whale would motivate me to finally sell Willy the Whale, the whale-shaped ice cream cake that had been sitting in the front-of-the-house freezer for ages. We'd found it buried in the walk-in in the back, and since it was way too old to be safe to eat, we put it on sale priced as an antique. Willy-shaped cakes had been off the market for years, so it may have been a one-of-a-kind collectible now.

And, of course, there was the very real possibility that he

just thought listening to *Moby-Dick* would somehow get me laid because it had the word "dick" in the title.

When my shift ended, I cruised around town for a couple of hours listening to the first two CDs. In that amount of time you can drive from one end of the Des Moines metro area to the other several times; I drove past George the Chili King, the state capitol, the three or four skyscrapers we had, all four malls, the sculpture garden, and just about everything else we had that we could possibly count as a landmark. Twice, in some cases. All the while, Ishmael, the narrator, rambled on through my shitty car speakers about how he came to sign up for a voyage on a whaling ship. I'd never read *Moby-Dick* before—honestly, I hadn't read anything all the way through in a long time—but I did read a Classics Illustrated version of it when I was about ten, and I was pretty sure that I remembered it ending with everyone except Ishmael dying.

Okay, so . . . Ishmael. Now *here* we have a talker. The man goes to church and repeats the entire fucking sermon. *And* the words to all the hymns. *And* the inscriptions on the gravestones of everyone in the churchyard who got killed by a whale. I wondered if he really remembered it at all, or if he was just making it up. He had to be making at least *part* of it up.

In fact, when he opens the book by saying, "Call me Ishmael," he's not exactly saying, "My name is Ishmael." He's just telling you to call him that. It isn't exactly the same thing, if you think about it. Fucker's real name was probably Bernie or something.

But you can tell he has a head on his shoulders, at least. He says right up front that the reason he got into whaling was that it was a "damp, drizzly November" in his soul, and all he could think to do on land was follow funeral processions through the street and hang around outside of coffin warehouses, and he was getting to a point where he couldn't see a guy walking down the street without wanting to knock his hat off his head. So he figured he ought to go out and kill monsters until he felt better. I respected that.

I kept waiting for him to bust out some big revelation that would make me understand life, or at least make me start to feel like the semi-intellectual person that I used to be again, but after two full CDs and more than two hours of talk about whaling and the sea, all that happened to me was that I got really hungry for seafood.

So I cruised back into Cornerville Trace and up to Cedar Avenue, where I went into Captain Jack's and ordered a Fish 'n' Fries platter with a Mountain Dew. To call what they served at Captain Jack's "seafood" wasn't much more of a stretch than calling my job "work," but it was either that or Red Lobster, and Red Lobster was too expensive. Plus, it was probably full of Valentine's Day couples, which was the last thing I wanted to see.

I sat down in a booth and wondered if Anna was eating fish-and-chips too, since she was in England and all, while I hummed along with the Billy Joel song on the radio. I was the only person in the whole place, except for the clerk, a middle-aged woman who was probably one of those fast-food lifers, and some guy who was frying up the food in the back. When I came in, they were yelling back and forth at each other over whose turn it was to clean the bathroom, and by the time my food was ready the fight had evolved into a really appetizing debate over whether men or women messed bathrooms up worse.

Happy goddamn Valentine's Day to me.

I was about halfway through my food when the front door opened up and Paige Becwar, the girl who'd come into the Ice Cave with Joey Brickman, stepped inside. She looked like shit compared to how she'd looked a few hours before. Like a damp, drizzly November in her soul had crept up to the surface and was smearing her makeup around.

My first instinct was to politely ignore her, but when she saw me she said "oh, thank God," and slid into the other side of my booth.

"Uh, hi," I said.

"I'm not mean to you, am I?" she asked.

"Not that I know of."

"Good. Because if I was ever mean to you, I'm totally sorry. I know I'm mean to some people, and I really need someone to be nice to me right now."

She grabbed a napkin and started dabbing her eyes. Up close I could see that she was wearing at least enough makeup to drown a monkey.

"So, uh, what's wrong?" I asked as I took a bite of fried fish and tried not to look at her cleavage.

"Joey's a dick."

"What did he do? Take you *here* for Valentine's Day instead of someplace expensive?"

"You mind not making fun of me?" she asked. "I'm in a bad place."

"It's not that bad," I said. "I mean, it's not Red Lobster or anything, but it's okay."

"Mentally, asshole," she said. "A bad place mentally."

"Sorry," I said. "Want some fries?"

She nodded and I pushed the tray over towards her.

I wasn't at all sure how to respond to a crying girl—especially one who had absolutely nothing in common with me. Was I supposed to pat her on the back and say, "There, there"? Suggest she go to sea and kill monsters until she felt better? Paige was a part of that crowd that went to parties with the football team, wore letter jackets, and all that shit. I was pretty sure she was a cheerleader, though I had never paid enough attention to know for sure. I had no idea how to talk to her.

"He broke up with me, if you wanna know," she said. "We had a fight, and he said he couldn't deal with my shit anymore, especially since Ashley Gilliam has been hitting on him and he could go be with her instead. He was going to drive me home, at least, but I stormed out of his car at a traffic light."

"So here you are?"

She nodded. "I've got snow in my heels now. And he hasn't even called or come after me."

"Did you want him to?"

She shrugged. "If a girl storms out on you, you're supposed to follow. But at this point I don't really care if he does or not. I'm done. I was going to break up with him soon anyway."

"Didn't really like him much?"

"Not really," she said. "But it should be, like, illegal to dump a person on Valentine's Day. Even if you hate their guts. It still beats being single on Valentine's Day. That's, like, proof that you're officially a loser."

I did a bad job of trying to look like I was focusing on

something out the window instead of responding to that.

"Sorry," she said. "Sensitive topic?"

"I'm used to it. You want any fish?"

She looked down at my tray and wisely opted to stick with the fries, and I quickly ate my hush puppies before she got any ideas about those. I was okay with being nice to her and all, but she wasn't getting my hush puppies.

"I guess I was really just with him because I'm used to having a boyfriend, and he was better than nothing. You know what I mean?"

"I guess."

She finished another fry and looked over at the window. In the glow around the streetlights you could see that the snow was coming down pretty good.

"What are you doing here?"

"Well, what's it look like?"

"I mean, you're not, like, meeting anyone here, are you?"

"No."

She held up a fry and sort of twisted it between her two fingers. "And you drove here, right?"

I could see where this was going.

"You need a ride home?"

She nodded awkwardly. "I hate to ask, but I live clear the hell out in Oak Meadow Mills and I really don't want to call my parents."

Oak Meadow Mills was one of those newer subdivisions full of white houses and cul-de-sacs out in the space that was farmland when I was little. Definitely too far to walk. There weren't any sidewalks on Cedar Avenue, anyway, so she would have just been trudging through drifts of snow and slush. In heels. And a skirt that didn't quite get to her knees. I don't think I hated anyone enough to make them do that. Even Stan probably wouldn't do that. Also, I felt kind of bad for making fun of her when she came in. We were both in the same sort of boat that night.

"Okay," I said. "Just let me finish eating this."

I ate the rest of my fish while she sat there looking uncomfortable, then I led her out through the snowy parking lot to my car, where I tossed all the junk from the passenger seat into the back. There was a lot of it: fast-food bags, homework I didn't do, laundry, empty Mountain Dew cans. I was afraid she'd be pissed about having to stand in the snow while I cleaned, but when I got into the driver's seat, she was smiling and sort of shaking her head.

"What's so funny?" I asked.

"It's just ironic, I guess," she said. "I never imagined that on my senior year Valentine's Day, I'd be happy to get a ride from . . . you know. Someone I don't even know."

I was glad she stopped herself from saying "geek" or "loser" or whatever she'd been about to say. That was very polite of her.

"I'm, like, such a terrible person," she said, as I pulled onto Cedar Avenue. "I've been in classes with you for years, but I don't know anything about you. Didn't you used to make a lot of movies and stuff?"

"Back in the day," I said.

"I know you don't play any sports," she said. "I'd know more about you if you did."

"I'm on the school crotch-kicking team," I said. "I'm a wide deliverer."

"The what team?"

"Crotch-kicking."

"Are you serious?" she asked. "There's a crotch-kicking team?"

I reminded myself that she was having a shitty night, and not necessarily thinking with her whole head. But I couldn't resist being a bit of a dick anyway.

"Sure," I said. "Cornersville Crushers. Went all the way to state last year. Almost got me a scholarship."

"What, do you just, like, run around kicking each other in the crotch?"

"Well, the idea is to kick the *other* team in the crotch, not each other."

"You're kidding, right?" she asked.

"Yeah."

She chuckled a bit.

In the old gifted pool days we actually submitted a proposal for starting a crotch-kicking team to the school board. The school ignored us, as usual. I don't know what we expected them to do. But it was a fun project, and a good excuse to talk about crotches in mixed company, which was quite a thrill in eighth grade.

Paige looked down at the CDs next to me as I pulled into the subdivision.

"Got enough CDs?"

"It's an audiobook," I said. "*Moby-Dick*. I just started it."

"English class?"

"Nah. It's kind of a long story."

She looked over the cover of one of the discs. "Is it any good?"

"It's okay so far," I said. "But I'm starting to think the guy who narrates it is sort of full of shit. He says he can't remember something very well, then he retells the whole story in total detail."

"You think he's lying?"

"Maybe."

We drove along for a while, and then, kind of out of nowhere, Paige said, "I've never been dumped before. This really sucks."

I didn't know what to say to that.

"You can do better than Brickman," I said. "That guy peaked in first grade."

"I know."

"And there are people in the world who can pull off the sideways baseball cap and look cool, but guys like him just look like they don't know how to operate a hat."

She giggled a bit and pointed me through the snow globe streets of Oak Meadow Mills. I'd never be able to afford a house like the ones we were passing on a retail salary, but that was okay by me. Those places all looked like they were made out of plastic. I got lost every time I went there—it was like a jungle of vinyl siding and brick that seemed to go on forever in an endless series of cul-de-sacs and blind roads that probably sprawled halfway to Waukee. Being in Oak Meadow Mills could be like being inside one of those mirror mazes that they had at the fair. Or at least in state fairs in movies. I don't think I've ever really seen one.

"Over here," said Paige. "The house with the SUV."

"Which one?"

She pointed at one on a corner. I pulled over, and she gave me a smile.

"Thanks again," she said.

"No problem."

For a tiny fraction of a second I almost thought she wanted me to kiss her. But then she unbuckled her seat belt and stepped out.

"I'll let you know if I need someone to kick Joey in the crotch," she said through the window.

I laughed, said good-bye, put *Moby-Dick* back on, and drove off back towards town.

I had just spent Valentine's Day night with Paige Becwar. Someone watching from a distance might have even mistaken us for being on a date.

This almost *had* to be a sign that the apocalypse was upon us.

4. THE ISLAND OF MISFIT TOYS

Rather than going home, where someone might nag me about homework or something, I drove back to the Ice Cave after dropping Paige off. Dustin Eddlebeck was working the counter, dealing with some couple who wanted chocolate milk shakes made with *real* milk and ice cream, not some crappy processed mix. Real shakes were one of our "off-menu" items; most of the time when someone wanted a shake we just gave them one from the machine, but if they asked, we could blend up a proper one for a few dollars more, though the ice cream was such low-grade stuff that it didn't make much difference. The Ice Cave was one of those places that goes against the idea that mom-and-pop places are better than chains.

"Anyone back there?" I shouted over the blending.

He nodded. "Bunch of people tonight."

I grabbed myself a handful of Reese's Pieces and made my way to the back, which was crowded to the point of overflowing with the sort of people who weren't likely to be otherwise engaged on

Valentine's Day. Stan, Big Jake Wells, Jenny Kurosawa, Danny Nelson, Edie the Communist, and a couple of people that I'd spoken to before but had no idea what their names were. The lights were low, as usual. The break room was a place of perpetual, glorious night.

Jenny waved at me from the couch.

"Is it true?" she asked. "Is Anna coming back?"

"I don't know," I said.

"You must be excited!" said Edie.

I just shrugged as casually as I could, and Jenny giggled. She might have been a bit drunk. There was a bottle going around, and a sip was usually enough for her. She and Edie were both fellow Gifted Pool vets who were now Ice Cave regulars, but they were at least still college-bound—Jenny was going to some place in California, and Edie was going to Grinnell, a small Iowa school popular with commies and anarchists. They hadn't turned the Cave into a lifestyle the way I had.

"Hey, Harris," said Stan. "You're just in time. We're having a contest."

"As long as it's not another game of Big Dick Malone," I said. "I hate that game."

"Nothing like that," Stan said. "Just a question and answer thing, and you're going to lose. Tell these guys how many times you got sent to the principal's office in grade school."

"None," I said.

Danny groaned. "I ought to kick your ass halfway up your butt," he said.

He got up and moved towards me, like he was actually going to do it, and I took a step back. Danny liked to hurt people. He wasn't a bully, exactly—"brute" would probably be a better word for him. He would never beat you up and take your lunch money, but he might beat you up just for fun. If this was the 1950s or whatever, he'd probably spend his nights either singing doo-wop on street corners or fighting in those low-down, no-good boxing clubs that you see in old movies now and then, but that I never saw in real life. Like mirror mazes, maybe they never existed in the real world, only in modern mythology.

"He made up for lost time in middle school," Edie said.

"Fair point," said Danny. "I'll allow it."

He sat back down, and Jake belched as loudly as he could. Of the lot of us, Jake was probably the most ambitious. He was always making plans for how he'd one day open a strip club on the east side; at one point he was going to call it Big Jake's Boobs and Butts, but Stan, in his wisdom, had pointed out that that made it look like it was *Jake's* boobs on show, which wouldn't attract the crowd he had in mind. So now his plan was to call it either Big Jake's Barbecue and Butts or Big Jake's High Class House of Ass.

He was never in the gifted pool, but he was an inspiration to us all.

Stan cracked open a fresh tub of Red Hots (red, for Valentine's Day), and we fell into this sort of bragging contest about which of us was the most fucked up, as we did from time to time. Often, being in the back room of the Ice Cave was like being on the Island of Misfit Toys from *Rudolph the Red-Nosed Reindeer*, only we weren't quite as emo about our lot in life as the messed-up toys were. We wore our troubles and failures proudly.

Danny Nelson said that his doctor had just told him he had

already messed up his liver pretty bad by drinking so much. He might have been lying. He usually was. Danny was full of shit.

Edie talked about how she was facing a suspension for punching a guy who was staring at her boobs instead of making eye contact, even though she'd already warned him twice. Danny, who was no stranger to boob-staring himself, offered to punch him too, if she wanted.

Jake said he hadn't made a payment on his car insurance in months. If he didn't come up with the cash, he'd be stranded out in Preston, the far-flung suburb about two miles north of nowhere where he lived, unable to make any more trips to the Cave.

Jenny was probably lying when she talked about how much pot she was smoking lately, and everyone knew it, but no one called her on it. Lies were not really frowned upon in the Ice Cave. It was generally known that she was only able to come to the Cave at all because her parents thought it was a study group.

I talked about how I needed to find some way to serve about two hundred hours of detention for cutting gym before they'd give me a diploma. I hadn't served any yet.

Stan talked about how he'd been cast out of Heaven by a vengeful god, and how it was harder to sneak his message into people's brains now that computers made it so easy to play "Stairway to Heaven" backwards.

This was our life. And it always would be. Even if I one day got a job, say, making training films for a living, if I ever ran into one of these guys, I would tell them that I made *fucked up* training films.

We all at least made a show of acting like it didn't bug us. I didn't tell people that I sometimes woke up in the middle of the night sweating and wondering what the hell I was going to do if my parents got a note or a phone call explaining things. There was a gnawing, hungry feeling of dread in my guts, that little cartoon monster that I could only ever ignore, not get rid of. The thought of Anna coming back only made me feel it more plainly, and I decided to change the subject before things got worse.

"So, speaking of trouble at school," I said, "Remember when we tried to talk the board into starting up a crotch-kicking team?"

Edie stood up and did a karate kick in the air. "Hell yeah."

"I just had Paige Becwar half-convinced that I was a wide deliverer on the team."

"Did you sing her the fight song?" Edie asked.

I shook my head, so she and Jenny launched into a stirring rendition of the song Dustin had written for our proposal, which was called "Till They Can Taste 'Em." I joined in on the lines I remembered, and Dustin stuck his head into the back room to sing out the last line. It was a beautiful moment.

"I fucking hate girls like Becwar," said Danny. "They get all pissed off and freak out if someone's wearing white after Labor Day. Say what you will about us, man, at least we don't judge people like that back here."

"What?" I asked. "You wouldn't pick on someone if he came back here in a polo shirt and a Nike hat?"

"I'd have to punch him," said Danny. "But I wouldn't *mean* anything by it. And we'd be cool afterwards."

He had a point. There wasn't a lot of judgment going on in the Ice Cave. We all met as equals. Then again, it wasn't like we had anything to test our tolerance. People like Paige and Joey almost never came to the back.

All the while, Stan was sort of staring at me.

"Where did you run into Paige?" he asked.

"She came into Captain Jack's while I was there," I said.

"And what were you doing at Captain Jack's?" he asked.

He'd caught me, and he knew it.

"Listening to *Moby-Dick* put me in the mood for seafood."

He nodded, like he'd known all along that listening to that damned book would lead me to eat at Captain Jack's, and that Paige would be there needing a ride home. And like he already knew what was going to happen for the next several months, too. It was times like this that I remembered why I tended to give him the benefit of the doubt on his stories about being the devil.

"All as I have forseen," he said. "Soon, there will come a great plague. The halls of your school will flow with the blood of the unbeliever. How's *Moby-Dick* so far?"

"It's okay," I said. "But what's the point? That I should go get a job on a whaling vessel so Anna doesn't find out I'm a loser now?"

Stan shook his head. "Commercial whaling has been globally outlawed since 1986," he said. "So you'd be fucked. My plans work a little better than *that*."

"She'd never think you were a loser, Leon," said Jenny. "She *loved* you!"

"Yeah, I had her totally tricked into thinking I was cool," I said. "But I'm not, and I don't know if I can fake it anymore."

Jenny laughed. "Do you know how much effort she put in to seeming all cool and intellectual and artsy for you? All that stuff you thought was spontaneous took *weeks* of planning."

"Right," I said.

"It's true," said Edie. "Like, how she used to wear that Kermit the Frog shirt that was long enough to cover her shorts, so it looked like she wasn't wearing any if she didn't move around too much? She practiced in front of the mirror."

"We used to get sick of her talking about you," said Jenny.

I had never heard that before, and I didn't exactly believe it. The idea of *Anna* doing something to impress *me* just seemed absurd to me. Jenny couldn't have actually known it if she did, anyway. She was barely allowed out of the house outside of school hours in those days.

Talking about Anna was just about the last thing I really wanted to do at the moment. I knew myself well enough to know that if I got started thinking about her, I'd get sucked back into the same misery I'd felt when she first left, so I took off for home shortly after that, quitting while I was ahead.

As I drove home I listened to another few minutes of *Moby-Dick*, and tried to think of whether I'd heard Ishmael say a single thing about women. I didn't think he had. Then again he hadn't said what put him into that "damp November" mood at the beginning in the first place. I would have bet a hundred bucks that it was a woman.

Or a guy, if that's the way he rolled. I think there was a really good chance that Ishmael and Queequeg, the cannibal guy, were fucking. I could imagine whaling, a job where you get shut up in a ship for years at a time with big beefy harpoon-wielding guys, probably attracted its share of nineteenth-century gays.

But I didn't really pay attention to what was happening in the book. I mostly just thought about Anna and felt like I was driving off of a cliff.

She was eighteen by now. That was the drinking age over there, so she was probably going to wine tastings and shit. She probably had a boyfriend, and he was probably the son of the Earl of Wigton or something. The two of them and her parents probably sat around talking about global politics while they ate gourmet food.

Meanwhile, my parents had probably spent their Valentine's night eating some sort of casserole where the recipe called for ungodly amounts of lard, canned vegetables, and ketchup.

My parents call themselves "food disaster hobbyists," which is a fancy way of saying that they get their jollies by buying up vintage cookbooks at flea markets, finding the most disgusting recipes in them, then cooking them and eating them so they can make fun of them. It's sort of like watching bad movies just to riff on them, only half the time you get diarrhea. For years—like, up until my sophomore year in high school—I thought that this was a real activity, and there were food disaster hobbyists all over the world. Then I Googled it and found out that it was pretty much just them. I didn't even like to think about where they were *really* going when they told me they were going away to conventions for the weekend.

I didn't participate too much anymore. My habit was to stay at work or at Stan's until I was pretty sure dinner would be over, then drive through Be-Bop's or Burger Box on the way home. Eating alone in my room or my car not only saved me from the food disasters, it saved me from getting nagged about how I was doing. Mom and Dad knew that I wasn't going to college right away, but they thought I was just planning to save some money first so I wouldn't have to work too much once I started. They had no idea that I wasn't sure how the hell I was even going to graduate in the first place. I was good enough at faking my way through classes that my grades hadn't suffered much, but I still had all those detention hours to work off. The less I spoke to them, the less likely they were to find out.

When I got in, they were sitting on the couch, watching TV.

"Hey, hon," said Mom. "How was work?"

"Same as any other night, really," I said.

"Anna called."

I grabbed the nearest sheet of paper I could find—a piece of junk mail from the table—and pretended to read it, so she wouldn't know I was sort of freaking out, even though I was relieved, on one level, that they'd said "Anna called," not "the school called."

"Did she?" I asked.

"She just wanted to see if you were around," said Mom.

"Did she leave a message?"

"She said she'd e-mail you her new number. She's picked up a tiny bit of a British accent."

Great. Something to make her even *more* out of my league.

I turned to head up to my room, but Mom caught me by the shoulder. "Not so fast," she said. "What's she up to these days?"

"Probably just studying all the time," I said. "I don't know."

"You two made the cutest middle school couple," said Dad, who hadn't gotten up from his chair. "You reminded me of your mother and me."

"Mom," I said, "if you could move your hand a few inches up towards my neck and squeeze until I go limp, I'd be very grateful right about now."

She pushed me away. "Not funny," she said. "Go check your mail, kid."

One thing my parents have not figured out is that you get to a certain age when teasing your kid just makes you *both* look stupid.

Sure enough, on my computer there was another brief e-mail from Anna. With a phone number. For a long time I just stared at it, and then at the dirt under my fingernails, and wondered what the hell I could say to her.

What if she'd, like, *waited* for me, and I'd repaid her by growing up to be a complete bum who screws around with really unpleasant girls at parties in Stan's basement? She might want to kill me, and I wouldn't blame her.

Or what if she hadn't thought of me in a long time?

It rang three times before she picked up. Her voice—the first time I'd heard it in three years—sounded groggy.

"Hello?"

"Anna!" I said. "It's Leon."

"Oh, wow," she said slowly. "Your voice changed."

I freaked out for a second, then realized she probably just meant that it was deeper now, not that she could tell I wasn't the same person I used to be.

"Did it?" I asked. "I guess it changes so gradually that you don't really notice it when it's happening."

She laughed. "You do realize that it's four in the morning here, right?"

"Oh, shit," I said. "I'm sorry! I didn't even think about the time difference."

"Don't worry. I'm up now."

She had, in fact, picked up a bit of an accent. Fuck. Even the kinds of British accents that people in England think make people sound stupid sound about 50 percent classier than any American accent. I couldn't possibly imagine anyone with a British accent in the Ice Cave.

"So, you're moving back to Iowa?" I asked.

"Well," she said, "as of last night we were thinking about coming back for a few days, at least, but I can't imagine we'll actually move. Mom mentioned that we could get a mansion south of Grand Avenue back in Des Moines for what we pay for a flat here, but I think it's about a thousand to one odds. And I love it here."

"Oh," I said. "Okay."

I didn't know whether to feel relieved or heartbroken. It was a bit of both.

"What have you been doing out there, anyway?" I asked.

"Working my ass off, mostly. I'm taking a lot of university classes this year. Any spare time I have I'm volunteering at the theater."

Of course. Volunteering at a theater. I instantly imagined her sitting around backstage chatting about metaphysics and Shakespeare with a bunch of guys from *Doctor Who*, even though it was probably just the theater at whatever school her dad was teaching at. Still—that meant she was hanging out with a bunch of British college guys. Way out of my league.

"Sounds like a good life," I said.

"It's not bad. I never get in trouble anymore, though, so I miss you guys. How's everybody been?"

"Getting by," I said. "Not too much to report, I guess. Edie has a girlfriend. So that's new."

"She's not with Brian anymore?"

"Nah, it was a pretty messy breakup. I haven't seen him around much lately. Hey, you didn't have fish-and-chips for dinner tonight, did you?"

She laughed. "I made chicken tikka masala," she said. "Why?"

"I had fish-and-chips," I said. "I thought it would be cool if maybe you did too."

"Yeah, it would have been," she said. But she said it awkwardly, like she was a bit creeped out, and I couldn't help but notice that she specified that she missed "you guys," not "you." My attempts at flirting and seeming all romantic and profound were clearly going nowhere.

"Hey," she said, "Sorry to cut this short, but like I said, it's four a.m. here. Will you be online tomorrow?"

"I have to work," I said, "but I'll be on when I can."

"Great," she said. "Talk to you then."

And we said "see ya" a few times, then hung up.

So that was it.

She wasn't moving back. If anything she would stop by just long enough to put my heart back inside my sternum, then rip it back out all over again. That was worse than never seeing her again, really.

And the way she reacted to my question about fish-and-chips made me think she was a little turned off by the notion that there might still be something between us. Maybe I was just being paranoid, but if I had to guess, I'd say that she was seeing someone else now.

Some British college theater guy.

And why shouldn't she? It wasn't like *I* hadn't been with anyone else.

I wandered over to my window to stare over the tree line. On winter days when the leaves were gone, I could see some of the lights of the signs for the restaurants on Cedar Avenue. Back in my more intellectual days I used to stare at the green light of the Wackford's Coffee sign and pretend I was the Great Gatsby.

Now the green light looked like it was flickering as the tree branches swayed in front of it. As I stared on, I became acutely aware of just how horrific the smell in my room had gotten. I was standing in a pile of empty pizza boxes, crumpled up sacks from fast-food places, broken speakers, dirty dishes, and crusty laundry.

But I felt at home. Like I belonged here, among the detritus and debris.

After a while I looked away from the light and saw that there was an SUV in the driveway.

And Paige Becwar was sitting at the wheel.

5. VALENTINE'S DAY & GARBAGE NIGHT

My first thought was that maybe Paige was in one of those groups like Active Christian Teens or something, and her whole thing at Captain Jack's had been part of some elaborate experiment. Maybe she and the other members had been going into one fast-food restaurant after another all night to see if anyone would offer to help a crying girl, and since I had, they were going to give me a prize. Like the SUV she was in. I could have used an SUV. To call my car a piece of shit would have been offensive to most turds.

But when I stepped outside, she got out of the driver's side, walked up to me, and said, "Hey."

"Hey," I said.

She came really close, close enough that our toes were almost touching, and I could still smell the fries on her breath. She stood there for a second, like she was nervous, or maybe noticing that *my* breath smelled like hush puppies, then inched a little closer. She looked . . .

relieved, I guess. Like she'd lost her keys and finally found them.

"Well," she said, "I'll bet neither of us saw this coming, huh?"

"What?" I asked.

Then she leaned in and kissed me hard on the mouth.

I was too surprised to pull back at first, but as she put her hand on my shoulder, I moved away from her and felt my knees shaking.

"What are you doing?" I asked.

"You can't tell me you didn't feel it."

"Feel what?"

"The spark!" she said. "When we had that *amaz*ing conversation in your car."

"Which one?"

"About, like, literature, and stuff," she said. "And about the school crotch-kicking team. You're *so* funny!"

I took a step away from her, but she ran a hand down my arm and held on to the end of my sleeve. I thought she might have started crying again, which is about what I'd expect from someone who had just kissed me, but she was smiling, so maybe it was just the snowflakes melting when they hit her cheek.

There had obviously been signs in the car that I hadn't picked up on. Maybe I'd be sending out a few of my own that I wasn't even aware of. That wasn't impossible.

"I'm kind of hung up on someone else right now."

The look in her eyes changed, like, instantly. All of a sudden she went from looking like a puppy to looking like a fighter who could have taken Danny down in one punch at a low-down, no-good boxing club on an old TV show.

"Who?" she asked.

"Anna Brandenburg," I said. "Sort of."

"That girl who moved to England?"

"Yeah," I said.

Paige's face went back to normal. She laughed, took a step closer, put her arms around my waist and kissed my cheek, then just sort of hugged me casually, like we were already an established couple or something, and comfortable around each other. I tried to turn my head away. Logically I should have run or pushed her away or something, but that would have made me look like a complete asshole.

"Wasn't she kind of a freak?" she whispered in my ear.

"In a good way, maybe."

"And isn't she gone now?"

"Yeah," I said. "But we never officially broke up or anything."

"But she's gone. If she's not with you on Valentine's Day, you're not really together."

She was still so close that her lips brushed my cheek some when she talked. Now she pulled her head back away from my face and seemed to get into position to kiss my lips again, but I took a step backward up the driveway and away from her.

"Listen," I said. "You're just upset because you got dumped. You don't want to hook up with me."

"I don't just want to hook up," she said. "I want to try something with you. Something more."

"No, you don't," I said. "We have nothing in common."

She took a step back. "Come on, Leon," she said. "I felt a *spark*. I never felt one of those with Joey, or my last couple of boyfriends, for that matter. We'll find things that we have in common."

"Look, I couldn't go out with you anyway," I said. "I mean, your friends would go nuts if you dated a guy like me, wouldn't they?"

"What, because you're a geek?"

"Geeks don't really just sit around dreaming of dating cheerleaders, you know. That's just in movies."

"I could be a geek," she said. "I'm wearing superhero undies right now." Then she gave me a smile that must have taken years of practice. "Can you honestly tell me you wouldn't like to see them?"

Okay. I'm not going to lie. I was tempted. Really tempted. She wasn't, like, a supermodel or anything—in fact, I could imagine her looking just like one of my mom's friends in ten or twenty years. But she certainly looked better than most of the girls who went around showing their underwear in the back of the Ice Cave or in Stan's basement. Seeing Paige's panties would have been among the top five or six most erotic moments of my short, miserable life. But even though I can't claim to *mind* seeing girls in their underwear, I always feel like an asshole for looking if I'm not actually making out with the girl at the time.

I continued my basic routine of saying the stupidest shit possible.

"I'm not really a geek, exactly," I said. "I don't have any comic books and I hardly ever go to movies."

"Well, I'm not really a cheerleader," she said. "Not since middle school. So we're not as opposite as we thought."

"You'd still be better off just patching things up with Joey."

For a second she didn't move a muscle. Her face stayed fixed in a crooked sort of smile. But then it slowly faded and she stepped back over to her car. I thought she was going to leave for a second, but instead she sat down on the front bumper and looked over at me. She motioned with her head for me to come over towards her, and for some reason, I did. I sat down next to her, in front of one of the headlights. It was still glowing, and warm.

"Now there's snow on my butt," she said. "I hate snow."

"I sort of like it."

She looked over at me.

"Are you gay?" she asked. "Is that it? Is Anna, like, the girlfriend you say you have in London so no one suspects?"

"No," I said. "I'm pretty straight."

"Then what the fuck is *wrong* with me?" she asked. "I just kissed you and hinted that I'd show you my superhero underwear and you totally blew me off."

"Nothing's wrong with you. I just . . . I don't think this is a good idea."

"Guys *never* say no. Not even when fugly girls throw themselves at them like that. They can't help it."

"Yeah, they can," I said.

"But they don't. Am I seriously *that* disgusting?"

Well, this was awkward.

I supposed that I could see where she was coming from. If you think guys never say no, but a guy like *me* turns you down, it's got to hurt. What if she went into some sort of shame spiral because of this? This was more pressure than I was used to having in my life.

"It's not that," I said. "But I don't think you're really into me. I think you're just upset."

"No," she said. "That's not it."

"If you hooked up with me tonight, you'd wake up wishing you hadn't. You'd probably say I drugged your fries or something."

"I'm a big girl," Paige said. "If I regret it tomorrow, I'll remember I wanted it now."

"And Anna might be moving back," I said.

"Might be or is?"

I paused. "She probably isn't. It's about a thousand to one."

Paige scooted across the bumper towards me, looked me right in the eye for a second, then put a cold hand on my cheek and kissed me again.

This time it was different than before, probably because I didn't instantly recoil. She slid her hand behind my head so I couldn't pull back. After a second I just sort of let it happen, if only out of scientific curiosity, because I realized I was being kissed in a way I'd never been kissed before. I mean, every kiss with Anna had been great and all, but we were a couple of middle schoolers trying to figure out how to do things like kissing. They were great because I was *kissing Anna Brandenburg*, the girl I'd liked forever, not because they were actually great kisses from a strictly physical sense. And the girls at Stan's parties tended to kiss you as though they were attacking you or marking you for death or something.

This was a kiss from a girl who really knew her shit. She probably read magazine articles about how to be a good kisser and stuff.

Eventually she pulled back, smiled, and said, "Well, think about it then, okay? Take a chance." She got off the bumper, climbed back into her SUV, smiled again out the window, and pulled away.

I had to admit that was smooth. She left at the one second of the whole encounter when I would have been most tempted to ask her to stay.

Once she was gone, I walked up to the front porch and sat on the bottom of the steps for a while. The wet from the sidewalk worked its way through my jeans to my ass and the wind made my lips chapped. But I could feel a bit of pressure on them, as though the weight of Paige's lips was still pressing against my own. Sort of like having vertigo after falling off a building. Or the way you feel like you're still going up and down when you're lying in bed after a day of riding roller coasters.

For a moment all I could do was sit there and wonder if maybe Stan's hangover cures caused hallucinations, and that the whole thing had never actually happened. It seemed more logical than believing that Paige Becwar had come to my house and pretty much thrown herself at me on Valentine's Day.

I drew a little pentagram in the fresh snow with my finger and decided to ask Stan for advice. I started to text him, but the story got so long that I ended up just calling and giving him a full recap. He sat listening patiently until I was done, but I couldn't help but feel as though I was telling him things he already knew.

When I finished, he said, "Leon, when a girl asks you if you want to see her superhero panties, *you say yes*."

"I couldn't, man," I said. "I felt kind of like a scumbag just for thinking about it."

"You *are* a scumbag," he said. "But you were being even *less* polite by telling her no."

"I don't know if that's logical."

I heard him exhale. "You hear any more about that girl in England?"

"I talked to her," I said. "Just before Paige showed up."

"Is she moving back?"

"Doesn't look like it. Probably not even coming back to visit."

"Hmm," he said. "Hmmm."

Just what I needed. Someone to quote from the wisdom of the walk-in freezer.

Then he said, "Intriguing."

And I said, "Most peculiar."

"Fascinating."

"Worthy of further study."

"Certainly one to put forth among the gentlemen at the academy."

"Shit, man," I groaned. "Paige fucking Becwar just threw herself at me. Maybe all this apocalypse shit is true after all."

"There are dark days ahead, young minion," said Stan. "There shall come a great plague. The high school hallways will flow with the blood of the unbeliever."

"Of course," I said.

I heard him exhaling. "Look," he said. "You've been thinking you need to clean up your act in the event that Anna came back, right?"

"Yeah, maybe," I said.

"You should at least clean out your car," he said. "And if I were you, I'd go out with Paige."

"Seriously?"

"Have you bothered to read *The Satanic Bible* yet?"

"No."

"Lack of style and aesthetics is one of the nine Satanic sins, and you've gotten to be a real sinner in that regard. Your car looks like an annex to the city dump, and the smell rubs off on you."

"Like you should talk," I said. "Even most rats with any self-respect won't go in your basement."

"Plenty of people who have their shit together better than you do come to my place," he said. "Paige will at least get you to start shaving those pubes on your chin."

I snuck a look over at my reflection in my window.

My whiskers *did* kind of look like pubes.

"Huh," I said. "Well, it's too late now, anyway. Tomorrow I'll probably get a message from her saying she'll kill me if I ever tell anyone about tonight."

"No. She'll be in the Cave tomorrow," he said.

"You think so?"

"She'll come for you. Trust me. I'm the fucking devil."

He hung up, and I sat still for a minute.

I needed to get my head together, and I couldn't do it in a room like this. I had almost convinced myself that there was something wonderfully noble about living in self-imposed squalor, but when I got Anna's e-mail, I was suddenly sick of feeling disgusted all the time. I was sick of that gnawing feeling in my guts that wouldn't go away no matter how many times I told myself I already had my dream job. Once Valentine's Day was over, and it sunk in that Anna was never coming back, I could probably get back to being happy with myself and my life as a burned-out loser, but I figured I should take advantage of this moment of clarity. I resolved to start serving some detention hours, and decided to start trying to make my room halfway habitable right then.

Getting all the dishes and glasses and silverware that were under my bed down to the kitchen took three trips.

Once I had bagged up all the trash from my room, I decided to clean out my car some too. I could probably get five more miles to the gallon if I got the junk out of it. I took a handful of plastic grocery bags from the bin in the garage out to the driveway and gathered up all the empty cans, sacks of fast-food junk, and shit like that out of the backseat. I peeled up the duct tape that was covering the stains and scrubbed them as well as I could. Then I started getting the crap out of the trunk—textbooks, dirty laundry, and a busted folding chair I'd found behind the Ice Cave and thought I could fix up. All the while the snow fell against my face and the night air stung my skin.

There was already a pile of trash bags on the curb, waiting for the garbagemen to come overnight. It was garbage night.

Valentine's Day, Garbage Night.

When I brought all the bags to the curb, the snow-covered pile of trash looked like a great white whale.

6. DREAD

Lingering dread. That's what that gnawing, hungry feeling in my guts was. The kind of feeling you get when you quickly wad up your ATM receipt and throw it out before you can see for sure that the balance is negative. The feeling that if you actually checked your grades, you'd be failing a class or two.

The feeling that you left your headlights on, or your door unlocked.

It's the feeling that you left a burner going on the stove.

Or forgot to clear the browser history.

And the certain knowledge that no matter how well you think you've kept it under wraps, pretty soon someone will figure out that you're a terrible person who shouldn't be allowed out in public.

It's the fear that the next phone call you get will be the one telling your parents that you probably won't be graduating on time.

That the next letter you get will be a note from the school about a test you cheated on a couple of years ago.

That the next e-mail you get will be from the Recording Industry Association of America saying that you're going to be the next person they randomly pick to sue for downloading music illegally.

That the next knock on your door will be policemen asking you about a City of Des Moines van that someone bumped into in a parking lot a while ago.

It's the feeling that the world is going to figure out you've been playing a straight flush with only four cards all this time.

It's the feeling that you left a fingerprint behind someplace.

It was with me all the time. Honestly, sometimes I think it's with everyone all the time. Everyone has a few stains on their soul.

I'd learned to live with it, for the most part. In the back room of the Cave, it was even a point of pride to have this gnawing feeling of lingering dread in my guts. It was proof that I belonged.

It had gotten stronger and more painful when I first got Anna's e-mail. The fact that she wasn't coming back was actually a relief.

The thought of going out with Paige really didn't help it.

But the thought of telling her no made it even worse.

7. YES

The last time I did anything to make a teacher—or anyone else—take much notice of me was in the first week of freshman year, when I had health class with Anna.

Our health teacher, Coach Humboldt, was a real jackass—one of those football coaches who get wrangled into teaching something else, since they're already on payroll, but don't know a thing about their subject. His whole method of teaching was to pass out Xeroxed magazine articles about health, which we'd take turns reading out loud while he sat at his desk.

All he ever did was add a comment or two; usually something about the evils of getting a divorce or being on welfare. I don't think he ever even read the articles himself, because if he ever did *any* reading himself, he would presumably know how to spell a little better. Coach Humboldt was not really spelling bee material; sometimes he'd pass something out that he'd written himself, and it was clear that he was one of those guys who didn't believe that one single way to spell a word should be enough. His spelling errors were not just the kinds of mistakes where you leave out a silent *M* or put the *I* before the *E* when it's supposed to be the other way around. He was misspelling words that any second grader should have been able to handle, and doing so with a real streak of creativity. You might even say he turned poor spelling into a sort of outsider art.

The longest handout was his list of classroom rules, which he passed out the first day.

My favorite was rule number seven:

> 7. USE THE BATHROOM'S BEFOR SCHOOL, AFTER SCHOOL, DURING YOU'RE LUNCH, OR BETWEEN CLASSES. IF YOU NEED TO GO MORE TIMES THAN THAT, WEAR A DIPPER!

It was a totally unfair, mean-spirited rule, and Anna and I decided to give him some hell for it. We thought about telling him we had some sort of health issue, like a spastic bladder or something, or just explaining that with only four minutes between classes on a campus a quarter of a mile long, no one ever had time to get to a bathroom.

But we decided to pick on the spelling mistake instead.

On the second day of class she and I both wore ladles—dippers—on strings around our necks.

Halfway through class, Anna raised her hand and said, "Excuse me, Coach Humboldt. My dipper didn't work. Can I go get a mop?"

It would have been a better prank if we didn't have to spend several minutes explaining it to Coach Humboldt, who was not exactly quick on the uptake. He sent Anna to the office for being a smart aleck, and I got to go along because I was wearing a dipper too.

Partners in crime.

When I got up the day after Valentine's Day and found that Paige had added me as a friend on various social media sites that I'd signed up for and never actually used, and sent a message through one that she would swing by the Cave that afternoon, just as Stan had foreseen, I could have almost used a dipper for real.

She arrived halfway through the afternoon shift, and neither Stan or I had said a word about our conversation from the night before. Not that we had much else to do; it was far too cold for most people to want any ice cream. A cold front had blown in at the end of the snowstorm, so the high temperature for the day was twelve.

But when Paige's SUV pulled into the parking lot, she stepped out of it wearing the same sort of short dress she'd had on the day before, only shorter, and with no coat. The sheer notion that she'd dressed up like that to look good for *me* made me feel like an asshole. I was flattered, in a way, but anyone who wants you to dress like that in twelve-degree weather is not really your friend.

Stan and I watched as she walked up to the door.

"I'll bet she's getting frostbite in some scandalous places," said Stan.

"Most likely."

"Lo, though your hands and ears freeze in the winter winds, I say rejoice, for Hell shall burn below to keep your feet warm."

I rolled my eyes.

"Go to the back, will ya?" I asked.

"You don't want me to tell you what to tell her?"

"I'll handle this."

"Say yes to her. Whatever she asks, say yes. Your Satanic master commands you."

"Just go to the fucking back."

Stan laughed and disappeared into the dark recesses of the break room.

The wind blew in from the parking lot and stung my cheeks as Paige stepped inside. I shuddered to think what parts of *her* it was stinging.

"Hey," she said.

"Hi," I said.

"I hoped you'd be working today," she said. "Otherwise I'd feel pretty dumb dressed like this."

"You're not even wearing a coat."

She smirked. "Girls have to suffer to look good."

"You must be freezing your ass off."

"I'm freezing lots of parts off."

She gave me a sort of pouty, suggestive look, and I just stood there for a second, looking stupid, until I thought to tell her we had a space heater in the back.

"Can we go back there?" she asked.

My knees were shaking, but I followed Stan's orders and told her yes.

For some reason, she didn't run screaming when I opened the back door and led her into the dim, fetid break room. She smiled and waved at Stan, who was stretched out on the couch, flipping through an issue of *Auto Trader*.

"Hey, guys," he said. "You want the room?"

"Yeah," I said. "Can you watch the front?"

"Yes," he said. He said it that way—like, italicized—to remind me that I was supposed to say "yes" to every question Paige asked. I nodded to show that I got it.

He crawled off the couch, and Paige and I sat down on it, even though I felt like I should spread some plastic over it first. Paige would never have sat on it with so much bare skin if she knew what went on there sometimes. But I didn't say anything. I didn't want to freak her out.

"So," she said, "have you thought about it yet? About us?"

I took a deep breath. I had.

I didn't actively *dislike* Paige. I'd even had a pretty good time talking with her the night before while I drove her home. And I didn't have a crush on anyone *else* who lived nearby. Maybe a relationship with someone else *was* what I really needed in order to get over Anna. In fact, it had to be. I'd never move on if I didn't have something to move on *to.*

Still, I had some reservations that Paige was the right person for the job.

"I don't know if I'm . . . like, *qualified* to go out with you," I said. "You'd probably want to hide me from your friends, right? Keep the whole thing a secret?"

She shook her head. "The worst of them will just think you have good weed or something," she said. "Or a giant dick. Haven't you ever seen a hot girl going out with a total douche bag?"

"I guess."

I took a deep breath as she moved closer to me on the couch

and tried to decide whether or not to be offended that she'd sort of just compared me to a giant douche bag. I guess I looked freaked out, because she gave me a reassuring smile.

"You thought I was a ditzy cheerleader, huh?"

"Yeah."

"And I guess I thought you were some geeky comic book guy."

I nodded.

"So the thing is, we're not really as different as we thought," she said. "And, anyway, those matchups always work in movies. Maybe they will in real life."

She was making some good points. I *had* had a pretty good time talking to her in the car the night before. And I wasn't really in any position to go around turning girls down if they were actually willing to take a chance on me.

And having heard from Anna again, I was heading straight for a fall. Maybe Paige could catch me before I landed on my ass.

Besides, I was under orders.

"So, what do you think?" she asked.

I took a long look around the room and felt my knees shivering, but I remembered my Satantic master's command.

"Yes," I said.

She smiled and moved in closer to me.

"Do you have much experience with girls?"

I was going to give her some detailed response, but I decided I was safer sticking to one-word responses.

"Yeah."

"Like, ones that are in the same country as you?"

"Yes."

"So you know what I want you to do right now?" she asked.

I frankly didn't, but I said yes again.

"So do it."

She smiled and leaned in just enough that I got the message. I moved in and kissed her once, then moved back. Her lips were still cold and my knees were still shaking.

"You can do it more than once, you know," she said. "Help me keep warm, okay?"

I did. I pulled her up against me and let her kiss my neck, even though it was ticklish as hell, and I wrapped my arms around her. Her dress was cut low in the back, and her bare skin was still cold. She kissed my neck softly and did something with her finger, like tracing the alphabet or something, on my thigh, slowly moving farther up towards my waist. She pressed her left breast into my shoulder.

I still felt weird about it, and like I maybe should have been saying no, but I can't say I wasn't enjoying it. It felt good. Really, really good.

And after a couple of minutes I stopped thinking about anything. I stopped telling myself it would at least help me get over Anna again if I went out with Paige. I stopped telling myself that I was just going along with it because I knew she'd feel terrible about herself if a guy like *me* turned her down when she was dressed like this. I stopped thinking I should say yes just because of Stan's orders. I just concentrated on kissing and got lost in the moment.

But then, just as I was getting comfortable, Dustin Eddlebeck came flittering into the back.

Literally. Flittering. That's what he did. He flittered.

Dustin was given to flittering. I almost expected him to sing out "tra la la" as he helped himself to some mix-ins from a tub.

Paige pulled away from me and looked a bit embarrassed.

"Hey, man," I said as Paige and I stood up.

The minute we were off the couch, Dustin took our place on it. He fell backwards, stared at the ceiling, and sighed, leaving Paige and me standing awkwardly above him.

"Oh, shit," I said. "Not again."

Dustin nodded. "I'm in love," he said.

I tried not to laugh. Dustin tended to fall in love more often that most people went to the grocery store. Every few weeks he'd be madly in love with some girl he met at a party or something, and he always went into this same "just got hit in the head with a mallet" mode when it happened.

It should be understood that Dustin Eddlebeck is a very sick person. He knows more dead baby jokes than any other man alive. He is the kind of guy who always, always refers to toilets as "shitters," even when he's talking about urinals.

But inside that greasy exterior beats the heart of a poet. He falls in love at the drop of a hat, and is the kind of guy who breaks into song and frolics about the break room when he falls in love. And he's good at it. The sick motherfucker knows a thing or two about frolicking.

"Who is it this time?" I asked.

"Jacqueline Hart," he said, the sound of the two names rolling down his tongue like balls on a Skee Ball ramp.

"I know her," said Paige. "She used to work at Casa Bravo with me. She's pretty nice."

"She's more than nice," said Dustin. "I met her at a gas station last night."

"Yeah," I said, "that's where a lot of classic love stories start. Under the soft lights of the self-service pump."

Normally he would have made some joke about the masturbation reference that is built into any mention of a self-service pump, but in his reverie he didn't even try it.

"I've been driving around trying to find her again all day," he said. "We talked for, like, five minutes, but then I just said I'd see her at school."

"You want me to text her for you?" asked Paige.

Dustin looked up. "Would you?" he asked. "I didn't get her number."

"I have it. A bunch of us are going to Hurricane's tonight. I'll see if she wants to come."

She pulled out her phone from her purse and went out to the front, leaving Dustin and me alone.

"So, you and Paige Becwar, huh?" he asked.

"I guess," I said.

"I thought I heard Anna was moving back."

"Nah," I said. "She might come back to visit, but she's not moving or anything."

Dustin turned on the stereo to add music to his reverie; KGGO was playing "I'm a Loser" by the Beatles, which made me think of myself *and* Anna. Myself for the title, and Anna because it was British. Five minutes of expert kissing had not yet cured me.

Paige came back in with a smile on her face a minute later.

"It's all set," she said. "Leon and I will pick you up, then we'll go get her and we'll meet everyone at Hurricane's."

Dustin practically leaped off the couch.

"Oh, fuck yeah!" he said. "What did she say about me?"

"That you helped her check her oil," she said. "And that you were kind of cute. She heard you were kind of a sicko, but I said you were nice. You are, aren't you?"

"Totally."

Dustin beamed and collapsed back on the couch in such a happy stupor, I sort of expected a squirrel and some birds to come sit on his shoulder. Or a rat, at least.

"You don't mind, do you?" Paige asked me. "I should have asked if you were free tonight."

"No," I said. "It's fine."

I wasn't used to being signed up for things in absentia, but being in a group with at least one familiar face would probably make it easier for me to dip my toe in the waters of whatever this was going to be. Paige told me to pick her up at six forty-five, then kissed me just hard enough to make me want more, and left.

She certainly knew how to make an exit.

8. TWENTY-TWO MINUTES

"I guarantee you I will find a way to screw this up," I told Stan towards the end of my shift. The gnawing feeling in my guts was working its way to the surface yet again. It hadn't been this noticeable since the day Stan showed me how to use a hair dryer and a toilet plunger to get dents out of my car before my dad could see them.

"You'll be fine," he said. "You afraid she's going to make you start acting like a prep or something?"

"Maybe."

"Or that you'll start liking her, but she won't want her friends to know about you?"

"Yeah."

"You think this is one of those teen comedies where a popular girl dates a dork?"

I considered this for a second while I spooned some vanilla ice cream into a cup of coffee.

"I could picture that," I said. "Our first date would be a trip to the mall, and there'd be a musical montage of scenes with me coming out of different dressing rooms wearing trendy outfits that Paige had picked out for me. One time I'd be in a dress."

"And you'd look like an idiot in all of them."

"Then we'd have a series of funny misadventures ducking behind bushes, covering our faces with newspapers, and wearing disguises so none of her friends saw us out together."

"Nice touch."

"And at first I'd be all offended that she didn't want to be seen with me, and I'd see right through her explanation that she just doesn't want anyone else to know her business. But then I'd learn something that highlights her own vulnerability and makes me understand, until she surprises me by kissing me in front of everyone."

"At the prom, probably."

"The movie would get an average rating of two stars, but it'll be a staple on ABC Family for at least ten years."

"You must watch a lot of shitty movies, Harris," Stan said. "But that sort of thing doesn't happen in real life. Her friends have all been out with worse people than you, and this is a group date, anyway. She's already showing you off."

"That's even worse. I'm not going to have anything to talk about with the kind of people she probably hangs out with."

Stan poured some hot water into a glass, then added a bit of lemon, a tea bag, and a dash of something from a bottle in a paper bag that he kept under the register. Leaning against the milk shake machine, he looked about as classy as a guy in an apron drinking a hot toddy from a paper cup probably could.

"Look," he said, "if you get stuck, tell them the story about the time Danny Nelson tried to keep one of his pet snakes in the back and why we had to get rid of it."

I looked at him to see if he was serious. He wasn't laughing.

"That story's kind of gross for mixed company."

"Trust your dark lord, Harris."

I don't know why I put so much faith in Stan's advice.

But sometimes I really did think he might be privy to all the secrets of the universe.

Back in the 1980s people honestly believed that bands were hiding secret Satanic messages in rock songs, and that you could hear them by playing the records in reverse. There are web pages where you can hear samples of them, and they all just sound like mumbling and jibberish to me. Most of the time, when the secret message is supposed to be something about Satan, it sounds to me like they're saying "Stan."

"Because I live with Stan." (Led Zeppelin)
"There's power in Stan." (Led Zeppelin)
"Stan is lord, he will give you 666." (Led Zeppelin)
"Stan, move through our voices." (Styx)
"Yeah, Stan, he organized his own religion." (The Eagles)
"Stan, Stan, Stan, he is God." (Black Oak Arkansas)

Sometimes I imagined all these bands having shadowy meetings with Stan at a lonely crossroads someplace, bartering their souls for rock 'n' roll stardom and sealing the deal with a handful of Skittles from an accursed barrel of mix-ins.

After work I cleaned myself up, finished cleaning out my car, and drove out to Paige's house to pick her up, listening to a few more minutes of *Moby-Dick* while I went. No answers yet.

When I knocked on her door, Paige stepped out. "Hurry," she said. "Let's not do the meet-the-parents thing." I was only too happy to oblige there, and the two of us practically raced down the icy driveway to my car.

"You cleaned up in here," she said, as she looked around.

"It's only fair," I said. "If you're gonna be spending any time in here, I could at least get rid of the fast-food wrappers and stuff."

She smiled.

As we got on the road to Dustin's house, Paige told me she waited tables two nights a week at Casa Bravo, the Mexican place on Cedar, and from then on we swapped stories about terrible customers and moronic managers. Casa Bravo sounded like a real shit hole to me. Her stories about getting yelled at and coming home exhausted only made me more aware of how lucky I was to work at a place like the Ice Cave. No one ever yelled at you there. George, the owner, didn't seem to care if we got bad online reviews, or even if he checked the browser history on the computer and saw that someone had been surfing for porn. Or if we ate our weight in mix-ins.

We picked up Dustin, then drove a few neighborhoods over to pick up Jacqueline, whom I'd never met. She was heavyset, but not bad-looking, with dyed black hair and lipstick that appeared to be dark purple. It was hard to tell in the dim light.

"Hi," I said. "I'm Leon."

"I've seen you around," she said.

Dustin just stared at her. "You have really pretty eyes," he told her.

"Uh, thanks," she said.

"I mean it," he said. "They look like glowing orbs above the sea."

She buckled her seat belt and thanked him again, but I could tell she was sort of weirded out.

All the way to Cedar Avenue, Paige and I enjoyed the spectacle of watching poor Dustin try to talk to Jacqueline. His attempts to charm her were well-intentioned, but most of them just made him look like a creep. At one point he even asked if she wanted to hear a poem he'd written for her.

"Uh, maybe later," she said. "Look, Hurricane's is right ahead. I don't want to make us late."

Throughout the evening Dustin's hopeless attempts to woo Jacqueline made my date with Paige seem better in contrast. We were the first of the group to arrive, and while Dustin kept trying to seem smooth, Paige and I chatted, just casually, for a few minutes about normal stuff, like that rumor about how chewing gum takes seven years to digest if you swallow it, and how nobody ever really went on "dates" anymore, it was mostly just big group outings that turned into hookups, and whether Coke was better than Pepsi. Stuff like that. There wasn't a lot of sarcastic wordplay, and nothing about the King of Prussia. It didn't feel at all like the nights I'd spent hanging out in coffee shops talking about jazz with Anna (who knew way more about it than I did—I just faked my way through it), but it wasn't bad. It was comfortable. I had no trouble holding up my end of the conversation, at least until everyone else showed up.

I recognized a girl named Monica from math class, and there was a guy named Keith who'd been in classes with me off and on since kindergarten, but most of the group were people I never would have dreamed of talking to before. No one made any cracks about Paige dating an idiot like me, but I started to feel more and more like I was in over my head as the evening went on. After a few minutes the conversation all became gossip about people I didn't know, movies I hadn't seen, and parties I hadn't been to.

Keith was polite enough to try to engage me in a talk about sports for a second, but that didn't go anywhere. They were all nice enough to call me "bro" and "buddy" instead of "fag" or "retard," which at least one of them had called me in the hall once or twice, but by the time we were finishing up the entrees, I was starting to feel like a piece of furniture.

Then I hit the bathroom and noticed a poster for an appetizer called Rattlesnake Poppers, which reminded me what Stan had said about the snake.

"Rattlesnake Poppers," I said when I got back. "That doesn't sound very appetizing."

"I think snakes are cool, actually," said Monica.

"Oh, they are," I said. "But they can be pretty nasty."

Dustin stopped looking awkward and laughed. "Oh, man," he said. "I had no idea those things were so gross until we got one at work."

Monica gave me a weird look. "Don't you guys work at that ice cream place?"

I nodded. "Ice Cave."

"You have a snake there?"

"Used to," said Dustin.

"It wasn't, like, running around loose," I said. "It was in a cage. Danny Nelson's dad said he couldn't have it in the house, so he thought he'd keep it in the back room at the Ice Cave."

"That's probably a violation of the health code," said Keith.

"That wasn't the biggest problem," I said. "The problem is that when it took a dump, you could smell it all over the store."

"And hear it from the front," said Dustin. "Snakes are the most incredible dump-takers in the animal kingdom."

Someone else pointed out elephants are pretty impressive defecators as well, and after that the conversation spiraled into a whimsical, somewhat disgusting, but mostly enlightened discussion about all turds, great and small.

From then on the conversation was easy for me.

It's an established fact that in the back room of the Ice Cave, the conversation will turn to the subject of excrement every twenty-two minutes. You could set a watch by it. I never would have imagined that the same thing would happen with Paige and her friends, but it did. Stan was right. We losers may have our differences from Paige's crowd, but that's one thing that unites all living things, from the snottiest cheerleader to the most introverted geek: Everybody poops.

At the end of the night we dropped Dustin off first, leaving Jacqueline with us. All night long Dustin had tried to be charming, and she'd looked as though she wished she could just disappear.

Paige turned around to face her. "I'm really sorry," she said.

"I don't know what to say," said Jacqueline. "He's a sweet guy. He's just sort of trying too hard."

"He means well," I said.

"I know. But . . . you know."

"Yeah," I said.

She shrugged. "Hey, he didn't text me any pictures of his scrotum, and when I wouldn't let him kiss me he took it well, so it wasn't the worst first date ever."

"People do that?" I asked. "They send you pictures of their nards on the first date?"

Both Paige and Jacqueline nodded. I thought this over, and out of instinct I tried to rationalize it.

"Well, maybe they think they're living the golden rule," I said. "They're doing unto you as they wish you would do unto them."

"They want me to send a picture of *my* scrotum?" Jacqueline asked with a laugh. "Girls don't have scrotums."

"You know what I mean."

We all had a good chuckle, and Paige put a hand on my shoulder. "See?" she said. "Leon is hilarious. And he's never texted me anything gross."

I was beginning to see what it was about me that Paige seemed to like. I might have been a loser, but I wasn't an *aggressive* loser, and I at least had enough sense not to start a date by texting her pictures of my scrotum or anything. Maybe I was a pretty good catch, by certain very low standards.

I had noticed over the course of the dinner that among this crowd, the one that circulated around the football team, Paige was sort of the shallow end of the pool. I mean that in the nicest possible way—not that she was shallow or a person of little consequence, but the other people in the crowd were just a bit *more* popular, a bit better-looking, and a bit better dressed than she was. She wasn't in over her head, exactly, but maybe she operated on the fringes of the group, the same way I did among *my* crowd. I fit right in with the burnouts and bums of the Ice Cave, but I wasn't *that* fucked up.

I didn't have a drug counselor or a parole officer. I didn't drink too much, and I hadn't committed any crimes. Not the kind you could get arrested for, at least.

Paige and I were both a bit out of our depths among our own crowds. Maybe together we could find a niche of our own.

After dropping Jacqueline off, I drove to Paige's house and we made out in my car for a bit. If we weren't in front of her house, we might have even moved to the backseat. But all the lights in the house were on, and she was fairly confident that her little sister was spying on us through binoculars.

The evening had gone well. For both of us. I'd been able to get a conversation about turds going, and she'd gone through a date without getting any pictures of balls sent to her.

Those may have been pretty low hurdles to clear, but at least we'd cleared them.

9. EXPERIENCE

After I dropped Paige off, I headed to Stan's place. His parents had never gone through with selling the house, so it was the same house I'd been to all those years before, but he'd long since moved out of the room where we'd played video games that one time and into the walk-out basement. This made the back porch into a private entrance to Stan's place, so I was never actually in the house itself, just the basement. I don't think I ever saw his parents once; sometimes I wondered if he even *had* any. The upstairs occupants might have just been a group of demons who used the old bedroom as an office now. How else could you explain the fact that he got away with making so much noise? Like the hangover cures, it defied rational explanation.

Stan's basement room was not so much a bedroom as a suite. In addition to his bed there was a couch and an armchair—his "throne"—that had been spray-painted black. The cushions were always kind of sticky, but being able to tell yourself it was just the paint was kind of reassuring. Adjacent to the main bedroom was a bathroom, a laundry room, and a storage room. It was, in many ways, a more spacious version of the back room of the Ice Cave. The wood-paneled walls were covered in posters for metal bands and newspapers from days when the headline was about some terrible disaster. There were stains on the walls and the ceiling that I never asked about. Here, we devoted our weekends to the pursuit of evil: playing video games, watching movies, and eating ungodly amounts of nachos.

When I arrived after the outing to Hurricane's, Stan was reclining in the chair, drinking one of his concoctions and playing a video game. The ashtray held a whole pile of cigarette butts.

"There you are," he said, like he'd been expecting me. "How did it go?"

I pulled up a chair from the little table off the side where he ran Dungeons and Dragons games, and took a seat.

"It went well, actually," I said.

He looked over at me. "Not so well that you got laid or anything, though, or you wouldn't be here."

"Well, her parents were home, for one thing. It was a good first date. That's all."

He focused on the game for a second, then nodded.

"How long has it been for you?" he asked.

"About a year."

"Was Brenda your first?"

I nodded.

Brenda.

Brenda was a regular at the Cave and in the basement for a while.

A peculiar thing about her was that when she had sex, she made noises like a cow. We all knew this, because she was not overly particular about who she slept with and wasn't above doing it in the break room while people were working, or in Stan's laundry room during parties, even though there was no actual door, just a burlap curtain that didn't exactly make the room soundproof.

Brenda got along *great* in the back room of the Ice Cave. Now and then she and Jenny would try to outdo each other and see which of them could be the bigger freak and, even though Jenny was very much into doing things her parents didn't want her to, Brenda always won. Jenny still had a filter in her head telling her when enough was enough; she might take off her shirt in the break room now and then, but the bra stayed on, at least, and she didn't sleep with just any guy who happened to be around when she got bored. She never sucked a guy off for half a bottle of vodka. I didn't know for sure Brenda had done that, but I heard that she did, and knew her well enough to believe it.

Jenny *hated* Brenda.

I didn't like her all that much myself, but somewhere along the line Brenda decided she wanted to fool around with me, and I wasn't in much of a position to say no to much of anyone at the time. I didn't have had the nerve to, really. So I started making out with her now and then. After a few weeks at second and third base, she dragged me into the laundry room in Stan's basement, stripped naked as nonchalantly as you would to take a shower, and told me to get to work.

She didn't really make it seem like I had an option, so I did as I was told.

I wasn't a very good worker, though.

For one thing, it took me forever to get it up. At home, in bed, just thinking about naked girls was enough to get me hard, but here was one in person, and it was like all the nerves and veins leading to that part of me had been cut off.

She should have cut me some slack. Given that I was only inches away from several pairs of Stan's dirty underwear, not to mention a litter box that hadn't been cleaned out in a while, it wasn't the easiest place to get in the mood. There are probably less erotic places to do it in the world, but I really, really don't want to do it in any of them. But rather than encouraging me or helping out, she rolled her eyes, reached out, took a hold of me, and tried a few tricks with all the enthusiasm of a repairman working on the engine of a car. I half expected her to give my nuts a quarter-turn and say, "Here's you're problem, right here. You should be having these rotated every six months."

I should have just put my pants on and left, but what would she tell everyone if I did? There wasn't much to do but close my eyes and try to focus and think about someone else.

Even after I finally got hard enough to get the condom on, it took way more effort than I would have imagined trying to get inside of her. I kept trying to, like, *slip* it in, and she kept saying, "Just *push*." And then I'd push at the wrong place and feel like an idiot. When I finally got it in, I couldn't imagine she was enjoying herself too much. I sure wasn't.

After about five minutes I went "Uhhhh" and shook around a bit, effectively faking my own orgasm before pulling out. Brenda either believed it or just didn't care—either way, it made me feel like an even bigger loser than usual. It was sort of a relief to me when she dropped out of school and moved to Council Bluffs with some thirty-year-old guy a few months later.

So that was my first time. My second wasn't any better.

For part of junior year I went out with Mindy, a girl I actually sort of liked—or, anyway, didn't actively *dis*like, at least at first. Some girls seem great when you're not going out with them, but as soon as they start kissing you, they turn really, really mean.

Mindy, for instance, was nice and occasionally funny when we were just hanging out as friends in the break room, but once we started going out, she started constantly telling me how big her ex-boyfriend Darren's dick was. Every time we were near a large, cylindrical object, like a water bottle, a tube of cookie dough, or a roll of paper towels, she would point it out and compare it to him. He was usually said to be bigger. Over time Darren's member began to take on nearly inhuman proportions in Mindy's stories. If they were to be believed, the guy must have needed underwear specially designed by a team of engineers just to walk down the street without getting curvature of the spine. He would have had to commission John Deere to make him a special wheelbarrow he could lug his nards around in. If he wanted to text someone a picture of his scrotum, he would've needed to set the camera up on auto-timer and then hike half a block away to get them to fit in the frame.

Needless to say, I did not measure up.

When she saw me with my pants down for the first time, she shrugged and said, "You'd probably be fine for most girls. I just kind of got spoiled by Darren."

Maybe I shouldn't have been so offended. It's not like I wasn't thinking to myself that her face wasn't as cute as Anna's, or that her hair didn't glow the same way, or that she wasn't as smart, or anything like that. I was spoiled too, having my first girlfriend be the girl of my dreams. But at least I had the sense not tell Mindy *out loud* that she didn't measure up.

By the time we actually had sex, instead of just fooling around, I had gotten to where I really didn't like her very much at all anymore. The first time we did it she rolled off me after a while and said, "Well, it's not what I'm used to. I couldn't really feel that much. But it's not your fault." I guess this was her being nice.

After that I just couldn't get it up around her at all anymore. Every attempt to do it was embarrassing and ended in failure.

This is something they don't put into brochures about why having teen sex is a bad idea: If you turn out not to be very good at it, you'll feel like shit. And if you're dating someone like Mindy, she might suggest that you should let her sleep with her ex, too, which won't make you feel particularly super. This gave me a whole new set of hangups that I'd avoided thinking about: What if Anna came back, wanted to go further now that we were older, and I couldn't do it?

Now I had to worry about it with Paige, too.

I sat and thought of all this while Stan drank and killed zombie Nazis, just a few feet away from the laundry room that had been the scene of my first great failure.

"You and Brenda weren't a good match, anyway," he said.

"Definitely not."

"Mindy, too. That wasn't any good."

"No. I think I might like Paige better than I liked them, but I haven't really gotten over how bad those last two were, you know?"

Obviously, I wasn't about to tell him I had performance anxiety issues, but you can't hide things from the dark lord. He probably already knew.

"So, you're worried that since you two may not have that much in common, you won't have anything to do with her besides make out, and if that's all you do, it'll end up like being with Mindy all over again."

"Exactly," I said. "That's exactly it."

The dark lord nodded.

"I'm going to give you guys something to do together," he said. "A mission."

"What do you have in mind?" I asked.

"Slushees," said Stan. "I want the two of you to find out every flavor of Slushee, Slurpee, and Icee you can get in the Des Moines metro area. Every kind of novelty shaved-ice drink they make."

"Uh . . . okay?" I said.

He paused the video game, lit a cigarette, stood up, and started pacing around the room. Wispy nicotine fumes trailed behind him and then surrounded him. I almost thought I saw Anna's face in the smoke, but it had to be my imagination.

"Most gas stations have three or four flavors," he said. "Mostly cherry and a couple of soft-drink flavors, like Coke or Mountain Dew or Dr Pepper. Sometimes you see blue raspberry. Piña colada comes up now and then. You should probably try them all, but I really want you to find this one flavor I saw once called white grape."

"So that's it?" I asked. "You want us to find the Great White Grape Slushee?"

"Every other flavor too. But mostly that one. White grape. Find it and bring me one."

"So, is that why I'm supposed to be listening to *Moby-Dick?*" I asked.

"Partly."

I thought it over. Going on a Slushee hunt sounded like fun. I have a collector's mentality in my DNA, I guess. My dad buys rare junk to sell online at thrift stores and the flea market at the fairgrounds all the time, and he's always on the lookout for old cookbooks to feed his food disaster habit. Sometimes in winter, when the flea market at the fairgrounds is closed and garage sales are out of season, he just gets the itch and starts driving around looking for pawnshops and stuff, hoping for a good score.

I liked to go along with him. I used to collect old record albums with embarrassing covers, and you could usually find a few at any given thrift store—my favorites were one called *Sex Education of Children* (which showed a smiling old priest sitting in a library on the cover) and a bluegrass album called *Satan Is Real* (which had two singers standing in front of a cardboard devil that didn't look real at all). Before I got into bad album covers, I was collecting old stereo speakers—enough to cover an entire wall of my bedroom. I wasn't into actual hunting, like shooting ducks or whatever, but I guess I had hunting instincts in my DNA.

So looking for a rare Slushee flavor sounded like fun, and it would give Paige and me something to do besides hanging out with her friends or fooling around. Not that I didn't *like* fooling around, but one thing leads to another, and my past experience in that realm hadn't exactly been encouraging. Just thinking of going much further than we had brought back that gnawing feeling in my guts.

"Speaking of gas stations," said Stan, "do you know which one Dustin was at when he met that girl?"

"No."

Stan grinned.

"Kum and Go," he said.

And we laughed.

If there ever comes a day when I don't think that gas station has a hilarious name, I'll know that my heart has died.

10. STEADY AS SHE GOES

The morning after our first date I found Paige in the hall at school and told her I was planning a quest to find the Great White Grape Slushee, and every other Slushee flavor, and asked if she'd come with me, starting that afternoon.

"That sounds sort of weird," she said.

"Yeah, but it'll be fun," I said. "Can we at least try it?"

"I guess. I have a yearbook meeting, but I can go after that."

So after her yearbook meeting we spent an hour or two in my car, listening to *Moby-Dick* and seeking out Slushees. She thought it was awkward just to go into a gas station, look at the Slushee machine, and then leave without buying anything half the time, but she went along with it the same way I went along with going to dinner with all of her friends at Hurricane's, I guess. We had three kinds of Slushees that day, but found no sign of a white grape–flavored one.

The next day, Tuesday, I went to Casa Bravo, since Paige was working that night. They couldn't get me a seat in her section, so I sat at the bar and she slipped me some free appetizers when she could get away from her tables. One of the other servers, a middle-aged woman that I think used to be a substitute teacher that I had once or twice, came over and congratulated me. "You're a lucky boy," she told me, in her raspy smoker's voice. "Paige has a great ass, doesn't she?"

I didn't know quite how to respond to that without looking like a complete douche bag.

I wound up sitting at that bar for several hours; about the only time Paige and I got to talk at all was when she came to the bar to roll silverware into napkins at the end of her shift. The nice thing about restaurant work is that you never know for sure when you're going to get off work, so she could be cut from the floor at nine thirty but tell her parents she was there until ten, giving us a solid half hour to fool around in my car without arousing suspicion.

On Wednesday after school we were back on the road, heading out to West Des Moines to go to a Quick Trip that I seemed to remember having a bigger Slushee selection than average. Paige seemed a bit baffled that I was really serious about the quest, but I was. I was under orders, after all. And if I filled up on Slushees in the afternoon, I could just get the soup or whatever the cheapest thing on the menu was at whatever restaurant we met her friends at later. It looked as though group outings to chain restaurants were going to be a regular feature of my life from now on.

Those first few days set a pattern that we stuck to for the next couple of weeks.

Most days we had about an hour between school and work to go out on Slushee hunts. On the occasion that neither of us was working, there was always some group of her friends going to one of the chain restaurants to hang out in the evening, but on those days we'd usually have several hours between school and dinner, and the hunt took us all over the Des Moines metro area. The gas stations with the most unusual flavors tended to be in the parts of town that needed a new coat of paint, where aluminum siding was the dominant architectural feature, and where you were always seeing busted cars and construction equipment by the side of the road. Those places were only about ten minutes down I-35 from Cornersville Trace, which by comparison looked so idyllic that you wondered how any kid in any house could ever have anything to complain about.

On the group outings that usually followed the Slushee hunts, I did what I could to hold up my end of the conversation, which was usually just a matter of turning the subject to poop, which worked most of the time, though now and then Paige would gently suggest that I should think of something else to talk about.

With so much to keep us busy, we didn't have too many chances to do anything I wasn't sure I was up to, sexually. Kissing and some minor groping were as far as we got until one day in early March, when what we hoped was the last snow of the year was falling, and the puddles that had formed on the ground during a brief thaw that melted most of the snow were turning back into ice.

On that day we were out in Paige's SUV and pulled into a Kum and Go in Waukee that we hadn't tried before. Inside they were selling a cherry limeade–flavored Slushee—a new one for us, which by then was a minor victory. We high-fived and took one to the parking lot, where I stepped on a patch of black ice, slipped, and fell on my ass.

The Slushee flew out of my hand, and I felt like I was watching in slow motion as the cup flew into the air, turned upside down, and emptied its dark red contents onto my chest.

Paige turned back and almost screamed as I fell. But once she realized that I hadn't cracked my head open or anything, she started to laugh.

"Are you okay?" she asked, as I got to my feet and let the goop drip off of me.

"Yeah. Just cold."

"Oh my God, you look like a murder victim or something!"

I looked down and saw that the cherry limeade Slushee had created a large red stain on my chest. It was spreading and dripping towards new territory by the second.

Paige started laughing as I stood up, and bits of the Slushee dripped down under my collar. I shivered and swore, and she gave me a sort of wicked smile. "We'd better find a place where we can get you cleaned up, baby," she said. "You're all messy."

I wiped myself down with the paper towels they kept next to the donut case, then laid out some of the free *Job Finder* newspapers over the passenger seat. I thought she'd drive to my place, so I could get changed, but instead she drove us into Oak Meadow Mills and up to her place.

I could hear music coming from what I assumed was her sister's bedroom, but her parents weren't home yet.

In the stainless-steel kitchen she took a few pages of the *Des Moines Register* off the table, set them on the floor, and had me stand on them.

"Okay," she said. "Now lift up your arms, Mr. Harris, so Nurse Paige can remove your shirt."

I raised my arms and she peeled my shirt off and set it down on the newspaper. My whole chest was stained red, and still cold. And sticky.

I had never had a naughty nurse fantasy or anything, but hearing her talk like one was totally hot.

She got a paper towel damp with warm water and started wiping down my bare chest, which felt incredible. Water dripped down my body and pooled at my feet. When my chest was reasonably clean, Paige looked up at me with a grin.

"Now, Mr. Harris," she said, "did any of that Slushee get into your pants?"

I started to panic. I hadn't been so turned on in years, honestly. There was no danger that I wouldn't be able to get it up.

But I was still nervous. What if I screwed up completely? What if I went one step too far and she got really pissed off? You can never tell with girls. Every sign she was giving me made me think she wanted my pants and underwear on the newspaper right that second, but what if she really meant for me to go into the bathroom and clean *myself* up? And what if she got my pants down and didn't like what she saw?

"I don't know," I said.

"I think some did," she said. "There was a trickle of it that went all the way down, Mr. Harris." She traced a fingertip from my belly button to the waist of my jeans. I squirmed, because it tickled like hell. She snickered.

"Are you ticklish, Mr. Harris?"

"A little."

"Well, don't worry; I'm a nurse. And I think we'd better get those pants off, just to check. We have to clean you very thoroughly so you don't get cherry lime disease."

"Isn't your sister right upstairs?"

"She won't come down. And if she does, she won't tell."

She took hold of my zipper and started to undo it, and I tried to decide whether to move her hand away. Any worries I had that she didn't really want them down were gone now, and it would be rude, really, if I stopped her. She'd probably be all upset and worry that I wasn't attracted to her or didn't like her or something, even though she had to be able to see the bulge for herself.

Still, I wasn't convinced that I wouldn't completely disappoint her if we tried anything.

My problems vanished when we heard the sound of the garage door opening.

"Oh, fuck!" she said. "That's probably my dad."

She stood back up and handed me my shirt. I started to put it back on, and she rushed to throw the paper towel and newspaper into the trash.

"Should I get out of here?" I asked.

"Probably not," she said. "It'll look worse if he sees you running away."

The door opened, and a middle-aged guy with gray hair and a tan stepped in. A tan. In February. In Iowa.

"Hi there," he said.

"Hi, Daddy," said Paige. "This is Leon."

"Hi, Mr. Becwar," I said.

"Gene," he said. "Just call me Gene."

He shook my hand and smiled. It did not seem like a sincere

smile to me. It was an "I just caught you alone with my daughter, but I'll act friendly to get your guard down" smile.

"You okay?" he asked, looking at my shirt.

"Yeah," I said. "We just had a little malfunction with a cherry limeade Slushee."

He laughed a sort of half laugh that was probably fake. "You look like somebody stabbed you." He leaned closer and whispered, "Which, incidentally, is what happens to boyfriends who misbehave."

Then he slapped me on the shoulder and offered me a can of Coke.

"We have to go, Dad," said Paige. "Leon has to work at five, and I'm meeting Leslie to go over yearbook stuff."

"Well, I'm sure we'll meet again," said Gene.

Paige took me by the hand and let me out of the front door and back to her car.

"Did Dad say he was going to stab you?" she asked.

"Yeah," I said.

"Pathetic."

"He never stabbed Joey, did he?"

"Well, he hated Joey. But he never *stabbed* him. He just threatened him a lot."

"He'll probably hate me, too."

"Probably. But he won't really stab you, obviously."

That wasn't really as obvious as it probably should have been.

Paige hadn't taken me to the mall and tried to give me a makeover or anything, but now and then, while we were talking during the first couple of weeks of being together, she had worked in some notes for me that gave me some clues on what she expected of me as a boyfriend. Perhaps the most memorable instance was when she told me about one of her exes.

"He lied to me," she'd said, "and that's one thing I can't stand. And I'm pretty casual. I could probably get over it if I found out that some slut got her hands in your pants at a party, you know."

"That won't happen," I told her. "I'm not like that."

"I'd be more upset if you were holding hands with one of them, honestly."

"That won't happen either."

"But if you ever *lie* to me, I'll come after you with a butcher's knife."

Then she'd given me a very serious look and started laughing. The laugh didn't make the look seem like it had been less serious.

That day had been the first time she threatened to stab me. I think it was the first time *anyone* did in my whole life. But one thing I never realized about adult relationships is that when you're in one, people threaten to stab you a lot.

The day after Paige first made that threat I ended up getting paired up with Claire Downing, who had been friends with Paige since kindergarten, to diagram the parts of a cell on a worksheet (now *there's* an activity that takes two people).

"Some people are saying Paige is crazy to go out with you," she said, "but I think you guys might make a good match."

"I wouldn't have thought we would be," I said. "But she's really nice, you know? We have fun together."

"Good," she said. "But just so you know, if you ever hurt her, I'll stab you in the eye with a butcher's knife."

Everywhere I went there was another threat of being stabbed. By the day of the cherry limeade massacre, when her dad threatened to stab me within the first few seconds of meeting me, I was starting to take it in stride.

I kept listening to *Moby-Dick*, off and on, all the while. Ishmael was talking about setting out on the voyage, the crew of the ship, and all of the ins and outs of the whaling business. But as much time as he spent talking about it, he seemed like he was leaving out some pretty basic stuff that maybe everyone just *knew* back when he wrote it.

Like, how did all the whalers have their own harpoons? Wouldn't those get lost a lot when you used them to fight whales? I would have thought whalers went through harpoons like guitarists go through picks.

And how the hell did they get the dead whales onto the ship, anyway? I got the impression that the way they fought the whales was that they spotted one, then loaded everyone into three small boats to go out and harpoon them. If your harpoon was attached to a dead whale, wouldn't it sink down and drag you to a soggy grave?

Every now and then I'd just listen and think, *Fuck. I don't know* anything *about commercial whaling.* Maybe Herman Melville could expect readers to know this stuff back in the day, but living in Iowa, the closest thing to a whale I'd ever seen in person was Willy, the whale-shaped ice cream cake. We didn't use whale oil to light our lamps.

But I picked up the basics over time by listening to Ishmael, just like I figured out the basics of being in a relationship by simply trying not to do anything particularly stupid during my time with Paige.

I was "going steady," as they used to say back when people dated casually and fucked seriously, instead of the other way around. Steady as she goes. Like the sailors in *Moby-Dick*, I managed my first weeks on the strange new voyage without having to be dumped into the sea as a mangled, bloody corpse.

I knew that they all died in the end, though.

11. SNOW

Being with Paige didn't make me stop thinking about Anna. The Slushee hunt, in fact, really only made that problem worse. See, most novelty shaved-ice beverages are about the consistency of snow after someone's stepped in it with a wet boot. And snow had a tendency to make me think about Anna. Lots of things did, but snow was one of the bigger ones.

When we were first starting to turn into a couple, Anna and I both had the same "move." We would write plays and scripts and stuff where we'd play characters who kissed. We acted out kissing scenes three or four times in eighth grade before we had one proper kiss where it was really just the two of us, not two characters that we were playing.

That one came on a snowy night when we were hanging around outside of Sip, the coffee shop a few doors down from the Ice Cave, waiting for rides home. I was holding the lamppost with one hand

and sort of swinging around it, and Anna was bouncing back and forth to stay warm.

When I saw that she was shivering, I stepped away from the lamppost and dared to put my arm around her. When she didn't shove me away, like I thought she might, I put my other arm around her too, so we were hugging. Then I looked at her and she looked at me. I wanted to ask if I could kiss her, but I'd read that you should never, ever ask for a kiss—you just move in confidently, slowly enough that if she doesn't want to kiss you she'll have time to say, "So, anyway," and fast enough that you don't seem too nervous.

For a second I stood there, worrying that she could feel my erection through my jeans, then I started to move in slowly.

She didn't say, "So, anyway."

She let me kiss her, and as I kept my lips on hers I felt myself warming up. You know how when you're cold and you slip into a hot shower you just feel this tingling in your head, like all of the cold molecules in your body have been led there to be burned up?

It was like that.

And I swear to God it started snowing harder the second our lips touched. The next morning there was a ton of snow on the ground and school was canceled. It was the fourth or fifth biggest snow in Des Moines since they started keeping track.

The kiss may not have been as well-executed as the kisses I shared with Paige; we were just a couple of eighth graders who knew nothing about kissing, pushing our faces together and hoping for the best. But it snowed so hard that they closed the schools for two days, and only a hell of a kiss can make it do that.

I couldn't imagine that I'd ever see snow falling in the glow of a streetlight and not think of Anna again. And the February that I started seeing Paige, it seemed like it was snowing all the time. Even in March, when the snows stopped coming, being around Slushees kept the feeling alive.

Paige seemed to know that she still had to compete with Anna, even though I told her she wasn't moving back. Sometimes when she kissed me she did this thing where she'd seal her lips against mine and sort of suck the wind out of me. It felt great, but a part of me felt like she was deliberately trying to suck every trace of Anna out of my body.

She even mentioned Anna once herself.

"Brent Flores asked her out in seventh grade, you know," she said.

"Yeah? I didn't know that."

"Either that or sixth. She called him something in French and walked away. And I'm sorry, but that's just rude."

I nodded a little. "Well, did he actually ask her out properly, or try to use some lame pickup line?"

"Knowing him, a lame pickup line. But still. Who tells a guy off in French?"

I was about to stick up for Anna, but then we came to a red traffic light and Paige kissed me some more. By the time she was done I had just about forgotten what she'd said.

Just about.

12. SCHEMES

One day in early March, I arrived at the Cave to find George and Stan poring over a large book. A yearbook, from the looks of it. George was chewing on a pencil and looking nervous.

"What's that?" I asked.

"Dustin's yearbook from last year," said Stan. "We're just doing a little work on the store's mailing list."

"Yeah?"

George looked up. "Just a new business initiative," he said.

"We're matching faces to the names in the database," said Stan. "Getting into the twenty-first century and shit."

"Very fancy," I said.

"All Stan's idea," said George. "All Stan. That's why I pay him the big bucks."

And he slapped Stan on the back and took off.

I wondered what the hell was really going on. There was no way they were making a database. If anything, George was probably just looking for names to add to a fake mailing list, like a crooked politician filling voter rolls with names from the cemetery, so he could tell his wife or the IRS or whoever that we actually had customers.

I was sure that the Ice Cave was not making a net profit. In fact, with his general encouragement that we eat all the mix-ins we wanted, I was almost certain that George *wanted* to lose money on the place.

Maybe it was a front for laundering drug money. Or gambling money, more likely. More than once George had come into the store and told us he was heading out to the horse racetrack in Altoona.

Or maybe it was just some sort of tax dodge.

Mine was not to question, in any case. I was just a lowly clerk. There was a chance that I was playing a part in some pretty ugly stuff, in an offhand sort of way, but so is everyone else with a job, if you think about it. Just about everyone who works is earning money for CEOs who may not be the world's greatest human beings.

While Stan flipped through the yearbook, I pretty much forgot about the whole thing and spent most of my shift texting back and forth with Paige. She was working that night too, and whenever she could get away from her tables to the smoking area out back, she'd text me about her dumb customers and how much she was making in tips.

I think she made more off one table than I was going to make all night, but she had to plot and plan and sneak around just to send a text, and I just sat back and messed with my phone half the night. The way I saw it, a relaxing job was more valuable than money, anyway. And if I was only a pawn in George's game of defrauding the IRS or something, so be it. He was beating the system. Good for him.

When George left, Stan kept browsing through the yearbook.

"You know," he said, "people at Dowling always said the public school girls were better-looking, but I don't really see it."

I looked up from the defrosting.

"We hear the same thing about Dowling girls," I said. "Catholic school girls have a mystique all their own."

"It's just the uniforms. And they don't issue pleated skirts anymore."

He flipped to one of the back sections, read for a second, and said, "Who's this Aaron Riley guy?"

"Doesn't ring a bell," I said. "Why?"

"Check out this poem he wrote."

I walked back to the counter and Stan passed me the yearbook, which was now open to a section of student-submitted poems. The one in question was all about the blood of Jesus. It was really pretty gory—the first two lines rhymed "blood for me" and "Calvary."

"I thought you guys couldn't do this shit in public schools," he said.

"If it went to court, they might say it couldn't have yearbook space," I said. "But no one really complained."

"Noted," said Stan. "Noted."

He slipped into the back with the yearbook and the mailing list, and for a while I heard him and Dustin talking and laughing back there. After an hour or so the two of them came back out to the front, and Stan said he had a new assignment for me.

"Yeah?" I asked.

He grinned.

"I want you to ask Paige to get you on the yearbook committee."

"Why?"

"You're going to help me get *my* message out the same way that Aaron Riley guy did for the Christians," said Stan.

Dustin handed me some pieces of paper—a collection of poems scribbled on the backs of discarded Ice Cave receipts and napkins. The first one was more of a fragment than a fully realized literary epic:

HERE'S TO MY SWEET SATAN
WHO'S THE LEADER OF THE CULT
THAT'S MADE FOR YOU AND ME?
WHO CAN HELP YOU GET A PERFECT SCORE ON SAT?
T-H-E
D-E-V
I-L THAT'S FOR ME!

"You," said Stan, "are going to get one of these into the yearbook."

"They're never going to take something like this," I said.

"They will if you sneak it in," Stan said with a smile.

I read through a few of them. They were awful. All of them.

Back in the gifted pool days Dustin and James Cole had tried to depress the hell out of the gym teacher by slipping beatnik poetry about how miserable the life of a gym teacher was into his office. The poems had titles like "Locker Room Mausoleum Sutra."

"Why don't you just submit one of the ones you wrote to Coach What's-his-name?" I asked. "Maybe that one about dodgeball. That was good."

Dustin smiled, and recited the first of what I remember as

being about a hundred stanzas of "Fortune Has Its Dodgeballs to Throw Out:"

It was October in the calisthenic Earth,
gray winds waltzing on raven wings,
crow's-feet growing ever more crooked
around your eyes
as you thought of catching
a Sunday subway
    to some
        far dodgeball game
        of the heart.

Stan snapped his fingers, as one does.

"Let me put that in," I said. "That's way better."

"I'm more interested in promoting my newer material," said Dustin. "I ain't no oldies act."

"But these suck."

"Lots of artists go through a phase of churning out crappy religious stuff."

I read a few more of the new Satan poems. The worst—or the dumbest, at least—was on the bottom of the pile, written on the back of a worksheet.

Sing a song of Cornersville Trace,
Amazing town, amazing place,
Town where we grow and learn
And work hard for the things we earn

Never fade from 'ere our hearts,
Relive all of the wondrous parts
Under our teacher's watchful eyes
Live we long, our hearts we prize,
Ever sing of this happy place,
Sing a song of Cornersville Trace.

Clearly, the only reason for the poem to exist was that it was an acrostic—the first letter of each line spelled out SATAN RULES. In terms of literary merit, it really sucked ass.

I looked at Stan. "You and your fucking hidden messages."

"It's dumb enough to pass for an actual student-written poem," said Stan. "I've never entered the hearts of the young through a yearbook before."

"I suppose metal songs and Harry Potter books get old after a while, huh?" I asked.

"Some things will never get old, but it's nice to try something new now and then."

I didn't think I could possibly get any of them into the yearbook, but I put the poems in my backpack, then sent Paige a text asking if it was too late for me to join the yearbook committee. I was spending most of the meetings sitting outside in the hall waiting for her, anyway. Signing up seemed like a logical move.

She eventually texted back that she'd try her best, and she escorted me into the yearbook room the next day after school.

Leslie, the president of the club, was one of those girls who acted like she was about thirty when she was twelve. She just had the air of someone who was at that phase of her life, not the one she was actually living through. Now, at seventeen, she seemed like a thirty-something CEO, and ran the yearbook accordingly. She looked sort of suspicious when Paige asked if I could join.

"You want to be in yearbook?" she asked me.

"Well, I can't join the Spanish club," I said. "And it's too late to take up sports, but I feel like I need to join *something* to help leave my mark on the school before I graduate."

She gave both of us a skeptical look. "You won't be allowed to approve pictures of yourself if I let you on staff," she said. "And we're almost done with them, anyway. So don't think you can turn the whole book into, like, a Leon fest."

"I won't," I said. "But Paige said there was a lot that still needed to be done."

She exhaled and flipped through a binder. "Look. We need someone to do layout on the computers. Everyone just wants to take pictures and interview people to get their favorite quotes and career goals and stuff. Can you do layout?"

"Probably," I said.

"Fine," she said. "Ask Mr. Perkins to show you the program."

Paige clapped her hands and kissed me on the cheek.

We found Mr. Perkins, the media specialist, in his office doing paperwork. His face lit up when I asked him to show me the layout program for the yearbook.

"You're going to do the layout?"

"Maybe," I said.

"Oh, thank God," he said. "I was afraid I would have to do it myself. You know it's a lot of work, right?"

"That's kind of what I'm afraid of," I said. "I've got a job and all.

And lot of detention time that I need to serve. But I said I could probably do it."

"I'll tell you what," he said. "Any time you spend on the yearbook layout can count towards your detention time."

I saw that I had an opportunity here, and I took it.

"Could it count double?" I asked.

"I'll see what I can do."

"Deal."

So I started going into the library during lunch to work on the layout. I'd work for maybe twenty minutes, fill out a card saying I'd been there for two hours, and Mr. Perkins would sign it without looking, giving me four hours of detention credit. At this rate, between lunch and the times I came in after school, I could easily work off all of my unserved detention hours by the time the layout was done.

I was going to graduate after all.

All because I'd obeyed my unholy orders.

13. DEAD CELEBRITIES

By the time winter fully melted away into spring, Paige and I seemed to have found just about every Slushee flavor in town. Days would go by without us finding a flavor we hadn't seen before. Still, there was no sign of white grape, and we began to believe that it was only a legend.

So we started hunting for Slushees less and less and spent more time going to movies and stuff, like normal couples. I had to spend more time around her friends, which was still tough for me when I couldn't steer the conversation towards poop, but I could sit through a movie with them as well as I could sit through one with anyone else. I just pretended I was one of those people who never, ever talk during a movie.

One day after a yearbook meeting I talked Paige into swinging by the Ice Cave just to hang out. She hadn't really spent any time in the back room yet, other than that first day, but I'd been to Casa Bravo a bunch of times when she was working, and after spending so many nights there and at various chain restaurants with her friends, I had started feeling like I was missing out on the action at the Cave. Part of why I spent so much time there, outside of working hours, was just that I didn't want to miss out if something really crazy happened, and by now I'd probably missed a lot.

As we drove out there I put on CD number six of *Moby-Dick*, and Ishmael said, "In old Norse times, the thrones of the sea-loving Danish kings were fabricated, saith tradition, of the tusks of the narwhale. How could one look at Ahab, then, seated on that tripod of bones, without bethinking him of the royalty it symbolized?"

I laughed and hit pause. "Easy," I said. "By not being the kind of guy who knew what the hell Danish kings made their thrones out of."

"Or not knowing a narwhal tusk when they saw one," said Paige. "This book is weird."

"Yeah."

"I keep waiting for them to say, 'Thar she blows, a hump like a snow hill,'" I said. "But maybe that's one of those famous lines that no one ever actually says in the book. Like, 'Elementary, my dear Watson.'"

"They never say that in Sherlock Holmes?"

"Nope."

"Weird."

That was one thing I guess I didn't pick up from the comic book version—*Moby-Dick* has got to be the weirdest fucking book of all time. Ishmael was always quoting conversations that happened when he wasn't even in the room and couldn't possibly have overheard. I wondered if maybe he actually died of kidney failure a week into the voyage or something, and just never mentioned that he spent most of the trip haunting the main deck and the captain's quarters.

He fucking *would*, too. It would be just like him to go on and on about whether or not whales were fish, which has nothing to do with anything, but not bother to mention the fact that he'd died, which seems like it would be *slightly* more important.

We rarely listened to more than a few minutes at a time, but all the rambling does get kind of oddly hypnotic after a while. It almost makes you feel like you're off in the middle of the ocean, slowly going mad with boredom and thinking that you see faces and symbols in the passing waves.

When we got to the back room of the Cave, Jake and Jenny and Stan and Dustin were all sitting around, and Mindy was standing up, leaning against the wall and smoking. I tried to avoid looking in her direction.

Paige looked pretty well out of her element in her academic letter jacket, but she sat down on an M&M's barrel and said hello to everyone. Once we'd all said our hellos Stan said, "Franklin D. Roosevelt's wheelchair."

Jake, who was sitting next to him, said, "An onion-based sauce known as a soubise."

Jenny, who was sitting on his lap, said, "Happy Meal toys."

Mindy said, "A tube of cookie dough."

And I said, "Whale blubber."

All this happened before I had a chance to explain anything to Paige, so there was a deadly silence in the room after I said that. It was her turn, and she had no idea what to do. She looked around the room for a second.

"Your turn, honey," said Mindy.

"Sorry," Paige said, "I . . . don't know the rules?"

"You ever play Dead Celebrities?" I asked. "That game where someone says the name of a dead celebrity, and the next person says the name of another one with a matching initial?"

"I guess," said Paige.

"This is *free-form* Dead Celebrities. You just say any random shit."

"The more random, the better," said Jenny.

"It's the sport of Danish kings," said Stan.

Danish kings. For shit's sake.

"Hey, Stan," I said. "Do you know what Danish kings make their thrones out of?"

"Narwhal tusks," he said.

Paige stared at him for a second, then Mindy said, "It's your turn. Say something. Anything random."

"Oh," said Paige. "Uh . . . gummy bears."

"Jaws 3-D," said Stan.

"Commemorative plates from the Franklin Mint with the *Family Circus* kids on them," said Jake.

Well-played.

"Those red phone booths they have in London," said Jenny, which I thought might be a subtle hint that she thought I should be thinking about Anna, and not going out with Paige.

"Cucumbers," Mindy said, looking right at me, and obviously thinking of all the times she'd compared her ex-boyfriend's dick to those.

"A female dog," I said.

"Sandals," said Paige.

I squeezed her hand. She was getting the hang of it, and holding her own, if not necessarily showing herself to be a real natural. There were no rules, but informally, there was an unwritten rule that saying something totally random was better than saying something inspired by what other people said. Like if Mindy said "cucumbers," it would have been a poor move to say "zucchini" next. But no one would have cared either way. We didn't keep score or anything.

I got Paige a handful of Reese's Pieces, and we stuck around until the conversation turned to poop, at which point we went back to my car.

"And that," I said to Paige when we left, "is life on the Island of Misfit Toys."

"How the hell did Stan know what Danish kings made their thrones out of?" she asked.

"He's probably reading *Moby-Dick* along with us," I said. "But he always knows shit like that. It's like he's memorized every book in the library."

"He's kind of creepy," she said.

"He's *really* creepy," I said. "But he's also a genius. You want to go look for Slushees? There might be some new flavors out."

She nodded, and we took off. It was raining now, and the drops plonked down hard in the deep puddles that sat where the snow piles used to be. At every dip in the road the car sprayed up a ton of water, which always looked like it would be fun to do in a car when I was kid, but now that I was actually doing it, it was kind of freaky. It's tough to control the car in that second when it's spraying water around.

We ended up at a Kum and Go on Hickman that had a blue

Mountain Dew–flavored Slushee, a new one for us. The clerk was a middle-aged guy who looked almost like a pirate—he had a receding hairline, but what was left of his hair hung down to his shoulders, and he had a mustache. All he needed was an eye patch and a parrot. And maybe an outfit other than a Kum and Go uniform. When we talked to him, we found that he used the word "shit" as a sort of vocalized punctuation mark.

"You that couple who's trying to find every flavor?" he asked.

"Something like that," I said. "You've heard about us?"

"Word gets around," he said. "Shit."

"We're looking for a flavor called white grape," I said. "Have you seen it?"

He just shook his head.

Paige leaned over me. "You think you could make some calls about it?" she asked. "Maybe ask your manager to order it?

He coughed and cleared his throat a bit. "Nah," he said. "I don't even know who decides how we get these things or what we get. It's a mystery. Shit. They change a couple of them out every now and then, though, so it might just be something they don't make no more."

He gave me my change, then turned up his radio and took a swig from a plastic bottle that had a Coca-Cola label on it but didn't look like any Coca-Cola I'd ever seen, and helped himself to a stick of beef jerky from our side of the counter.

"I mean, white grape?" he went on. "That doesn't even sound real. What in the hell is a white grape? Shit. One of the other stores I work at has cherry lime or something, though."

"Yeah, we've had that one," I said.

"That's some good shit," he said. "Cherry lime. Shit."

As I turned to leave, I suddenly wondered if this guy was an older version of me, time traveling back to give me a warning or something. I mean, his was just the life I had been setting myself up for. He was working a job that mainly required him to sit around eating and drinking all day. He could have been me in twenty years. I just hoped I didn't lose my hair like that.

We moved on to a Grab 'n' Go on Merle Hay Road that we hadn't hit yet, but they didn't have anything we hadn't seen a hundred times. The clerk was a girl about our age or a few years older.

"Hey," I said. "We've been trying to find a Slushee flavor called white grape. Have you ever heard of that?"

She smiled but shook her head. "We have white grape cigarillos but not Slushees."

I sighed and looked wistfully into the distance at the restrooms. "Maybe we'll never find it," I said. "We're destined to spend our lives in search of the Great White Slushee."

She giggled, and Paige dragged me back to the car. The rain shower was starting to turn into a thunderstorm now; there was a flash of lightning every few seconds.

"You were totally flirting with that girl," Paige said as she buckled up.

"I was just joking around," I said. "Like I do all the time."

"You need to not be doing it with cute girls, though," she said. "Not in front of me, anyway."

I guessed that if you looked at it from a certain angle, my joking with the clerk might have seemed like flirting. I thought I was just being friendly and all, but I guess there's a fine line between being friendly and flirting, and I suck at reading signs. Even the ones I'm sending out myself.

As I pulled back onto the wet road, she said, "It's not that I don't trust you, but I know you still think about that girl in England."

"Less and less," I said. "I'm trying not to."

"Thanks."

Thunder crashed across the sky, and we drove along listening to Ishmael for another block or two, then she put her hand on my knee. By the time I came to the next light, she had moved it to my inner thigh. Then she went for my zipper.

"Whoa," I said. "I'm driving here."

"The windows are all rainy. No one'll see."

"But I have to concentrate on the road."

"You wanna pull over, then? I know a place we can go."

"I don't know," I said.

She sighed out loud.

"Jesus, Leon," she said. "*This* is what I'm talking about. You always seem like you've got one foot out the door. Like you don't want to do anything that'll make it seem like we're a real couple."

"It's not that," I said. "It's not that at all."

"Is there something wrong with me, then? We've been going out for a month now, and you've barely even felt me up yet."

"I always screw things up by going too fast," I said.

"You can screw it up by going too slowly, too, you know."

I forced a smile. "Isn't that usually the *guy's* line?"

She sighed again. "I just feel like . . . if you really like me, you should *want* me to touch you."

"I do," I said. "I'm just . . . I'm nervous, is all. I'm afraid I'll disappoint you or something."

"You won't," she said. "I promise."

I kept driving along. For a second I thought I heard tornado sirens going off, but it was just an ambulance going by on a road up ahead.

"You told me you had a lot of experience with girls when we first started going out," she said.

"It wasn't a lot of *good* experience," I said.

"Who all have you been with?"

"Did you ever meet that girl Brenda?"

"The one who dropped out and moved to Council Bluffs with an older guy?"

I nodded. "Her and Mindy. That girl who was back there today."

"And it was bad?"

I turned the *Moby-Dick* CD off and just drove down the road to the next stop sign, letting the car hit some big puddles to make giant splashes. Even being in the car didn't feel private enough for a conversation like this. I wanted the windows covered with water so no one could see in. It didn't work very well; the water hit the sidewalk instead of the car. But the rain did the work well enough.

"I guess you could say that," I said. "Brenda was pretty mean, and Mindy made it very clear that her old boyfriend had left . . . uh . . . some big shoes to fill. That's why she was saying things like 'a tube of cookie dough' in free-form Dead Celebrities back there. That's how big she said he was."

"Bitch," said Paige. "For the record, guys who make a big deal out of how big their dick is are usually terrible in bed."

"I always hear it doesn't really matter."

She nodded, but looked like she was choosing her words carefully. "Every girl I know says it matters," she said. "But it's more about how you use it. And, like, the rest of your body."

It occurred to me that I didn't really know how many guys Paige had been with. I knew from little things I'd heard her say, mostly to her girlfriends, that she'd slept with Joey, and I knew that he wasn't her first. Any sex ed teacher would probably tell me I should find out her whole history if we were going to go any further than we already had, but how do you ask a girl something like that without seeming like you're calling her a slut or something?

She kept her hand on my inner thigh. Her pinky finger, and just her pinky finger, was tapping ever so lightly between my legs. At the next traffic light she kissed me hard on the mouth, then pulled back and licked gently at the corner of my mouth with the tip of her tongue. I forgot to watch for the light to change and got honked at by the person behind me. The rain kept coming down, and her face was lit by lightning.

"Where's that place we could go to that's private?" I asked.

"Behind that hippie store between Sip Coffee and the Ice Cave," she said.

"Earthways?"

"Yeah. They have this nook thing."

"A nook?"

"It's, like, two brick walls jutting out from the back. You can just barely fit a car between them. It blocks up the windows so no one can see."

"Okay."

And as we drove along, I hit another big puddle, and Paige moved her hand behind me and started rubbing the nape of my neck, which gave me a bit of that tingling "just got warmed up" feeling I had gotten with Anna that night in the snow. Maybe it was never really anything more than acupressure or something in the first place.

It was about a five-minute drive back to Cornersville Trace from where we were normally, but it took twice as long to navigate my way through the hard rain. Sure enough, back behind Earthways, the hippie store that sold candles shaped like wizards and stuff, there were actually a couple of random brick walls jutting out from the back of the place, serving no practical purpose that I could figure out, and far enough apart that when I pulled the car in between them, there were walls on either side of the car. It was like a miniature garage without a door or a roof. A cubby hole for cars.

"You're right," I said. "It's a perfectly car-sized nook."

"Supposedly they actually built these walls just to make a place for people to park and fool around," said Paige. "Because, you know. They're hippies."

"Sounds like the kind of thing hippies would do," I said. "Looks more like a place to keep a Dumpster to me, though."

"Don't mention Dumpsters now," she said. "It's not a turn-on."

"Sorry."

I also didn't mention just how badly I had to pee right then.

"Almost everybody I know either lost their virginity here or in the cemetery," she said.

"The cemetery?"

"There are some secluded spots there, too. But it's in the dirt, so it'd probably be too muddy today. I don't want to have to call my dad and explain how we got stuck in the mud on somebody's grave."

I tried not to look like I was nervous about going any further than we'd been. Or intimidated by the fact that Paige seemed to know all the semipublic places to get it on. I almost wondered if she was just making stuff up, like when I pretended to be on the crotch-kicking team, and I was supposed to laugh, but she seemed pretty serious. For a second I thought up all the perfectly good excuses I could think of for being in a cemetery if we got stuck there, but I forced myself to focus on the moment for a second.

I looked over at her. "Was this where you first . . ."

"Oh, no," she said, with a laugh. "My first time was with Mark Hatfeld. We were watching *Mean Girls* on his parents' couch."

"How was it?"

"The sex or the movie?"

"The sex."

"Not as good as just watching the movie would have been. Not the first time, anyway. We got better at it later."

"Well," I said, "I'll take a couch or a cemetery or right here over my first place any day. Mine was on the floor of a laundry room, two feet away from a pile of Stan's dirty underpants."

She laughed out loud. "Oh, you poor baby," she said. "Come here. Nurse Paige will make it all better."

I *did* love it when she called herself Nurse Paige.

She leaned over and kissed me, then took my hand and guided it under her shirt.

Then, without moving her face from mine, she undid my pants and put one hand inside, and with her free hand she undid her own jeans and slipped my other hand inside of them. I moved over and kissed her neck while I tried to concentrate on doing different things with each hand, which took my mind off having to pee, at the very least. The sound of water rushing down a nearby drain pipe wasn't helping at all.

We didn't go to the backseat. I didn't even unbuckle. We just kissed and touched. The only time we paused was when she pushed my pants and shorts down just enough to have them out of the way, then took a minute to examine what she could see by the flashes of lightning coming in through the back windshield. She couldn't see too well, probably, but she seemed to approve. Brenda hadn't exactly disapproved, but she hadn't bothered to look, really. The novelty of seeing naked guys had long since worn off for her, I guess, and seeing another dick was all in a day's work. It was nice to be with someone who seemed to be enjoying herself, for once.

And everything worked just like it was supposed to. We didn't really do much that required it to, just kissed and touched, but still. I didn't have to apologize or assure her that it wasn't her, it was me. We just had fun.

We fooled around until the rain stopped and (though I didn't tell her this part) until I got to the point where I had to stop making out and start taking steps that would lead me to getting to a bathroom soon. After I dropped her off at home, I drove to the first grocery store I found and went in.

I was clear back to my car before I realized that the Beatles song playing in the grocery store hadn't made me think about Anna at all.

14. HELL

The next time I convinced Paige to come to the Ice Cave, the only person in the whole place was Big Jake, who was leaning on the counter, and sipping something from a plastic cup.

"Where is everyone?" I asked.

"Got too crowded," he said. "So they all went to Stan's."

I looked over at Paige. "You want to go over there? There's probably a party going on."

She nodded, but there was doubt on her face.

It wasn't exactly misplaced, either. Stan's basement could get a little crazy when enough people were there. As we drove over, I tried to warn her about what might be going on there—public drunkenness, perhaps the odd live sex act, etc.—but she didn't seem concerned.

"I've seen it all before," she told me. "It can't be worse than what goes on at football parties."

I was almost offended by this. I'd never been to a football party, but I took it as a matter of faith that a heavy metal vomit party was a very, very different sort of atmosphere. At the very least it would feature dimmer lights, different music, and a decidedly different odor. No one in Stan's basement wore half as much body spray as the people Paige hung out with.

Some of them probably could have stood to try some, though.

When we arrived, Stan, Dustin, and Jenny were sitting at a table, smoking pot and playing Dungeons & Dragons. About eight more people, only about half of whom I recognized, were lounging in front of the TV, watching one of those "wild college party" porn videos where a bunch of guys in backwards hats pound girls who are supposed to be real students, but are probably really porn stars, in dorm rooms. It was Stan's old, boxy TV that we'd played video games on years before; it still got all the colors wrong, which made the porn sort of psychedelic. It was like watching overgrown, douchey Smurfs do it.

At least two more people were in the laundry room, presumably acting out scenes from the DVD. You could hear them moaning over the Megadeth CD that played on the stereo.

Paige surveyed the place like a prairie dog who'd just tunneled up out of the ground into a toxic waste dump, but she squeezed my hand and managed a weak smile.

Mindy was sitting on the couch. For no reason that seemed obvious, she had stripped down to her underwear, which probably should have made the place seem a bit more debauched, but somehow it just made her look sort of stupid. She wasn't wearing *fancy* underwear or anything; just a very plain bra and a thong that looked kind of like a jock strap and gave her the general air of a person who was too lazy to put clothes on in the morning. Looking at her and remembering having been with her made me feel kind of sick.

She was the first one to notice us, though.

"Hey," she said, when we walked in. She sat upright and sort of showed herself off. I ignored her and led Paige through the room, past a cooler full of beer bottles, to the table where Stan was sitting.

"What's happening?" I asked.

"Not a lot. Help yourself to some drinks."

Paige, ever the social butterfly (at least compared to everyone else there) did her best to make conversation.

"What are you guys playing?" she asked.

"D and D," said Stan.

"Is that the game where you, like, roll dice and kill goblins and stuff?"

"Yeah," said Dustin. "That's what we're doing. We're rolling dice and killing goblins and stuff."

"That's pretty much it," I said. "In a minute someone will fire a cannon at Dustin's character point-blank, and he'll roll the dice to see if it hurt."

"My character can handle it," Dustin said. "He's an eight-hundred-year-old warlord."

"And now that you're playing him, he'll be dead in six months, tops," I said.

"That's true," said Stan. "You guys do realize that your characters were better off without you, right?"

Dustin looked at me. "Stan is the most evil dungeon master ever," he said.

"Well, yeah," said Stan. "I'm the fucking devil. Go get some drinks."

We wandered over to the open cooler that sat against the wall, but there was nothing in it that Paige would drink, so the two of us ended up just standing by a wall.

"This isn't good party music," she said.

"It's good for *this* kind of party," I said.

For a while the two of us just stood there, watching the crowd milling around, idly banging their heads to the strains of early Megadeth in the dim light of the oddly colored porn, charming faces all aglow. One of the guys who was watching the DVD got up and said he had to take a piss, and the girl who was sitting next to him on the floor followed him into the bathroom.

Mindy, meanwhile, kept looking over at Paige and smiling, like she was just waiting for her to freak out and shriek or something. Paige completely ignored everything that was happening. Soon, she was looking through her phone, and I figured that she was desperately checking social media sites for some other gathering we could go to. After a few minutes, right when I think we both realized at the same time that the guy and the girl hadn't come out of the bathroom yet, Paige got a message saying a bunch of people were going to Leslie's to watch a movie, and asked me if we could go.

Having subjected Paige to seeing Mindy in her underwear, I figured I owed it to her to go someplace she'd like better.

"That wasn't nearly as shocking as you said it would be," she said as we left. "It was just kind of gross down there. Your friends are kind of disgusting, you know."

"They aren't so bad," I said.

"And what's Stan's thing with pretending to be Satan all the time?"

"He's been doing that since he was at least nine or ten," I said. "And I'm not really even sure he's pretending. His hangover cures defy science. And I don't think I've ever seen him fall asleep."

"Are his parents out of town?"

I just shrugged as I got into the car. "I haven't seen either of them in years. I only ever saw his mom once, and that was just for five seconds when I was about nine."

She shook her head. "Weird."

I didn't much want a lecture on how bad my friends were, so I put *Moby-Dick* back on as we drove off to Leslie's, where about twenty people had gathered in her living room to watch a really awful comedy that was still in theaters, but that someone had downloaded off a torrent site. It was a camera recording that looked like shit, and you could hear people talking in the background, but I don't think a better quality file would have made the movie any better. The one thing it had going for it was a scene where an old lady gets diarrhea and says, "Oh, merciful Heavens!" while she explodes. It was stupid, but I laughed.

And when I did, some asshole turned back to me and said, "Do you know that is the *only* time I've heard you laugh at this entire movie?"

Some guy on the other side of the room looked over towards us. It was dark and he couldn't see me, but he said, "Is it that Leon guy? I told you, man, all this guy ever talks about is turds! I'm just saying, bro."

I laughed along with everyone else—you've got to be able to laugh at yourself when someone makes a realistic point. I'd brought it on myself. I was the Poop Guy.

At the end of the movie Paige and I drove off to the nook and did a little more fooling around. I noticed that sometimes she didn't seem to be kissing back, like what she really wanted wasn't to make out, but just to be kissed. That was all right.

Once I dropped her off at home, I headed back to Stan's place, where everyone was watching a Japanese horror movie. These were my people. And no matter how good I got at hanging around with Paige's friends, they probably always would be.

This, of course, made me wonder again what the hell Paige saw in me, beyond the fact that I had the sense not to go around sending people pictures of my balls when they hadn't asked for them. But she saw something. Out of all the guys at all the restaurants and living rooms in town, she'd chosen me. The Poop Guy.

In fact, the next morning she asked if I'd like to have dinner at her house and meet her parents.

15. DANCING

Paige had never tried to get me to shave the pubelike whiskers that I'd cultivated on my chin. I suspected that she liked them, actually. They gave me sort of a rugged air that I think some women are biologically programmed to dig—it's a mental remnant of the days when tough-looking guys could bring home more woolly mammoth meat or something. But the day I was supposed to meet her parents, I shaved them off using disposable razors and shaving cream that I picked up down at the dollar store. I looked about twelve years old without them, and even less like I could ever kill a woolly mammoth, but I wanted to be halfway presentable.

When I knocked on the door, Paige opened it up and immediately covered her face with her palm when she saw my smooth face.

"Oh my God," she said through her hand.

"Go ahead, you can laugh," I said. "I look ridiculous."

She put her hand down and just chuckled, then did this thing where she put her hand on my shoulder and traced it down my arm before holding my hand.

"You look nice," she said. "But now I feel like a cradle robber."

"I'm older than you," I said.

"Girls mature faster than boys."

I shuffled my feet and took off my shoes. The carpets were all white, and everything about the house made me want to rethink any plans of cleaning myself up. When I get a house, I'm getting brown carpet so I can track mud around, spill stuff, whatever. I'd be afraid to fart in a room with white carpet.

A man should be able to fart in his own house. I'd rather live in some hovel, like the pirate guy from the Hickman Avenue Kum and Go probably did, than live in Oak Meadow Mills.

"Is that him?" came a voice from the kitchen—Paige's mom, I assumed.

"He has a name, Mother," said Paige.

Her mom emerged in the hallway, smiling. She was rich, all right. Most of my friends' moms look like brutally normal women in their thirties and forties in their mom jeans and sweatshirts. Paige's mom looked like she'd spent a lot of money putting herself together. I imagined that she was probably a Botox user.

I gave her my most charming smile.

"Hi," I said. "I'm Leon."

"I'm Renee, Paige's mom," she said. "Come in. Make yourself at home!"

Paige and I followed her into the kitchen, where Paige's twelve-year-old sister, Autumn, was sitting at the table already, staring at her phone. Their dad, Gene, whom I'd already met the day he threatened to stab me, was cooking something on the stove.

"Hi, Leon," he called out. "Have a seat. We're casual here."

Nothing weird had happened, but I could tell Paige was totally embarrassed already. She gave this *Oh my God, I'm* SO *sorry* look as we sat at the table, with me across from Autumn, who was wearing so much makeup that if you pushed the edge of a quarter against her cheek, the makeup probably would have held it in place.

The family all prayed before dinner. I kinda felt like they should have made sure I wasn't Jewish or anything first, but I suppose Paige would have told them if I was.

After they said "Amen" and we all started on our salads, Autumn said, "Is it true that everyone who works at the Ice Cave worships the devil?"

"Autumn!" said Renee. "That is not polite!"

"Natasha said they did!" said Autumn. "I'm just curious. God."

Autumn did that thing you hear from girls a lot where she added an "uh" at the end of every sentence. Like, she pronounced "God" as "God-uh."

Paige did it occasionally too. It kinda bugged me, but I was learning to live with it.

I dodged the question, of course. There was a woodcut print of the Little Brown Church in the Vale, one of Iowa's few landmarks, on the wall, so I obviously wasn't going to score any points by trying to explain that it was mostly agnostics and pagans back there. I was not going to mention Stan under any circumstances.

I was just turning myself off and faking it, the way I sometimes did in group outings, and the way I did just about any time I had to talk to a teacher or my own parents. It's about like going to someone else's church: Stand when they stand, sit when they sit, and hope you don't end up getting sacrificed with a big knife or something.

"Did you ever think about one of the other ice cream places?" Gene asked from the stove. "We like Penguin Foot Creamery."

"I worked there for a while," I said.

"It's supposed to be a great place to work," he said. "They made some list in *Forbes*. Something about the best employers or fastest growing companies."

"They talk a big game," I said, "but I get more hours at the Ice Cave, and I have a better chance of moving up to management sooner. All of the managers at Penguin Foot have to go to college first."

"Well, there's nothing wrong with that," said Renee.

"Yeah, but I can't really imagine going to college just to go into retail management," I said. "I'm probably better off getting into it now and getting it on the résumé ahead of time."

"Smart," said Gene. "Didn't I tell you he was smart, Renee?"

"You did," said Renee. "You sure did. Which college are you going to, Leon?"

The answer, of course, was *nowhere*. But I had rehearsed for this by telling my stock lie to my parents over and over. I was on autopilot, not even thinking about what I was saying now.

"Just junior college for the first year or two," I said. "So I can work more and save money while I get the requirements out of the way. You don't do anything in your major the first couple years anyway."

"What's your major?"

"Undeclared for now. I haven't quite decided. But the requirements are the same for a lot of them."

Gene set the food down on the table—steaks. Nice ones. Mashed potatoes, too.

"Can I grab you a beer, there, Leon?" he asked.

I looked up, thinking, *Hell yeah*, but not knowing whether I ought to say that. But then he slapped me on the back and said, "Just kidding! Ha!"

Har de har har.

There were only two particularly awkward moments over the course of the dinner, really, but they were big and notable ones.

The first was about halfway through the main course, when Autumn looked me right in the eye and said, "Do you guys have sex?"

I didn't have to answer, because Renee shouted, "Autumn! This is the dinner table. That is very rude."

"I was just asking," said Autumn.

Paige fixed her with one of her serious glares, only *way* more serious than the ones she gave me, and her dad started asking if I ever played golf. Which, of course, I did not. I hadn't even played *miniature* golf in a long time. He offered to take me out to play the back nine at the country club some time, and I said it sounded great.

I felt like kind of a chump saying that, but it's not like I could *say* it sounded awful, and that I knew it would give him a good chance to get me to a secluded place to give me a sex talk. Stand when they stand, sit when they sit.

The next big, notable, awkward moment came when Paige's mom asked me a question for which I was really, really unprepared. One that I could not have prepared for and couldn't handle on autopilot.

"So," said Renee, "you're escorting Paige to her debutante ball, right?"

"Oh, God, Mom, you can*not* bring that up," said Paige.

"Debutante ball?" I asked. "They still have debutante balls?"

At first I tried not to laugh. I'd seen debutante balls in, like, cartoons now and then, but I thought they were one of those things that *used* to exist, and maybe still did, but that I'd never meet anyone who'd been to one. Like 4-H Club meetings. Or low-down boxing clubs and mirror mazes.

If those were real, she might as well have asked me if I was going to the moon or something.

Paige was sort of blushing. "They still have them," she said, "but the only people who care are the debutantes' moms."

"Well, technically, it's not a *debutante* ball," said Renee. "It's a *scholarship cotillion* that the Harvester Club puts on every year. But we call it the debutante ball. I'm surprised Paige didn't tell you about it. Lots of her friends are going."

The thought of actually *going* to one brought about that same familiar gnawing feeling in my guts that had been less noticeable since I got the detention dealt with. I didn't know shit about debutante balls, but something told me I couldn't count on the fact that everyone poops to help me make small talk at one of them. I went straight to looking for a way out. Paige didn't seem excited about it, so I didn't feel obligated to go along with it.

"I'd need a suit, wouldn't I?" I asked.

"Every man should have a suit," said her dad. "I'll take you shopping myself."

Sweet Satan, this guy was desperate to get me alone. I was starting to think maybe he was a pervert or something.

"I think I have one," I said. "I just don't wear it much."

"Don't tell me you spilled a Slushee on it." He laughed as he picked up his fork. Renee gave him a weird look, and Gene said, "Didn't Paige tell you about that? The two of them go driving around looking for some weird Slushee flavor," before putting the steak in his mouth.

"They do not," said Autumn. "They probably just park the car and have sex."

"Shut *up*, Autumn!" said Paige. "We drive around town and, like, explore."

"Explore sex," said Autumn.

"That's enough, Autumn," said Renee. "Didn't you also say you were listening to an audio book together, Paige?"

"Uh-huh," said Paige. "Leon has been listening to *Moby-Dick*."

"See? Dick!" said Autumn.

Gene put his silverware down, swallowed the food he was chewing, and gave her a stern, fatherly look.

"Autumn," he said, "I'm sure they aren't doing anything I wouldn't want them to do."

He gave me a very quick *you'd better not be* look.

"And that's a real classic book, isn't it?" asked Paige's mom. "It's very famous." Then she looked at Autumn and said, "And it's very old, so there's no sex in it."

"Not so far," I said. "I'm only about halfway through, though."

I'd been making a point of listening to it more lately, now that I'd calculated that if I didn't hurry up, I could be listening for months. I usually had it playing while I was working by myself, and any time I was in the car. And I was more and more sure that Ishmael and Queequeg were more than friends.

Paige, meanwhile, was clearly getting desperate to leave before anyone said anything else about sex.

"Don't we have some yearbook work to do, Leon?" she asked, the second I finished my steak.

"Yeah," I said. "We'd better get going, huh?"

Autumn opened her mouth, obviously to say we were going to go have sex, but both parents stopped her with another look. I did all of the necessary hand-shaking and talking about how good the food was (which at least wasn't a lie—that steak could have been the food of Danish kings), and we hustled out the door into my car.

"You want to go to the Ice Cave?" Paige asked.

"Yeah, I think I need a squalor fix."

"Sorry about my sister," she said. "That kid is *obsessed* with sex. You guys probably don't talk about sex in that back room as much as she does."

I pulled out of the driveway and shook my head. "The people at Casa Bravo talk about it way more than we do."

"Huh," she said.

I'd been at Casa Bravo enough now to know that Paige's coworkers were at *least* as sick as mine, and probably more so. They were mostly older than us, so when they talked about sex, which they did constantly when there weren't any customers around, none of them were as likely to be lying about it as we were.

"So," I said, "to change the subject . . . what's the Harvester Club?"

"It's one of those service organizations," said Paige. "Like Rotary or Lions or whatever. And every year they have a debutante ball."

"Is there any chance of me getting through one of those without making a complete fool of myself?"

"It's no big deal," she said. "All you have to do is get through a meal and a cocktail party, then escort me down a runway to a dance floor."

"Cocktail party?"

"With Shirley Temples."

"That doesn't sound *completely* impossible."

I kind of turned this over as we drove along, until she reached over and slipped her hand into my pants. Her fingers were chilly from being against the window, and I sort of cringed.

"Cold!" I said.

"Sorry," she said as she took it back out. "Could that, like, give you shrinkage?"

"Probably."

"I normally want it to go the other way," she said. "But I always wondered what they looked like with shrinkage. Just . . . you know . . . medical curiosity."

I suppose I should have been more turned on. But with her talking about me getting shrinkage, her little sister pretty obviously imagining the two of us naked right that very second, and her dad being suspiciously eager to get me alone (even though that had to be all in my head), I felt kind of . . . violated, in a way. Like her whole damned family was picturing me naked, and she was picturing me, like, extra naked. Naked and shriveled.

So I changed the subject and asked the first question that came to mind, even though I already knew what the answer was.

"So, Iowa State," I said. "Are you going to stay in the dorms, or are you just going to commute out to Ames?"

"Dorms," she said. "As much gas as my car eats, driving an hour and a half every day would probably cost even more than the dorms."

"Makes sense," I said.

"Are you really going to junior college? I thought you were waiting or something."

"I don't know, honestly. I've been telling my parents I'd wait until second semester or next year, but I'm really not even thinking that far ahead. I haven't even taken the SAT yet."

"You really should," she said. "Time's running out."

"I know. I'll sign up for it tomorrow."

We made it to Cedar Avenue, then turned onto Seventy-sixth Street and went past the pond and the middle school. There was still a bit of ice on the pond, but a couple of ducks had come back from their winter trip south and were lounging around in the water. The fountain hadn't been turned back on yet, though.

"I didn't really know you before last month, but I always thought you were, like, a genius," Paige said. "And that you were going to MIT or something. Or film school."

"Nah," I said. "I planned to do stuff like that when I was kid, but I kind of let myself go."

"How come?"

I drove over a speed bump, then said, "You know. After Anna moved."

We got quiet for a second. Then another. The streetlights came on, and Anna's name just kind of hung in the air. I sure as hell didn't mention that when we passed Horton Street, you could actually see her old house out the driver's-side window if you looked down the road.

Then Paige said, "Steering wheels."

"Huh?"

"Free-form Dead Celebrities. I said 'steering wheels.' Your turn."

"Oh. Narwhal tusks."

She smiled. "My sister's cheap makeup."

"Golf."

"Care Bears."

"Fireworks."

"The birthplace of Herbert Hoover."

"Spray-on tans."

And so we went on like that, all the way to the Ice Cave. Inside, Dustin was working the counter, but other than that it seemed quiet.

"Anybody here?" I asked him.

He shook his head. "A bunch of people went to Stan's house."

"I don't suppose you want to go there?" I asked.

Paige shook her head. "We can just hang out in the back room here," she said. "Sounds like we'll have it all to ourselves."

I nodded, and we walked back and had some gummy worms. She set the stereo to radio mode and found a hip-hop station.

"I don't really care about the debutante ball," she said, "but it's a big deal to my mom. Can you take me?"

"I guess so," I said.

"I'll owe you big-time," she said.

"Oh, yeah?"

She sat next to me on the couch and smiled. "I tell you what," she said. "If you promise to take me to the ball, then I'll fuck your brains out."

"You mean right now?"

"No, some place where I can be naked and not get a rash. And not tonight, anyway. It's my period. But sometime soon."

I tried not to look like I was panicking a bit, and not just because I didn't want her to think I was all weirded out by her mentioning her period. We'd done a lot of fooling around by then, but actual sex still seemed like a disaster waiting to happen. I couldn't put it off forever, though.

All at once the answer came to me.

"I have an idea," I said. "We'll do it the day we find the white grape Slushee."

She giggled. "If it doesn't take too long."

"Okay."

"That or the night of the ball," she said. "Whichever comes first."

"All right," I said. "Let's shake on it."

She shook my hand with great dignity.

"When Captain Ahab orders everyone to get Moby Dick, he nails a gold coin to the mast," I said. "I wish we had one we could nail to the wall."

We laughed, and we kept shaking hands for a second, then she went over and messed with the radio until she came to something slow, then held her hand out in front of me.

"Stand up," she said.

I took her hand and got up, but didn't know what she had in mind. Then she put my hand on her side and grabbed the other one.

"Come on," she said. "If you're taking me to the ball, you need to be able to dance."

"Hey, no one said anything about dancing," I said. "You just said I had to escort you down a walkway and mingle with people."

"The more you dance, the less mingling you have to do. Did you cut gym the weeks they did ballroom dancing?"

"Yeah.

"Do you know how to dance at all?"

"No."

"Then I'm going to teach you."

And she did.

And I guess Dustin must have been listening in and relating all of this back to Stan. There's no other logical explanation for the fact that I went in to work the next day and found a gold-colored coin with a hole in the middle—a five-yen piece from Japan—nailed to the wall in the back room.

16. HAIR

The very next morning I went to see the guidance counselor, a woman named Mrs. Smollet who, according to well-placed sources, slept in a coffin and sprinkled rats' assholes on her oatmeal in the morning.

She was in charge of the gifted pool program for a while when I was in middle school, and scaring the shit out of her was one of our greatest pleasures. When she saw Anna wearing devil horns, it seemed like it took all her willpower not to drag her by the ear into the nearest bathroom and baptize her in the toilet.

We'd hated each other back then, but she was very professional with me when I came to her office now to look at upcoming SAT dates. That was kind of a relief, but it felt *wrong* to me, somehow, to sit there talking to her and not say anything to frighten her. There are some enemies you should just *keep* as enemies. Being courteous with her just made me feel like I'd gone soft and given up.

So after I'd arranged to take the test the day after the debutante ball, I asked if I could pick up a few condoms while I was in the office.

Mrs. Smollet just looked at me like she was trying to figure out if I was serious or just messing with her. It was a little of both, really.

"You *know* I don't give out condoms," she said. "I don't run *that* kind of counselor's office."

"Come on," I said. "I'm going to have sex anyway, right? Don't you want me to be safe?"

"The only safe way is not doing it, Leon."

"I'll bet I know what's *really* going on here," I said. "You *want* girls to get pregnant. You probably think that eating the placentas of teen mothers will keep you young or something. That's why you don't give out condoms, right?"

She made a face like she was about to gag, and I felt, for just a second, like I had been born again.

"Seriously," I said. "*That's* why you don't like birth control or abortions. So you can get your grubby mitts on regular helpings of locally grown teen placenta."

She started to say something, but I kept talking.

"So, do you glug them straight out of the bucket, or do you mix them in with a shake every day for breakfast and lunch, and then have a sensible dinner?"

She gave me this look like a caterpillar had just crawled up her ass and she was trying not to react.

"I'd thought you'd matured past this phase, Leon," she said.

"Nope."

She was probably the only person on the planet who felt like I was more mature now than I was in middle school.

If I had matured at all, really, besides just in the sense of starting to grow facial hair and all that shit, the only real evidence was that I had pretty much come to grips, psychologically, with the fact that I really wasn't any cooler than my father.

My father was a dork. A complete dork. There's no nicer way to say it. But he was no slacker; after a long day of being the bad boy of the accounting firm, he'd come home and mess around with his various collections, cook up a "food disaster" with mom, or get to work on one of the inventions he was always working on. I hated his posters with dopey motivational phrases on them, which he plastered all over the house, but they seemed to work for him. He was no slacker, at least. He was cooler and more ambitious than I was, honestly. Accepting that was about as hard a thing as I ever had to do.

I wasn't quite as embarrassed by him or my mom as I had been in middle school, but I was still dreading letting Paige meet them. For one thing I couldn't really trust them not to mention Anna. And I couldn't just ask them not to, because then I'd get the old "it sounds like you're not really over her" lecture.

Furthermore, Paige wanted to come over on a food disaster night. She had thought they sounded hilarious when I made the mistake of telling her about them.

It wasn't as simple as just cooking a bad meal. When they did a "food disaster," they actually dressed up in appropriate attire for each particular disaster meal. If the cookbook they were using was from the 1950s, Mom would wear a poodle skirt and talk about Eisenhower. Dad wore hideous leisure suits that he bought at thrift stores for stuff from cookbooks from the 1970s.

When I was in eighth grade, they found a stapled-together,

hand-typed-and-photocopied cookbook called *True Americans Are Grilling Americans*. For that they had taken on the roles of Lester and Wanda: Grilling Americans—a couple of white trash hicks who wore muscle shirts and talked about *Wheel of Fortune* and killing bears a lot, in between talking about food (which usually consisted of well-done meat and enough ketchup to choke a whale). They liked being Lester and Wanda so much that they'd kept playing them occasionally, even when they moved on to other cookbooks.

Now, after four years, the saga of Lester and Wanda was like one of those epic Viking poems that goes on for eleven thousand pages. They had backstories; there were subplots, recurring characters, and everything. Probably even some symbolism. I took on the role of Americus, Lester and Wanda's no-good son. I didn't say much at the meals—I mostly just grunted and acted like a total bum, which wasn't exactly hard. A lot of nights I was really just playing myself.

On the night in question, when Paige was coming, my mother made something called a Pop Art Pineapple Casserole from a 1967 book called *Kitchen Freakout*, which was supposed to be "hippie food" but was probably written by people who'd only seen hippies in cartoons. The picture of it in the book looked like something you'd normally see in a petri dish.

When I left to pick Paige up, Mom and Dad were sitting at the kitchen table, dressed in grungy clothes and pretending to be Lester and Wanda reacting to a hippie cookbook.

"You don't s'pose eatin' this stuff will make us into no godless commies, do you?" asked Mom/Wanda.

"Don't worry," said Dad/Lester. "If it does, I know a fella we can call to come shoot us."

"You guys think maybe you can turn it down a bit tonight?" I asked.

"We'll try," said Dad, in his normal voice. "But isn't this what people in Oak Meadow Mills think we slobs on August Avenue act like, anyway?"

Mom laughed and socked Dad in the arm.

"Don't worry, Leon," she said in her own normal voice. "We've got our embarrassing stories about you carefully picked out. We won't stay in character for long."

I had told Paige that they were doing a hippie cookbook, and when I arrived at her place she was wearing a peasant shirt, faded jeans, and one of those dream-catcher necklaces that they sold at Earthways, with a single braid tied into her hair. She looked pretty hot, really, but I had neglected to tell her that they weren't actually being hippies tonight.

I tried to explain about Lester, Wanda, and Grilling Americans. Paige said it sounded fun, and like real family bonding, but there was the same doubt in her voice that I detected when she agreed to go into Stan's basement. It may have occurred to her that this was going to be weirder than she'd imagined.

"I'm in the wrong costume then, huh?" she asked. "Should we go back so I can put on a flannel or something?"

"Nah," I said. "They'll just pretend that Americus brought home a hippie girlfriend and make it part of the scene. I'm not going to promise it won't be really embarrassing."

"It can't be worse than having Autumn at my place," Paige said. And she bravely followed me to my car.

This was a milestone I don't think I'd reached before: doing something with Paige that I'd never done with Anna, even though I knew Anna wanted to. Anna was always asking about the food disasters, but I was so embarrassed by them back then that I wouldn't have let her come to one even if she'd offered to let me watch her change into whatever outfit she wore for it. Not even if the cookbook that week had been *Cooking for People in Swimsuits.* I had been fully confident that if she saw a food disaster, she'd never speak to me again. Unless she thought that they, and my parents, were awesome, which would have been like a knife in my back.

Now, maybe it wasn't so much *maturity* as simply giving up, but the idea of someone else seeing a food disaster didn't fill me with so much dread. I realized that I wasn't too cool for them. Not even close. And a part of me was curious as to how Paige would react to something like this. I'd seen her among squalor and filth and even a bit of geekery, but not among pure dorkiness.

Mom and Dad were nice enough to talk like regular people when Paige and I first arrived, but as soon as they served the Pop Art Pineapple Casserole, which contained both chicken and marshmallows in addition to the pineapple, they ceased to be my parents and became Lester and Wanda: Grilling Americans. They pretended that Paige was an actual hippie that I'd brought home for their approval, and of whom they were trying to be understanding and tolerant, in a hillbilly sort of way.

"Is this what your people eat, Paige?" asked Mom/Wanda. "Down on the commune?"

"Uh . . . yeah," she said.

"They mostly eat granola, Ma," I grunted. "They got better sense than to eat this crap."

"Tastes okay," said Dad. "But it needs some ketchup and red meat."

"It tastes like garbage you'd find in the Dumpster outside of a candy store," I said. "And I'll bet it can defy gravity. Look."

I scooped up a spoonful of the stuff and threw it at the ceiling, where it stuck like glue. Paige squealed—I guess I should have known that throwing food at the ceiling wasn't something that went on very often in her house. It wasn't unknown at mine. Many food disasters were better thrown than eaten.

"See?" I said. "Groovy."

"Oh, lord," said Mom. "He's smoking the weed. I knew it! She corrupted him!"

"You're cleaning that up later, Leon," my dad said, in his normal voice. But I could tell he wasn't mad. He was probably too busy thinking of ways he could modify the casserole recipe and invent an edible glue or something. Then he laughed, and mom laughed, and after that we gave up on trying to stay in character.

"You've eaten plenty of things that were worse than this, Leon," said my mother. "And I'm not talking about the food disasters."

My dad snickered. "Did we ever tell you about how you once ate some of Beethoven's hair?"

Paige smiled and grabbed my arm, then looked at my dad. "Do tell," she said.

I stared at both of my parents, whose faces were so full of glee that I could tell they were sitting on a story they'd waited years to break out.

"Beethoven's hair?" I asked. "As in Beethoven the dead composer?"

"That's the one." Dad smiled.

"At what point did I ever eat any of Beethoven's hair?" I asked. "I'm pretty sure I'd remember eating a piece of a dead person."

"It was when Leon was a baby," Dad said. "I'd just gotten a job at the accounting place, and I was hoping I could invent something to make me rich enough to quit the job before he started school."

"That certainly worked out," I said, sarcastically.

"Can it, Leon, I'm telling a story," Dad said with a laugh. "Anyway, I was having trouble coming up with ideas. Then I found a catalog for a place that was selling tiny, quarter-inch strands of Ludwig Von Beethoven's hair. And I thought that having something like that, something that came from the head of such a great genius, might inspire me."

"You let him buy something like that?" I asked my mother.

"Well, it was either that or let him fly a kite in a thunderstorm like Ben Franklin. That was his first choice," said my mother. This did not surprise me for a second.

Paige grinned and nibbled at the psychedelic casserole.

"How did you know it was really Beethoven's hair?" I asked.

"It was real, Leon," said my mother. "Believe me, I made him check into it before he spent any money on it. Some guy bought a whole lock for tens of thousands and defrayed the cost by selling little bits to people like your dad."

"So, I bought this tiny strand of Beethoven's hair," Dad went on. "And when it arrived, I got it out of the little case that it came in, and I was holding it on the tip of my finger, just seeing if some of his genius would be transferred into me via osmosis or something. I remember I even had a recording of his Fifth Symphony playing."

"But no inspiration?" I asked.

"Oh, it was inspiring, all right," he said. "I was so moved that I brought it over to your high chair to show it to you. And I was saying, 'Leon, this is a bit of one of the greatest geniuses who ever lived,' or something like that, and holding it up to your face. Then you opened your mouth and bit my finger, and that was the last I ever saw of Beethoven's hair."

"Ew!" said Paige. She covered her face with her hands and laughed.

"You have got to be kidding me," I said.

"Boy, did we panic for a minute there," said my mother. "We were ready to call an ambulance."

"From eating a tiny bit of hair?" I asked.

"Well," said my father, "we looked up some info on Beethoven, and it turned out he died of lead poisoning—and the reason they know that is because they found traces of it in strands of his hair."

"Luckily for you, you can't get lead poisoning from a tiny, two-hundred-year-old piece of hair," said Mom. "But I was still sure you were going to keel over dead any second for days."

"Maybe it helped me build up an immunity," I said. "That explains why I've been able to stomach all these food disasters."

Paige laughed and laughed, but she laughed even harder and said, "Oh no, oh no," when I said I was going to have some business cards printed up that said LEON HARRIS: CLASSICAL CANNIBAL. I thought that having eaten a bit of Beethoven was kind of awesome, really. It's not everyone who can go around saying he ate a bit of a famous dead composer.

All in all the dinner could have gone a lot worse. At least Mom didn't break out the naked baby pictures or anything; there had been enough picturing me naked at the last "meet-the-parents" event. But afterwards, as I took Paige back home, I got the distinct impression that the whole night had sort of weirded her out. She tried to cover it up, but I could tell.

"It was . . . interesting," she said.

"Hey, I never said my parents were normal."

"I know you wouldn't remember something from when you were a baby, but do you think your dad is serious about that story about Beethoven? Or is it just, like, one of those stories you tell like being on the crotch-kicking team?"

I thought about that as we came to a stop sign on a pockmarked intersection. "Mom wouldn't have gone along with it if it wasn't true," I said. "And buying up a piece of famous hair is *exactly* the sort of thing Dad would do."

"You're just like him, aren't you?"

I didn't answer. I may have accepted that I was a lot like him in my mind, but saying it out loud was another thing.

And I wasn't totally sure what she wanted me to say.

This is the thing about relationships: When you meet the parents, you have to think about the possibility that you'll end up with this person forever, and that dinner with the parents might be a preview of what your future would be like together. And I couldn't blame Paige if imagining a life like the ones my parents lived freaked her out a bit. It was one thing to be with the Poop Guy for a while, but quite another to be with a guy who might be forty years old and pulling out "Classical Cannibal" business cards.

Of course, there was always a chance I'd end up living like Paige's parents myself, even if it wasn't what I wanted. Maybe I'd even end up in one of these mirror-maze subdivisions full of vinyl siding and ride-on lawnmowers and everything else that made punk rock necessary in the first place. Staying in the suburbs is what happens to pretty much everyone from the suburbs, right?

Obviously, Paige had never imagined living among the cannibals any more than I had imagined living among stainless-steel kitchens.

But that's life, I guess.

17. PERMISSIONS

I came to realize that the yearbook staff was a regular hotbed of Machiavellian maneuvering. Paige kind of thrived there; there was something about girl-world drama that really brought out a different side of her than what I usually saw, but which sort of made her come alive. If someone said something about someone else, she would get right up, pick a side, and start fighting.

At the yearbook meeting after the dinner with my parents, there was an argument about whether they should include a couple of pictures that showed two different girls wearing the same outfit. It seemed like a stupid thing to be concerned about to me and a few other people, but I didn't want to get involved. It meant a lot to Paige.

"They'll both want to kill us all," she said. "They'll go down in history as people who copied each other. Is that how any of us want our class to remember us in fifty years when they look at the old yearbook?"

"Well, it's their fault for dressing like that," Leslie said back. "We're not here to create a legacy, we're here to create *memories*, and we have to tell the truth about people, or we're just creating *false* memories."

"So what? No one's going to want to remember the way things really were. That's why people like my dad think high school was great. They blocked out the way it really was."

I just ignored this. I wasn't there to make decisions. I just laid out the pictures they chose.

This sort of shit *consumed* the yearbook staff. Paige would be fuming about it for hours. And I would smile and nod and try to tune it out, because she got really upset when I laughed or tried to tell her that in fifty years our yearbooks would mostly be gathering dust in storage lockers and basements, not inspiring memories. They weren't going to be a source of real nostalgia and no one would think of them as a legacy. Not really. It was just a bunch of bullshit, if you get right down to it. I suppose yearbooks always are.

For instance there was this one picture of Mr. Larson, the science teacher, and the caption the committee picked was (get this): "Mr. Larson imparts his daily dose of wisdom to a batch of eager minds."

I could think of two things wrong with that caption. First, you've got your "eager minds" shit. Then, you've got the very notion that Mr. Larson had any wisdom to impart in the first place. The man wasn't even wise enough to get his nose hairs trimmed before operating a Bunsen burner. The day when his nose hairs caught fire was bound to come one day; I always imagined that the flame would work its way up the hair, like a fuse, and then there'd be a little explosion and he'd end up standing there with his face covered in soot, like a cartoon character who'd just bitten into a carrot that turned out to be dynamite. *That* was the kind of event I'd want to commemorate in a yearbook.

Really, though, if I looked through the thing years down the road, I'd probably just see Mr. Larson and realize that his nose hairs weren't any longer than *mine* had gotten to be, and younger generations who had heard me tell the legend of Mr. Larsons's hairy nostrils would realize that I was no more a reliable source than Ishmael.

As the Battle of the Matching Dresses raged on, I excused myself to go to the library and do some layout work. I'd made it to the "Senior Class Through the Years" section, and had to scan in all the pictures of us from the last twelve grades that the committee had scavenged, and figure out how to set them up to look their best on a page.

Sifting through the photos, I came across a shot from the middle-school days showing a group of kids walking down the hall. Anna was with them. It was back when her blond hair was down to her butt.

I found a place for it, and then, to keep my mind off her, found a place to slip in the "Satan Rules" acrostic. It fit right in with the other student-submitted artwork.

Once it was in place I filled out my time sheet for two hours. Mr. Perkins signed it without looking at it, as usual, and I headed out to work. Paige said she'd come see me there after the meeting ended.

At the Cave, Stan was behind the counter, giving a girl with dirty-blond hair a lesson in how to pronounce "sorbet."

"It's sor-*bay*," he said. "It's French."

"Oh, shit," she said. "And I've been calling it sor-bit all this time. I'm so embarrassed!"

"Oh, don't be," said Stan. "Most Americans call it that."

"But we shouldn't," she said.

I ducked around the counter and saw that she was wearing one of those vintage anti-George Bush shirts that were popular among the protest crowds lately (at least among the ones who couldn't find an old anti-Reagan shirt, which was the real trademark of quality in that scene). If there was one thing Stan liked more than annoying religious customers, it was messing with liberals. As a Libertarian, he really couldn't stand outspoken liberals, unless they were cute enough, in which case he'd pretend to be on their side for a while.

I had learned not to mention politics around him years before. Back in the day when I was with Anna, I would have argued with him toe-to-toe on point after point, but now I just didn't really care enough. I didn't follow the news much at all anymore. I usually just let Edie Scaduto handle the arguments with him.

"You like foreign stuff?" Stan asked the girl. "Like, Euro-trash and J-pop and all of that? Bollywood?"

"Yeah," she said. "Totally."

"Well," said Stan, "I'll tell you what I'm going to do for you. We just started serving this drink that's really big in Japan right now."

"For real?"

"Let me whip you up a sample. No charge."

She smiled at him, and he grinned over at me.

"I had to bug the manager and bug the manager to start serving this," he said, while he pulled supplies from the cabinets. "He keeps thinking that we should stick to just serving American stuff."

"Heh," she said. "Like sorbet?"

"And apple pie. Which is actually German."

She smiled. "Typical."

The apple pie we served was probably made in China, actually.

While I got my apron and hat on, Stan poured some milk into a glass, then mixed in a bit of soda water, the kind we used for Italian sodas, and put it on the counter for the girl.

"There," he said. "Carbonated milk."

"Really?" she said. "This is big in Japan?"

"Everyone there drinks it. I spent a year living there, and we had it with every meal."

"Seriously?"

"Hai, Brianna-san."

He bowed a little and said something else in Japanese. The girl, Brianna, smiled, stared at the glass for a second, then took a sip. I nearly gagged.

"Mmm," she said.

"See?" he asked. "The Japanese believe that carbonating a normal beverage infuses it with vitality."

"Awesome."

I started scrubbing down the counters and helping myself to food while Brianna drank her carbonated milk.

Stan flirted with her for a bit, then turned back to me. "Anything to report?"

"The poem's in the yearbook," I said. "The acrostic."

"Excellent," he said in his best Mr. Burns voice (which was a dead ringer for the real thing). "It's all falling into place. Find the white grape Slushee yet?"

"No."

"Finish *Moby-Dick*?"

"Jesus, man, you nag worse than my parents. I'm just over halfway done."

"How are things going with Paige?"

"Pretty good," I said. "As long as I keep my head down and ignore all the girl drama stuff."

"Oh, God!" Brianna said. "Girl drama. Ugh."

"Yeah," said Stan. "We keep this store a drama-free zone. The back room is, like, a temple of meditation, in a way."

"Oh, really?" Brianna took another sip. Either she was actually enjoying it or she was a heck of an actress.

"Yeah." He smiled.

"Hey, did I tell you I have to take Paige to a debuntante ball?" I asked.

Stan turned from Brianna to me and smiled a very different smile before he turned back towards Brianna.

"Do you hear this?" he asked. "A debutante ball! Like, in a Tennessee Williams play or something. With big fancy dresses and ballroom dancing and rich assholes who don't pronounce the letter *R*!"

"That sounds awful," Brianna said. "I didn't even know they still had those."

"They do," I said, "but the only people who really care about them are the debutantes' moms. It's something to do with the Harvester Club raising money and scholarships and stuff."

"Raising money for rich people?" asked Brianna.

"Dude," said Stan. "You *have* to go. No matter what. You *must* go to that ball."

"I am," I said. "I already told her I'd take her."

"So you have to get a tux and everything?"

I nodded as I poured myself a cup of coffee and lopped in a scoop of the Superman ice cream, which tasted like vanilla but was red, yellow, and blue.

"I work in a suit place," said Brianna. "McIntyre's, downtown. I'll hook you up."

"Noted."

Stan grinned and drummed his fingers together. He kept talking to Brianna for a few minutes, then asked if she wanted to see the "temple of meditation." She followed him into the back, but she didn't get far. After one step in she turned right back out.

"There's a girl with her shirt off back there!"

"That's just Mindy," said Stan. "She won't mind."

"Won't mind what?" asked Brianna. Then she looked down at the half-empty cup in her hand and her face changed from one sort of grimace to another as she put the pieces together. "Oh, fuck," she said.

"I wasn't, like, planning a threesome," Stan said. "I just mean she won't mind if we're back there with her."

"What did you tell her to get her back there?"

"Nothing. She just strolled in," said Stan.

"And took her shirt off?"

Stan nodded, and I had no choice but to back him up. "She does that all the time," I said.

"What the fuck?" asked Brianna. "What, did you tell her it was popular in Sweden to sit around topless?"

"No," said Stan. "I just told her she could take her shirt off if she wanted to."

"Playing Permissions?" I asked.

Stan nodded. "Permissions."

This was one of the most exciting games that had developed in the break room.

"Forget it," said Brianna.

And she stormed out of the place.

"Some Tempter of Humanity you turned out to be," I said.

"Hey, you can't win 'em all. Even Faust got away eventually." Then he grinned and said, "I should have told her Mindy was topless because she's breast-feeding. Protest chicks love that stuff."

"That might have bought you nearly thirty more seconds before she figured out there wasn't a baby back there," I said. Then I laughed a bit. "You should have just told her about Permissions. She might've been into it."

Stan slipped into the back to attend to Mindy just as a car pulled into the driveway. Paige was in it, accompanied by Catherine and Leslie from the yearbook committee. As they came through the front door, Paige gave me a look that translated to, *Fair warning: This is gonna get ugly*.

"Hey, guys!" I said.

Paige smiled and came up to kiss me, then whispered, "Sorry to bring this in here, I just wanted to see you," in my ear.

Before I could even reply, she'd zipped to a table with Leslie and Catherine, and started in on a massive argument about some drama that I couldn't even figure out. A combination of yearbook stuff and girl stuff. I don't know. There was yelling.

This kind of argument, which came up from time to time, brought out a side of Paige that I would have preferred not to see. It would consume her for hours, and would be all she talked about for the rest of the day. About every twenty minutes she'd say, "But I don't even care. It doesn't even matter. I'm done with it," but she never really would be.

The Ice Cave truly was, if nothing else, a low-drama zone, just like Stan said. There were disagreements and all, but most of it could be solved either by Danny punching someone or Stan mixing up a glass of something. If the UN had a grubby break room where everyone could just eat candy and hit each other in the shoulder over a few drinks or a joint, the world would probably run a lot more smoothly.

After a few ugly minutes Paige stood up from the table.

"That's *it*!" she said. "I'm through with this. I don't even care. Whatever."

She walked around behind the counter and took my hand. "Come on," she said. "Let's go to the back."

She tugged my arm, and before I could say anything, she'd opened the door. She took one look in, then pulled her head straight back out. She was blushing bright red.

"I was going to tell you not to go back there," I said.

"Oh my God, I wish you had," she said. "I just saw Stan's butt."

"He's naked?" asked Leslie.

"No," said Paige, "but his pants are down, for some reason."

"They're playing Permissions," I said.

"What's that?" asked Catherine.

"It's pretty much the same thing as truth or dare." I said. "One time we were back there playing that, and someone asked what the consequence was if someone didn't do a dare. And we realized there sort of wasn't one."

"Right," said Leslie. "The reason you do the dares is because deep down, you *want* to."

"Uh-huh. So instead of saying 'I dare you to,' you say 'I give you permission to.' And you can either do it or not. It's kind of liberating, in a way."

"Huh," said Catherine. She had a serious look on her face, and kept staring at the door instead of the people who were talking to her, like she was so busy turning something around in her brain that she didn't have any spare synapses available to send the signals to her neck to get it to move.

Catherine was what I guess you'd call a girl-next-door type. Cute, but more "math tutor" cute than "stripper" cute, if that makes sense. She seemed friendly and sort of innocent when she wasn't yelling about yearbook stuff, and as far as I knew she lived up to that image. She wasn't the sort of girl who got in trouble. She was the sort who would say "shit" now and then, though not usually the f-bomb, and even when she did say words like that she normally didn't say them right out loud; she was the sort who whispered her swears, then giggled and looked around the room, like she was afraid Jesus was going to show up to wash her mouth out with soap.

But now she stared at the door to the back room.

"Can anyone play?" she asked.

"I'm sure you'd be welcome if you wanted to," I said.

Catherine stood up with steely determination and said, "I'm going in."

And she boldly did, leaving just me, Paige, and Leslie standing there. They'd forgotten all about whatever the drama was. I guess nothing ends a fight like someone seeing someone's naked butt.

That's another tip for the UN.

Show your ass, save the world.

"She doesn't strike me as the sort of person who would go back there," I said.

"She normally isn't," said Leslie. "When she used to play The Nervous Game people wouldn't get past her shins. But she's been blogging about how she's sick of being all goody-goody."

"Yeah," said Paige. "I feel like she's been looking for a chance to start her 'doing whatever my parents don't want me to' phase."

"Stan claims another soul," I said.

Meanwhile, Leslie herself was just staring at the door to the back room. "Maybe I'll go back there and just watch," she said. "Someone should keep an eye on Catherine." And she slipped into the back, leaving me alone with Paige. I wouldn't have thought Leslie was the type for that sort of depravity, but I guess everyone knows that dark desires lurk behind the shuttered windows of suburbia.

"You don't want to go back there, do you?" asked Paige.

I shrugged. "Stan's playing Permissions with a bunch of girls, two of whom have never been back there. I almost feel obligated to go be a moderator."

"They can take care of themselves," said Paige. "Leslie's probably done everything that might come up already, and she won't let Catherine do anything she'll regret too much. But you know what?"

"What?"

"Now I've seen *Stan's* butt, and I've never seen yours."

I nodded a bit. "I guess not," I said.

"Every time I get your pants down, we're in the car and you're sitting on it, so I can't see it. I've touched it, but not seen it, unless you count side-butt. That's weird."

"I was halfway sure my mom was going to break out pictures of it from when I was a baby the other night," I said.

"I'll bet it was adorable," she said.

"Modesty forbids."

She smiled. "I give you permission to show it."'

I nodded, turned around, and undid my jeans. If you didn't drop trou in the middle of a shift now and then, it was hard to say what working at the Ice Cave was all about.

When I lowered the back of my boxers, Paige whistled.

Just as the front door opened.

I raced to get my pants back up and turned around. Paige was cracking up, and Big Jake was standing in the doorway, covering his eyes.

"Boy, am I glad it's just you," I said.

Paige was laughing so hard, she had to sit down in one of the booths.

"It's not funny!" I said, even though I was laughing too. "What if that had been some customer with kids or something?"

"Like any of those ever come here," said Jake.

"We just *had* a girl in here who didn't know what it was like," I said. "If *she'd* been the one who saw that, she could probably get us shut down."

"Someone probably *should,*" said Paige. "This place is out of control."

"Not to mention out of the health code," said Jake.

The back door swung open, and Mindy ran out into the store in her bra, waving her shirt above her head like a lasso. She ran around the counter three times, then ran back into the back room.

"Permissions, I presume?" asked Jake.

"Yeah," I said. "Stan and a bunch of girls."

"And me," said Jake, as he bolted for the back room, leaving Paige and me alone again in the cool quiet of the front of the house. Sunlight beamed in through the windows and lit up the freezer, where the antique Willy the Whale ice cream cake kept its lonely vigil.

"Spring is in the air," said Paige. "When everyone wants to get naked and a young man's fancy turns to love."

Love.

I'm pretty sure that was the first time either of us had said that word out loud in front of each other.

She looked at me for a second. She'd tossed the word out as bait and wanted to see if I took it. I waited for a bit to see if she said anything first, and for a second I was panicked all over again and thought she was going to say she loved me. I wasn't sure I ready for that sort of thing.

I didn't get the same frantic feelings about Paige that I used to with Anna.

But this wasn't the same sort of relationship, either. This was a *real* one. An adult one. Maybe saying that word was the logical next step. The next phase.

Maybe falling in love is just about finding someone who is willing to put up with most of your shit if you put up with most of theirs. Making two puzzle pieces fit together, even if they weren't exactly from the same puzzle. Maybe all of that "my whole world is on fire" thing is something else.

Paige and I were still letting the word hang in the air when Stan stepped into the front—fully dressed, but with his boxers tossed casually onto the top of his head, like a beret.

"Debutante ball," he said. "I command you to go to the debutante ball. This is not negotiable. You'd just be fighting with fate."

"We're going," said Paige.

He turned to me, balancing the boxers on his head. They started to slip, so he readjusted them—instead of just resting them on his head, he put them on like a crown, the elastic waistband circling his infernal brow. The legs stuck up above him like rabbit ears.

Or, you know, horns.

Big, floppy horns that probably smelled like ass.

"You're getting a suit?" he asked.

"Yeah," I said.

He bowed, then stood up perfectly straight. "Very good, sir."

A puff of smoke came through the crack in the door to the break room. Stan turned and walked back in, with the greatest amount of dignity and pomp I could possibly imagine for a guy with underpants on his head.

I looked at Paige and she looked at me and said what may have been on both our minds.

"I think you need to find a better place to work, baby."

18. SUITS

Most days when Paige was working at Casa Bravo, I'd swing by for a while at the start of her shift. If it wasn't busy already, I could grab a table in Paige's section and she'd slip me some fries or something.

But some days, when it got busy early or when the manager was being nosy, I was exiled to the little outdoor space by the Dumpsters where the servers came to smoke, and I'd stand around talking with them until Paige found a chance to come out and say hello. This could take a while, but if I left before I saw her, she'd be pretty upset.

On the day my dad was taking me suit shopping, I went straight to the restaurant with Paige after school to wait for him to pick me up. They were already slammed inside, so I headed right for the Dumpsters, where I found myself talking to Chris, a balding server in his midthirties who looked like a washed-up professional wrestler, about *Moby-Dick*. The night before, I'd listened to the section about whale genitals, and I was dying to talk about it with *someone*.

"The whole last three or four CDs have just been the guy going on about whale anatomy and shit," I said. "I didn't think he'd ever get around to talking about whale dicks, but he finally did."

Chris gave this a thoughtful nod as he puffed on his cigarette. "Bet those aren't small."

"Nope. Apparently the sailors used to call that part the 'grandissimus.' They're roughly the size of a whole person."

"So's mine," said Chris.

I almost asked him if he knew a girl named Mindy, but instead I just went on. "Some guy in the book actually takes the skin from one and goes around wearing it like papal robes or something."

"Weird."

"And then when the boat washes up on a desert island, all the natives see him dressed like that and think he's a god. That's what gave George Lucas the idea for the Ewoks and C-3PO."

"Yeah?"

"Nah. I made that last part up."

He flicked his cigarette lazily at the Dumpster. "Paige *said* you were kind of weird," he told me. "What's she like in bed?"

The most obvious response here was, "None of your fucking business, baldy," but before I could say anything, a bunch of other servers showed up at the smoking area, and one of them, a middle-aged woman named Jane, announced that they were about to have a contest to see who could make their mouth look the most like a butt hole. One by one, they pursed their lips together so that they looked like anuses.

The conversations out by the Dumpster were often way, way nastier than anything we ever got up to in the Cave. They had the same pissing contests over which of them was the most fucked up, but there was a bit less pride in their voices. They were older than us, and dealing with stuff like custody issues, getting thrown out of apartments, and shit like that. I think that pretty much every restaurant is like this; all the people your parents don't want you hanging out with in high school seem to grow up to work in food service.

But the smoking area behind Casa Bravo wasn't a permanent den of sin, like the back of the Ice Cave. It was just a little one that existed for five minutes at a time when enough people could sneak away from their tables long enough to smoke, then ceased to exist when the cigarettes were tossed out. Most of the night the space by the Dumpster was just a space by the Dumpster.

The anus-mouthed servers finished smoking and went back inside just as Paige slipped out.

"Hey, baby," she said. "Sorry it took me so long. My tables are all pains in the ass."

"No problem," I said. I kissed her, then asked if she realized that her coworkers were probably actually sicker than mine.

"Yeah," she said. "But I don't smoke, so I'm hardly ever out here when they really get going. I just do my work and go home. At least they work their butts off before they come back here."

She gave me a quick kiss and a squeeze on the ass, then ran inside to get back to her tables. Every minute of downtime was something she had to fight for in her job. The servers at Casa Bravo may have been fucked up, but you couldn't call them slackers. Their jobs were way, way harder than mine.

A minute later my dad texted me to say he was out front in the Casa Bravo parking lot. He was so enthusiastic about seeing me in a suit that he'd offered to buy me one, and I couldn't really afford to say no.

"So, run this by me again," he said as we drove towards downtown. "It's a debutante ball?"

"Technically I guess it's a scholarship cotillion," I said.

"That's even worse!" said Dad. "Do you have to know what kind of fork to use on your grapefruit?"

"I just have to escort Paige down a walkway or something, then mingle and dance around."

"I didn't realize Paige's family was in that kind of circle," he said. "I didn't know we *had* high society in Iowa."

"That's because you and I spend our time at thrift stores, flea markets, and B-list ice cream parlors," I said. "You don't run into the country club set at those."

"Hey, your mother and I go to fancy places sometimes," he said. "We went to the West Egg Steakhouse a while ago."

"When?" I asked.

He thought for a second, then said, "About two years ago, I guess. But in a couple of years when you're out of the house, we'll probably go more."

"What's stopping you now?" I asked. "I'm not home that much as it is, and it's not like you need a babysitter for me."

He didn't have an answer for that, but he nodded for a bit rather than just admitting that he and Mom had turned old and lame.

Mom and Dad were barely into their forties. They were still young, really. At an age when a lot of people these days are just starting to think about settling down and having kids, they were about to enter the kid-free phase of life. They were young enough that they could still probably go to rock concerts and night clubs and stuff and not look completely stupid.

But would they? Nope. Maybe they planned on that when they got married young and had me in their early twenties, but instead they'd probably just bought themselves ten or twenty extra years of playing shuffleboard and watching game shows.

Suckers.

I directed Dad through downtown Des Moines to McIntyre's, the place where Brianna worked. I sort of wanted to talk to her and make sure she wasn't going to organize a protest against us or something.

Inside the store, she was sitting at a counter, wearing a plain black blouse and with her hair in a bun. Seeing her dressed like that, instead of like she was going to a protest rally, made me think about how most of the hippies from the 1960s ended up becoming yuppies in the eighties. But I suppose you shouldn't look too hard for symbolism in people's work uniforms.

Before she noticed us, I was whisked me over to some slick-looking asshole with a tape measure in his hand. My dad put his hand on my shoulder and said, "I have a young man here who needs a suit for a debutante ball."

"You've come to the right place," said the salesman. "The Harverster Club one?"

"That's the one."

He flashed me a no-cavities smile, and I looked around the store and felt sick to my stomach. I wasn't a suit kind of guy. I was so far out of my element in a place like this that I almost wanted to pee on the wall just to make the place seem more agreeably squalid. The suits on the rack seemed like they were closing in around me, ready to swallow me up and spit a yuppie version of me back out.

But I shook the salesman's hand. "Do you have anything made from the skin of a whale's grandissimus?" I asked.

He didn't quit smiling, but I could tell he thought this was going to be a long afternoon.

I waved at Brianna while Dad and the salesman talked about what sort of suits were hot this year (plain dark colors and shades of gray, of course), and she sort of smirked when she saw me. I pretended I was looking at some ties and walked over to her.

"Hey," I said.

"Getting ready for the ball?" she asked.

"What else?"

She smirked again. "You know your coworker is insane, right?"

"Of course I do," I said. "He's been claiming to be Satan since he was at least nine."

"Did he ever really even live in Japan?"

"Not that I know of."

She just smiled and shook her head a bit. "Cute," she said. "I guess he thought he was seducing me or something, right?"

"He probably just wanted to get you to hang out and join in the game they were playing in the back room," I said. "But I sort of feel like I should apologize on his behalf."

She shook her head. "Let me guess," she said. "He spent the next hour talking about what a bitch I was for leaving."

"No," I said. "He can take no for an answer pretty well."

She tilted her head to the side and played with a pen that was on the counter. "Guess I'll give him that, at least," she said.

"Yeah," I said. "I hear that if a guy takes no for an answer and doesn't text you pictures of his scrotum, he's probably ahead of the curve."

"Unfortunately, that's about right. And that carbonated milk was really fucking good."

I leaned in closer and motioned my head toward the salesman. "This guy strikes me as a scrotum texter."

She nodded and leaned in even closer to me to whisper in my ear. "That's Avery. He would probably send me pictures of his asshole as a morning pick-me-up if he didn't know I'd sue him."

"He could just send a shot of his face," I said. "Same difference."

She smirked, and I walked back over to the suit racks, where dad and Avery the salesman started having me try on suits, one after the other.

While we went through suit after suit, each of which looked alike to me, I developed a theory that we think of shopping as a women's activity because it's got to be more fun to shop for women's clothes than men's. Women get to pick out a dress style, the color, the accessories, all kinds of stuff. There are a million kinds of dresses in the world. Suits for men are all pretty much the same. They don't even have plaid ones anymore. I looked. I liked the idea of showing up for the ball dressed up like a used-car salesman from an old movie and telling all the country club people that I owned Crazy Leon's Used Car and Antique Hair Follicle Emporium, just to see how they reacted. Dad probably would have gotten a kick out of that, but he was determined not to walk out of there without getting me into a decent, "for realsies" suit.

I shrugged my way through the whole ordeal, and after a while my dad started getting frustrated.

"Come on, Leon!" he said. "Clothes make the man!"

Avery the Asshole went into what I assume was his standard pitch for no-good teenage slobs.

"Women can't resist a man in a suit," he said. "You put on a well-cut suit, and that shows women you're a man of power, class, style, sophistication. A man of the world."

"I make just over minimum wage," I said. "I haven't been out of Iowa in a couple of years, I haven't got any power, and I'm about as sophisticated as your average baboon."

"That's why you need a suit," said Avery. "You have to fake it 'til you make it."

I was just about to make some sarcastic remark about what it was that I was supposed to make when he leaned over and whispered, "And by 'make it,' I mean make it with your girl."

Then he patted me on the shoulder.

Over at the counter Brianna smirked again and rolled her eyes, like she knew exactly what he'd just whispered in my ear.

"What do you think of Brianna?" he whispered.

"She's nice," I said.

"She's *real* nice," he whispered. "And I happen to know she likes men in suits."

I somehow doubted this, seeing as how she wore protest clothes outside of work. I also doubted that she'd like having her manager, or whoever Avery was, hold her up as a possible prize that you could win if you bought just the right suit.

Avery was wearing a gray suit, so I decided then and there not to get anything gray.

"Fine," I said. "I'll take a black one."

"The popular color this year is really more of a charcoal gray or a midnight blue," said Dad. "Weren't you paying attention?"

"It's the women," Avery said with a wink. "They find *almost*-black less threatening and more comforting than plain black."

"Hey, Brianna," I called out, "do you find men in black threatening?"

"Yes," she said. "Men in gray suits are comforting and approachable. Men in black look like they're coming to take me away."

"See?" asked the salesman. "No one wears all black anymore, unless they're going to a funeral. And you'll scare Brianna."

"Brianna could kick *my* ass," I said, raising my voice enough that she could hear from across the store. "Couldn't you, Brianna?"

"The customer is always right," she called back.

"See?" I asked. "If I'm going to wear a suit, I want to look evil in it."

Dad and the salesman looked at each other.

"Kids," said Dad.

This from a man who once accidentally burned off most of his hair testing a new invention and dyed what was left of it green.

I ended up getting a black suit with a red vest, even though I had to admit that I didn't really pull the look off. Stan would have looked good and evil in it, but I sort of looked like a raggedy butler. That still felt better to me than looking like the asshole who sold it to me, though.

Back in the car, Dad told me that he thought Brianna was flirting with me.

"I doubt that," I said.

"I think she was," he said. "Is that why you wanted to come here? To see her?"

I shrugged. "She and Stan had a bit of a fight yesterday, and I thought I should apologize for him."

"She seemed nice," he said. "Are you and Paige okay?"

I nodded. "Sure."

"Your mom and I thought you and Paige were an unusual match," he went on. "But if it works for you, it works for you."

"That's what I've been thinking," I said. "Relationships are all about taking two puzzle pieces that aren't even from the same puzzle and making them fit."

I suppose I hoped Dad would talk about what a wise young man I'd become when I threw a line like that out, but he just nodded a little.

Paige and I were back out hunting for Slushees the next day. Now that we'd established exactly how we'd celebrate getting the white grape one, she was much more into the whole quest than she had been before. In the days since the five-yen piece appeared on the wall, we'd searched for the Great White Grape Slushee everywhere: among the subdivisions of Ankeny, the split-level houses of Clive, the brick bungalows of Beaverdale, the stately mansions of Sherman Hill, and the neatly ordered streets of downtown Des Moines.

By this time we'd found that we could usually predict what they'd have in each gas station. Casey's General Store usually had the same three flavors at every location, Kum and Go usually had the same four, and Quick Trip had the same six.

But now and then there'd be a wild card, and on that day we found two new flavors: Strawberry Citrus Freeze, and something called Purple Vanilla, which was tasty as hell. "Purple" is a reliably good flavor to start with, and adding vanilla made it practically a gourmet dish, as gas station grub goes. Rather than sharing one, like we usually did, we each got our own. Paige hadn't had a whole one in a long time; she usually just had a sip of mine and got a bottle of juice, if anything. But one makes exceptions for purple vanilla.

When we got to the car, I called Stan.

"We found purple vanilla," I said. "Is that it?"

"Why would purple vanilla be the same thing as white grape?" he asked.

"Well, purple usually means grape, and vanilla-flavored stuff is usually white, right?"

"You've got a fine understanding of junk food semiotics, Harris," Stan said. "But you still haven't found the Great White Grape."

Whether it was the right one or not, purple vanilla was a great discovery. We were both on sugar rushes by the time we adjourned to the nook, where we did a couple of things that we'd never done before. We began with purple mouths, and by the time we finished, other parts of us were purple too. Parts that I'm pretty sure had never been purple on either of us before. We both probably looked like we had leprosy or something, but making each other look like lepers turned out to be both fun and romantic. So much fun that for the first time I felt like I was actually *ready* to go further. Like finding the white grape Slushee was nothing to be afraid of anymore.

And it was still out there, hiding in some far-flung convenience store, as mysterious as love itself.

19. THAR SHE BLOWS

Just before spring break, I finished the layout for the yearbook, and Mr. Perkins officially absolved me of having to serve any further detention hours. As long as I kept coasting through my classes and didn't fail any of them, I was going to graduate right on time.

There was a party at Stan's place that night, and I felt like I'd earned a bit of celebrating. Paige was reluctant to go, though, and peppered me with questions as we drove towards his house on Sixtieth Street.

"Is Molly going to be there?"

"Who?"

"Molly," she said. "You know. The drug. Not the person."

I almost snorted. "There'll be some pot, but you'd probably get laughed at if you asked for Molly."

"I wouldn't ask, I'm just wondering what to expect."

"Just imagine a party that someone might have thrown after a Black Sabbath concert in 1974, if you can."

"Will there be anything to drink besides beer?"

"What do you usually have at football parties?"

"Wine coolers. Stuff like that."

Now I imagined Stan with a blender and slices of real fruit, mixing up frozen pink drinks, and I laughed out loud. We weren't fancy down there. It was a working-class place with wood-paneled walls and an earthy aroma.

"They probably won't have those."

She moved her hand to my thigh. "Are you sure you don't want to go on a Slushee hunt instead?"

I thought this over. I'd been looking forward to the party, but it wasn't really going to get going for a while, and we'd been having so much fun on Slushee hunts that it was hard to say no. Better to at least start out doing something I knew we'd both like instead of something I had to talk Paige into.

So I changed course and headed south down Merle Hay Road, and turned onto University Avenue. Paige smiled and took my right hand and played with my pinky finger while I steered with the left one. Ishmael rambled on, as usual. We only had a few CDs to go by now. Most of the time I didn't pay much attention to him.

We wound up near Waukee, and as we sat at a red light, it happened. The guy on the audiobook said the most famous line from the book: "Thar she blows! A hump like a snow hill! It is Moby Dick!"

"Holy shit," I said. "They really *do* say that!"

"Go back, let's listen again," said Paige.

I scanned back a few seconds.

"Thar she blows! A hump like a snow hill! It is Moby Dick!"

The sky split open wide, golden beams rained down from the Heavens, and a gathering of angels appeared above our heads, singing songs of hope. That's what it felt like, anyway.

I rolled down the windows and Paige shouted, "Woooo!"

I honked the horn and flashed the headlights.

When we got to the next traffic light, Paige leaned over and hugged me. We kissed until the light turned green, and I felt like I was the King of the Audiobook Listeners. Like I had truly done something great. Something I could be proud of. I guess it's not the same as curing a disease or putting out a fire or getting into Harvard, but finally making it all the way to the most famous line in *Moby-Dick* really feels like a magnificent accomplishment. I'd had to listen to a whole *lot* of Ishmael rambling on and not making any sense to get there. But we'd made it to "Thar she blows, a hump like a snow hill, it is Moby Dick," and now the end of the book was in sight. And Paige and I had done it together, more or less.

"This calls for a Slushee," I said. "Any Slushee. Have we been to this gas station up ahead?"

"I don't think so."

"Let's go. Maybe they'll at least have that Purple Vanilla one again."

She smiled. "You want me to turn you purple before we go to the party?"

"I'll turn *you* purple, baby."

"Now *that's* what a girl wants to hear."

A Kum and Go loomed ahead of us like Camelot. The Promised Land. Mecca. The Emerald City. Whatever.

"We should get some candy bars too," she said as we stepped in. "This calls for a celebration."

"Candy bars, hot dogs . . . everything they have on sale. Nothing in the gas station is too good for my baby."

I looked over to the counter and realized that the clerk was that same pirate-looking one who had been at the store on Hickman, the one who seemed like a time-traveling version of myself. I was about to go say hello to him when Paige grabbed my arm and said, "Uh, baby?"

She pointed over to the Slushee machine, and there it was.

Three flavors. Cherry limeade, blue Mountain Dew, and white grape.

I fell to my knees on the dirty ground. Our quest was at an end.

We kissed again, filled two cups, and took them to the counter.

"So it was real after all," I said to the guy.

"Yeah," he said as he took my money. "Thought of you guys when I saw it. Shit."

I threw all of the change into the "take a penny leave a penny" tray, as a sort of offering, and we took the fabled Slushees out to my car. They were delicious. The fact that white grapes may not have been an actual fruit didn't matter—no grape-flavored product tastes like anything that occurs in nature.

I felt like we could have driven all the way to Chicago and harpooned a whale at the aquarium that night.

But we hardly talked as we sat in my car. We just looked at each other and smiled and slurped at our straws.

Neither of us had forgotten what we'd planned to do the night we found the Great White Grape Slushee. I finally broke the silence by saying something stupid.

"Too bad we're not wearing white," I said. "Then if anyone saw us doing it, they could call it a hump like a snow hill."

"If you keep saying things like that, I won't want to do it anymore."

"Fair enough," I said. "I assume your parents are home?"

She nodded. "And Autumn's having a slumber party, too, so going there is totally out, unless you want to give them a lesson."

I didn't seem to me like there was a lot Autumn didn't already know.

"Would someone rent us a hotel room, or do you need a credit card?"

"I have my dad's, but I don't want to have to explain the charge," she said. "We could just use the nook at Earthways, though."

"You really want to do it in the car?" I asked.

"I don't care," she said as she pulled her hair back into a ponytail. "I just want to do it tonight. A car's better than Stan's laundry room, at least. We can do it better some other time."

I took another sip of my Slushee, then went back into the Kum and Go to buy a thing of condoms (which, by the way, struck me as a hilarious thing to do).

Paige put her hand on my knee as we drove back through the west suburbs to Cornersville Trace. The sun was down now, and the pavement stretching out before us glowed like gold under the orange haze of the street lights. The sky was the color of a purple vanilla Slushee above us, and it complimented Paige's eyes when I looked over at her, which I did whenever we came to a stop sign. By the time we got to Earthways, it was dusk.

Everything seemed beautiful. It was a new-made night.

But I don't mind saying I was still nervous as hell. Part of the reason I'd agreed to do it when we found the white grape Slushee was that I wasn't sure we ever actually *would*. Paige probably wasn't going to want to pretend to be Nurse Paige the first time we did it—she'd want it to be just the two of us, Leon and Paige, our souls touching, and all of that shit.

I still wasn't sure I could live up to what she wanted.

But a deal was a deal, and I felt like I was ready to give it a try.

There was just one minor complication: When we got to the back of Earthways, a car—Leslie's, according to Paige—was in the nook, rocking enough that the edges bumped into the brick walls now and then.

We sat there and sort of laughed for a second at the general absurdity of the whole night.

"I wish we had one of those lovers' lanes, like they always do on TV," Paige said. "Every town like this on TV has some place where you can park on a cliff and look out over the whole city."

I nodded, then took a sip of my Slushee and had a minor epiphany. "Hey," I said. "I've been thinking white grapes weren't a real thing, but if they aren't, what do they make white wine out of?"

"Huh," she said. "Maybe it's just another name for green grapes."

"So this is, like, a chardonnay Slushee," I said. "Class and a *half*."

"A nonalcoholic wine cooler."

We toasted with our Slushees and thought about driving around the block, but if we did, some other car might come and snatch up the nook the second Leslie left. We ended up waiting until her car backed out and pulled away.

It was a tight enough spot that we couldn't open the doors, so we clumsily climbed over the front seats to get to the back, got as comfortable as we could, and started making out. Our mouths were cold from the Slushees, and so was her left hand, the one she'd been using to hold her cup and was now using to touch me. But then we rotated a bit; her right hand, the one that had been by the heat vent in the car, was warm.

And pretty soon, the rest of her had warmed up too.

The windows fogged up, we took off our shirts, and then, for the first time, all the rest of our clothes. We'd shoved them out of the way before, but never taken everything off. Undressing in a crowded car required some regular acrobatics, and took a couple of tries, but at least laughing at our own inability to get undressed without elbowing each other in the head kept the mood light.

When we were naked, I held her against me as she sat facing me on my lap. Her skin felt fantastic against mine. There's no feeling in the world like feeling someone's skin against yours.

She looked into my eyes while she moved her hands up and down my bare sides.

"I love you, Leon," she said.

For a second I panicked, but then I heard myself saying, "I love you, too."

She kissed me hard on the mouth and I moved my hands up to her breasts, then slid them down her body, and we slowly progressed from there.

I did my job about as well as anyone probably could, under the circumstances. The actual sex was awkward, sweaty, a little painful, and hampered a bit by the added pressure of knowing that another car had pulled into the back of Earthways and was waiting its turn to use the nook.

But we took our time.

And it isn't saying much, but whatever might have been wrong with it, it was the best I had ever had.

I think she was lying, but she told me it was the best she'd had too. Even if she *was* lying, it was a lot better than saying, "Well, it's not what I'm used to." There are some times when you just don't want the other person to be completely honest with you.

As we drove off, I felt . . . accomplished. I'd made it clear to "Thar she blows," found the mysterious white grape Slushee (which turned out to be the ideal precoital iced novelty beverage), and managed to hold up my end of the deal sexually, even without her pretending to be a nurse or anything. Just knowing I was capable of having sex at all made me feel like a huge burden had been lifted off of my back and was now floating away towards the stars that shone down in the central Iowa skies.

It was only late that night, when I got home, that I turned my phone on and saw that there was a voice mail from a UK phone number.

20. MIDNIGHT

The fact that I'd first had sex with Paige about fifty feet away from the spot where Anna and I kissed in the snow had not escaped me. I wished it had, but it hadn't.

Neither had the fact that Anna probably would have liked my "hump like a snow hill" joke, or at least pretended to, even though it was pretty awful. Or the fact that Paige's remark about the "non-alcoholic wine cooler" might have symbolized me becoming more like the kind of people *she* normally hung out with and less like I fit in with all the old gifted pool hooligans who circulated among the Ice Cave and went to parties in Stan's basement.

I had made a point of not programming Anna's new number into my phone, but I knew that the voice mail had to be from her. My instinct was to delete it without listening to it. What good could come of it? I was with Paige now. I was in love.

But at two in the morning, as I lay awake in bed, I couldn't shake the voice in my head saying that the kiss with Anna had been way better than the sex with Paige.

That wasn't fair. All of the conditions were right for that kiss. It was an event that I'd prayed would happen, and never quite believed would, and everything in the environment had made it seem more romantic and monumental. There's no reason that a first proper kiss in conditions like that *shouldn't* seem more earth-shattering than sex in a car parked in a place that was designed to hold a Dumpster. Especially with someone in another car behind you, waiting for you to finish and flashing their lights like assholes.

And it's not like Anna and I *really* changed the weather that night. The snow would have kept falling and shut the schools down whether the two of us had kissed or not. If she had said, "So, anyway," and pulled back, it just would have seemed like a storm had come to bury all my hopes and dreams under the thick blanket of snow.

I thought of going back to Paige's house and trying to sneak into her bedroom, where we might be able to do it better.

I thought about going to Stan's. I had almost forgotten that there was a party going on.

I thought about getting some bottles from the cabinet and using them to help me get to sleep.

Then I gave in and pushed the button on my phone to listen to the voice mail.

"Hi, Leon, it's Anna. Can you give me a call when you get this? Sometime when it's not the middle of the night, preferably. See ya!"

I listened to it five or six times in a row, then calculated that it was about eight in the morning in the UK.

That was probably late enough that she'd be up. I could get this out of the way.

She knew who it was right away when she answered.

"Hi, Leon!"

"Hey," I said. "What's up?"

"Just catching up," she said. "My dad got an offer for a job at Drake."

"Yeah?"

"For about five minutes we actually talked about moving back to Des Moines."

My heart rose and sank all at the same time. It moved sideways, I guess.

"But just for about five minutes?" I asked.

"Yeah."

"So you're not coming back?"

"Doesn't look like it," she said. "He'll probably go in for a meeting, but that'll be it. I'm probably going to Oxford, anyway. Are you springing for something out of state, or sticking around Iowa?"

"I don't know," I said. "I'm going to wait a semester or two first, and save money. I didn't even sign up for the SAT until a few days ago."

"Really?" she asked. When I didn't answer, she chuckled a bit. "Remember when we did that whole thing with the Gradgrind test in eighth grade?"

"Yeah, that was a kick."

That was our last truly great gifted pool initiative, the one we referred to in our notes and e-mails as "Operation Take This Test (and Shove It)." We told the school that we'd throw the test—like, fill in random circles on the Scantron sheets—if they wouldn't cut us in for a chunk of the funding they'd get to reward our high scores. We were the gifted pool, after all. They needed us to get the average scores higher. Of course, they ended up just threatening to expel us all instead of offering to pay us, but it was worth a shot.

"Have you guys pulled any more big pranks like we used to do?" she asked.

"Nah," I said. "Not really."

"Really?" she asked. "Nothing?"

"I slipped a poem with a Satanic message into the yearbook," I said. "And the other day I accused Mrs. Smollet of eating the placentas of teen mothers to preserve her youth. But that's about it. Nothing anyone's noticed."

"Huh," she said. "I kind of imagined you guys being the terror of Des Moines."

"We mostly just hang around in the back of the Ice Cave these days," I said. "Remember that place? Right next to Sip?"

"I think I only went once or twice," she said. "Has it gotten better?"

"No. And there's a Willy the Whale ice cream cake in the freezer that I'm sure was there before you moved."

"Huh," she said. "And you hang out there, not at Sip?"

"Well, Dustin and I work there," I said. "And the break room is sort of a hangout now. The coffee isn't as a good as Sip, but it's free."

"Huh," she said again.

I felt as though she was pretty disappointed in me. She probably figured we were out occupying the banks or something.

We talked for a few more minutes, then she had to head off to class. I collapsed onto my bed, still fully dressed and now feeling almost exactly as bad as I had the last time I'd spoken to her.

My head was spinning, though maybe not in the same directions as it had been before.

Anna was going to Oxford, probably. And I was just thinking that maybe I could get into community college.

All at once I was fourteen again, wondering if I could ever possibly be cool enough to be with Anna, or if she was completely out of my league. She sure was now.

But what did it matter? She was gone, she wasn't coming back, and I had just told Paige I loved her.

Maybe it was time I just broke off ties from everyone from middle school and started hanging around more with Paige's friends. There was no reason to go on feeling sick with myself for not acting like a person who wasn't even me anymore. Who's still the same person at eighteen that they were at fourteen? Who the hell *should* be?

Suddenly, I found myself fretting about what I'd be doing with Paige for the rest of the school year. Our Slushee-hunting career was probably over—even if there was another flavor we hadn't tried, hiding in some far-flung gas station, I didn't think Paige would be into the quest anymore.

When they found the great white whale, the sailors in *Moby-Dick* all went off to die. What would *I* do after finding the white Slushee?

The one other activity Paige and I tended to agree on was fooling around. The thought that there was probably a lot of sex in my future *should* have been encouraging, but somehow it wasn't.

Eventually I gave up on getting to sleep, crawled out of bed, and drove clear back to the gas station in Waukee to get another white grape Slushee. I put it in my cup holder and drove to Stan's house. With everything else that had happened, I'd almost forgotten that there was a party going on.

Things were well underway by the time I got there. The air was thick with at least three kinds of smoke, music was blasting, and a Dungeons and Dragons game was sitting abandoned on the table next to a large pile of lunch meat packets and a thing of mustard.

In the flickering light of the TV screen I could see that a couple of people I didn't even recognize were dry humping on the couch, and I watched for a minute to see if I could pick up some pointers or something, but they didn't really seem like they were having much fun. They were just kind of attacking each other. The kind of sex that any idiot can have if they've had a few energy drinks.

Three girls sat around a bong near the TV in the back corner where a couple of guys I didn't recognize were playing video games. Dustin Eddlebeck was huddled against a wall by the table, talking and laughing with Catherine, who was doing a bad job of trying not to look at Mindy and a naked guy who were dancing across the room. Catherine had survived her game of Permissions, and was now hanging out in Stan's basement. She and Dustin were eating plain lunch meat out of a bag that they shared. Her journey towards the dark side was complete.

Stan was sitting on his throne. He surveyed the whole scene with a smile, and laughed triumphantly when I presented him with the white grape Slushee. Red lights flashed on the TV screen and lit up his face.

"Well done, young minion," he said, as he took it from my hands.

"I guess we need another task now," I said.

"You want another one?"

"I need something I can talk to her friends about besides turds."

"So? That works, right?"

"Yeah, but now I'm starting to get a reputation as the Poop Guy."

He nodded and took a long sip of the Slushee. "It will pass. Soon, there will come a great plague and the halls will flow with the blood of the unbeliever."

"Right."

"Indubitably."

"Naturally."

"So let it be written, so let it be done."

Paige was probably asleep by then, in her comfortable bed, with the stuffed turtle that she always slept with. I wished I was there with her, instead of getting a contact high and a headache in a filthy basement. The stains on the ceiling—the ones I didn't dare ask about—took on cryptic and threatening shapes above me, and a sick feeling gnawed at my spleen. Or maybe it was my liver. I coasted through biology.

Staring at the stains is the last thing I remember before I fell asleep. I don't remember having a drink, but I woke up with a splitting headache on Stan's floor.

A few other people were asleep in chairs and on the floor, and some others were awake, in various states of undress and sobriety. Those who were awake were stumbling slowly around the basement like zombies in a graveyard looking for brains.

21. POISON

Over the rest of spring break I tried to work as many extra hours as I could, just to have enough money for the time I spent with Paige. Those places with crazy crap on the walls and cheese sticks on the menu weren't cheap.

Even sex cost more than you'd think. There were bribes to pay.

Paige's parents both worked outside of the house during the day (unlike my mother, who worked out of a home office), so the only real obstacle to us getting any privacy at her place during the day was her sister, who was pretty hard to get rid off. On Monday afternoon while Paige and I were watching TV on her couch, Paige got up and walked over to Autumn, who was sitting at the kitchen table, talking on the phone.

"I'll give you five bucks to get out of the house for an hour," she said.

"Where would I even go?" asked Autumn.

"Outside. Go play at the tot lot or something."

"I'm almost thirteen," said Autumn. "I don't play in tot lots."

"Then go sit on the swings and talk with your friends. I don't care. Just go."

Autumn rolled her eyes. "Look," she said, "I know you guys are going to have sex. Just go ahead. I won't tell."

"But you won't give us any privacy, either."

"I won't peek."

"But you'll be sitting outside the door, taking notes and probably recording everything on your phone."

"So what?"

She eventually got out of the house for fifteen bucks, and Paige and I took full advantage of the privacy. Beds really are much better than cars or piles of laundry.

That day was my first experience with serious, post–sex cuddling. You can only do so much of that in a car with someone flashing his lights at you, and all I wanted to do after being with Mindy and Brenda was leave. You never want to stay on the field long after you lose a game.

In Paige's bed we just cuddled up to each other. Her hair tickled my shoulder and smelled fantastic, and her down comforter was cool against my skin.

And even though her boobs were *right there,* I found myself staring below them at her stomach moving up and down as she breathed. Lying there with her next to me, calm and breathing, was a whole new kind of feeling.

We did it in her room again on Tuesday while Autumn was at the mall, then used the nook on Wednesday.

Thursday morning, Stan and I were working when Autumn and a bunch of her girlfriends came into the Cave.

Middle-school kids tend to be a big pain in the ass as customers. Half of them just order water, and the other half are really picky and demanding about exactly how they want their sundaes made. They stay for hours, make a giant mess, and never tip. I made a point of not getting too upset, since I did the same kind of thing in middle school myself, but Autumn and her friends got on my nerves, and every second around them inched me closer to being an old bastard who sat around complaining about how kids today are different, with their skatin' boards and their velcro shoes.

At least *my* friends in middle school had been smart. Autumn's friends might have been smart individually, but together they seemed to be dumber than the sum of their parts.

They showed up in a group of five, and we saw them coming.

"Looks like we're in the soup now, old sport," Stan said.

"We should drill for this sort of thing," I said.

Autumn pointed me out from the doorway as soon as they came in.

"That's him," she announced. "That's the guy who has sex with my sister."

"Is that true?" one of them called to me.

I just said, "Welcome to the Ice Cave. What do you want?"

"See?" asked Autumn. "He doesn't even deny it."

They lurched towards the counter like bears coming up to a parked car in the forest looking for picnic baskets.

"Is her sister good in bed?" one of them called up to me.

"Does she, like, wipe down his forehead first?" one of them asked the others, as though I couldn't hear them. "He has a really greasy forehead."

"I wouldn't want to see him naked," said another. "The rest of him's probably greasy too."

They all giggled and poked each other and made jokes about the zit that I had on my nose. Like *they* didn't all have a million of them under the metric ton of makeup they wore.

I couldn't help but think that if it was a *girl* behind the counter and a bunch of *guys* came in talking like that, everyone with any sense would agree that the guys were being complete assholes.

I wasn't getting any sympathy from the devil, though. Stan was laughing his ass off at me.

"And my sister said he's kind of a cannibal, too," Autumn said.

"You mean he eats *her*?" asked one of the friends.

When they stopped cracking up, which took a while, the group converged into a circle, and Autumn explained that I once ate a bit of Beethoven's hair. I couldn't believe Paige had told her that story. Stan listened in eagerly, occasionally glancing over at me.

"Is that true?" one of the girls asked me.

"So I'm told," I said.

"Now the real question," Stan said, loud enough to make it clear he was really talking to *them*, not to me, "is this: Are you sure it was a bit of hair from his *head*?"

The girls all erupted in giggles and shrieks. Shrieks, mostly.

"What do *you* think it was?" I asked.

He shrugged. "Maybe the undertaker was like, 'Hey, I want a souvenir. Pull down his pants and give me the scissors."

The girls howled. I thought about going to the back and just letting Stan handle the giggling horde himself, but Mindy was back there and I sure as hell didn't want to be alone in a room with her. I stood there and stuck it out.

"Even if they aren't pubes, that's disgusting!" one of them said. "Who buys pieces of dead people to start with?"

"My dad," I said.

"Your dad must be a freak," said Autumn.

"That means you probably are too," said one of the girls. "Everyone grows up to be just like their parents, even if they hate them."

"You better break them up, Autumn," someone said, "or you'll get a weirdo for a nephew or something."

"He uses condoms," said Autumn. "I found one of the wrappers in Paige's room."

I looked over at Stan with pleading eyes. This was getting *way* out of hand. He nodded and put a hand on my shoulder.

"I've got this," he whispered. "Don't worry."

Then he jumped up onto the counter.

"So, girls," he said. "Enough about Leon. Which of you would like to join the Nontoxic Club?"

They all just sort of stared at him.

"Come on," he said. "The Nontoxic Club. You get free ice cream for joining."

"I'm in," said one of them.

He grabbed some cash from the register, handed it to me, and said, "Go to Target and get some tempera paints and paint brushes. Make sure the paint says 'nontoxic' on the label."

I took off, avoiding the leers I was getting from Autumn. I'm sure I heard her say the word "thingie" as I walked past. Christ, my friends never talked about sex *that* much in middle school. And I hung around with Dustin Eddlebeck.

When I came back, the girls were all sitting at the largest of our few tables, with sugar cookies in front of them. Stan presided over the scene, taking questions and making sure they didn't eat their cookies ahead of time.

"Yeah," he was saying. "It's *kind of* like the Clean Plate Club, only it's not for idiots. Leon, you want to give all of these ladies paintbrushes?"

I did, and Stan grabbed the multicolored tempera paints I had picked up and poured some of each color into paper cups. The Ice Cave was starting to look like the arts and crafts cabin at a summer camp or something.

"All right," said Stan. "Your first job is to decorate your cookie. Paint it up however you want. Express yourselves."

And the girls all set to work. In a few short minutes the five teenyboppers had produced really girly looking cookies, with hearts and the names of their favorite singers and stuff.

I could imagine how my friends would have decorated cookies at that age. Anna would have probably done something truly artistic, a cookie suitable for framing. Edie Scaduto probably would have painted on a hammer and sickle, like on the Soviet flag. I probably would have done the Metallica logo, and maybe my best attempt at the bloodstain and hammer from the *Kill 'Em All* album cover. It wouldn't have come out as well as I'd imagined it.

Paige, meanwhile, probably would have made one like her sister was making. That was kind of scary to consider, but I pushed it out of my mind.

"Everybody done?" said Stan.

"Yeah," said one of the girls. "Can we have our ice cream now?"

"You're not in the club yet," said Stan. "First you have to eat the cookie you just decorated."

They all went, "Ewwww."

"That's not safe," said one of them.

"Sure it is," said Stan. "This paint is nontoxic. Only an idiot would market poison in a container with a cartoon bear on it."

The girls all sort of shook their heads and giggled nervously.

"Jesus," I said. "Not to sound like an old geezer, but when I was your age, my friends and I would have eaten them."

"Then *you* do it," said Autumn.

Well, that was it. The gauntlet was laid down.

"Fine," I said, "just give me a cookie. I'll eat one if you guys do."

Stan gave me a cookie, and I got to work painting a Metallica logo on it. In black, with a red background. I covered the whole surface of the cookie.

"All right," I said, while Stan dealt with an actual customer. "Give it a minute to dry, and I'll eat it. But you all have to promise to eat yours, too."

"All of us?" one of them asked.

"At least one of you, or no one gets free ice cream."

They all kind of discussed it among themselves, daring each other. After a minute I blew on the cookie to make sure it was dry, then wolfed it down. It just tasted about like any other sugar cookie, really. The paint didn't get on my tongue at all.

"Mmm," I said.

I could have done something lame like falling to the floor and twitching around and playing dead, but I didn't. I needed the kids to know I was serious. I had to set a good example and act like a proper, mature paint-eater.

"See?" asked Stan. "He didn't keel over and die, and now he's a member of the Nontoxic Club, worthy of all benefits and privileges pertaining thereto. Now, which of *you* is going to join the club?"

"You think we're going to survive something just because a greasy guy who eats pubes did?" one of them asked.

It was a fair question, but Stan went into full-on temptation mode.

"I don't think you want it spread around that you're a bunch of wimps," he said. "Or that you're not worth partying with. That's the kind of reputation that could follow you to high school."

And he went on like that, telling them all the wonders of high school parties and popularity that could all be theirs if one of them just ate a painted cookie, and how unpopular they could become if they didn't.

"Fine," said Autumn. "I'll do it if you'll shut up. But you all owe me!"

There was hardly any actual paint on her cookie—just a swirly pink line or two. When she took one bite, she might have gotten a tiny bit of paint in her mouth, but not much. Still, she looked like she was going to puke.

"There," she said. "Is that enough?"

"Whole thing," said Stan.

She cringed, then another girl, one I didn't think had said a word the whole time, picked up her own cookie and slowly, methodically, ate the entire thing.

"Welcome to the Nontoxic Club," said Stan.

They all got their free ice cream, but they left as soon as they finished eating—kind of fleeing the scene, I guess. The same way you want to leave the laundry room after an embarrassing sexual episode.

"Once upon a time," said Stan, "I took Jesus on top of a mountain and offered him the world and everything in it if he'd worship me. Now I'm just offering teenyboppers help getting into high school parties if they eat nontoxic paint."

"Seems like you could have found an easier way to get rid of them," I said.

"Maybe. But this was more fun."

An hour or so later Paige came flying into the store, looking pissed.

"Did you make my sister eat paint?" she asked.

I shrugged. "It was just a painted cookie. It was nontoxic paint."

She gave me a nasty look. "What the *hell* were you thinking?"

"I ate one too," I said. "And mine had a lot more paint on it than hers."

"Look," said Stan. "It's my fault. But they were in here talking about sex and what Leon looks like naked. All it takes is *one* of them to go home and say we were talking about sex with them, and next thing you know the story turns into Leon flashing them or something, and half the people in town will believe it, and they'll shut this place down."

"So you made her eat paint?"

"I changed the subject and did something to get them to leave," he said. "I'm in favor of all forms of sin and perversion, but I'm not going to do anything stupid."

"He saved my ass," I said.

Paige glared at us. She was clearly trying her best to remain calm, but she wasn't succeeding. It was the same look she got when yearbook and girl-world drama got into her head.

"Look," she said, "no one thinks that Autumn is more annoying than I do, but she's my sister. And now she's crying and freaking out and saying she needs to go have her stomach pumped."

Just then, Mindy strolled out of the back room.

"Hi, hon," she said to Paige.

Paige gave her a nasty look, then gave me a nastier one. The stabbing look.

"And *she's* here?" she asked.

"Hey, I didn't invite her," I said.

She reached out and held my hand, but not with much affection or anything.

"My love," she said, "I think you're starting to understand now that we belong together."

I gulped, but I nodded.

"Well," she said, "I'm not going to be stuck with a loser who hangs out with other losers forever. I don't want to spend my whole life cleaning up your messes."

"You won't," I said.

"Or bailing you out of jail when these idiots talk you into doing something stupid."

"You won't," I said.

"Or listening to you apologizing when I catch you with some skank you didn't know you were flirting with."

"Look, I didn't invite Mindy over, and I haven't even gone back there all day. If I had, I would have been able to avoid your sister and her pervert friends."

Paige took a deep breath. "I know that," she said. "But don't you think you should find a better place to work than this?"

"I like it here," I said.

"But if you worked someplace else, you could make more money and not have fucking *Mindy* show up all the time," said Paige.

Mindy smirked, then said, "Well, fuck you too."

Paige ignored her.

"Also," she went on, "I wouldn't have to reassure my idiot sister that she isn't going to die because some dumbass made her eat paint because she *might* have been talking about his dick."

"She *definitely* was," I said.

"So?" she asked. "What are you worried about? I told her you were above average."

I wished Stan would snap his fingers and turn the whole store into a lake of fire right about then. I didn't dare to look at Mindy to see how she reacted to that one.

"You *told* her that?" I asked.

"What's the big deal?"

"Is that even legal?" I asked. "Talking about stuff like that with a kid her age?"

"Sorry, okay?" said Paige. "It's not like you haven't told all the people back there about fucking me."

"No, I haven't," I said.

"You haven't told them we did it?"

Stan and Mindy snickered like a couple of seventh graders.

"I told you," I said. "Guys sound like douche bags when we talk about sex."

"Yeah," said Stan. "Girls sound liberated, guys sound like douche bags. That's just the way it is."

I nodded. "We may be a motley crew of damned and forsaken souls around here, but we aren't *douche bags*."

"Whatever," said Paige. "If it bugs you so much, I won't talk about it anymore. But that's no excuse to make my sister eat paint."

"Sorry," I said. "We won't do it again."

"Do you have enough money to take me to dinner and a movie tonight?" she asked. "And pay for both of us?"

"Not really," I said.

"You *need* a better job," she said. "This place is shit. You might as well just turn in pop cans for nickels, like a fucking eight-year-old."

And she walked out, leaving me feeling like a complete asshole.

So this was love.

I remembered the night she'd first come to my house excited to be with me even though I was a complete bum. I wouldn't have believed that someone like her could ever love someone like me.

Now, I was starting to realize that love is like one of those songs where you have to play the whole thing backwards to hear all the hidden messages.

22. LOVE

Love is like a middle-school dance: You're supposed to be having a good time, but mostly you just stand around questioning your value as a human being and thinking that maybe you should have stayed home.

Love is also like a Slushee: It's so sweet, but so, so messy, and deep down you know, from the first sip, that the smooth texture won't last, and after a few sips your tongue will be too numb to taste much, and pretty soon there'll be nothing left in the cup but some shaved ice that takes more work than it's really worth to suck through the straw at all.

Love is like a blanket on the bed in a cheap motel you check into when the rainstorm gets too hard to drive your leaky car in. It's warm and dry and feels like just what you needed, but you can't help thinking that it might very well give you a rash.

Love is like a maze of mirrors. No map can help you through it because you can never quite tell where you're going. Also, you're likely to see sides of yourself that you normally don't.

Love is like putting on a new pair of glasses that makes you experience the whole world differently. You hear birds chirping and bells ringing, and you feel soft breezes and notice that the flowers on the trees smell like Heaven. But sometimes you also notice the weeds growing up through the cracks, the noisy floorboards, the rattle in your engine, the hole in your shoe, the stains on the ceiling, and everything else that never bothered you before, and now it drives you nuts.

Love is the feeling that your life is finally about to begin. But that's one thing when you're younger and think being an adult will be awesome, and another when you know it's all about busting your ass to have a stainless-steel kitchen and shit.

Love is a whole new gnawing feeling in your guts. And it doesn't replace the old one. You just have to hope that it compliments it.

Love is something you get by without for a long time, but once you find it, you can't imagine life without it anymore. Which seems like a good thing, but you could say the same thing about a colostomy bag, probably.

Love is like fitting two puzzle pieces from two different puzzles together. You try not to think about the fact that the original puzzles they came from will never be quite the same, or that the new picture they'll make might look all wrong.

Fuck.

23. MARKETING

By the time I got home from work that day, Paige had sent me links to about fifty restaurants in town that let you apply for jobs online. They all said they were looking for people who were self-motivated, friendly, and detail oriented.

I wanted to just write "Fuck detail orientation, you bigoted scum" right into the name field, but I didn't. Paige was right. I was never going to amount to anything worth being if I just kept working at the Ice Cave forever. I still didn't mind the idea of not amounting to anything so much, but if I was ever going to move out of my parents' house, and have enough cash on hand to get cheese sticks and things now and then, I was going to need a job that paid better. It's one thing to be broke and living in a tiny hovel with cars up on cinder blocks in the yard if you're single, but having a girlfriend isn't cheap. So I filled out the applications.

None of them asked what my grades were like, so I had *that* going for me. Most just wanted a résumé. A few had a box in which you were supposed to answer the question "Why do you want to work on our award-winning team?"

I usually just put "so I can gain real-world experience with a successful organization." That was bullshit, of course, but it sounded better than "for the cash." A lot of would-be employers hate to hear that, for some reason. You'd think they'd like honesty, but people seriously expect you to say you always dreamed of being a fry cook.

I couldn't resist messing around with a couple of them, though. One was a place clear out in Altoona, which was farther than I wanted to commute. With that one I added a part in my résumé saying that I was a wide receiver on the school crotch-kicking team. A wise manager would look at that and think, *Let's hire him! A guy who can be a wide receiver on a crotch-kicking team can probably take a lot of torture.*

On another one, for a place clear the hell in Indianola, I even added a bit about how I had led the crotch-kicking team to the state championship, despite the notable handicap of only having one leg. "The guys who are making a movie about me say I'm a hero," I wrote. "But I'm just an ordinary, detail-oriented young man who won't let adversity stand between me and my love of kicking people in the crotch."

At the West Egg Steakhouse there was another question: "Describe a time when you've utilized outstanding leadership skills."

That just about made me want to barf. I was applying for a job working in a restaurant, not rallying armies to cross mighty rivers into battle or bossing whale hunters around.

I figured that the West Egg Steakhouse was *way* out of my league, being a fancy downtown steakhouse, so I decided to have some fun with my answer:

Last year in school I took a class on marketing. My group had to develop a new product idea and then make a commercial for it. The other people in my group were slackers, but with my leadership, we developed a concept for a breakfast cereal called Nards. The commercial we made was so good that everyone in the class wished they were eating Nards right then! I was fascinated by the psychology behind it, and how marketing could make people get so excited about Nards. Maybe I can make it for real sometime, and you can sell it at the West Egg. You could even put it on the sign. WEST EGG STEAKHOUSE: EAT NARDS HERE!

That, of course, was the one application that got a response.

The day after I sent it in, the West Egg Steakhouse called me in for an interview. I halfway thought they were kidding, but I cleaned myself up as well as I could and drove out there after school.

The manager there was a younger guy, maybe thirty or thirty-five, who had his hair slicked back. He was wearing a midnight-blue suit and a red bow tie, and his nametag said BRAD. He seemed a little less slimy than the salesman back at McIntyre's, but not by too much, and the nonblack suit didn't make him seem comforting or approachable to me. But I did my best. Stand when they stand, sit when they sit.

"You must be Leon?" he said, offering his hand.

"I am," I said, taking it. I shook it hard and looked him in the eye, like you're supposed to.

Brad glanced down at a printed-out version of my application. "I see you're interested in marketing," he said.

"Yeah," I said. I managed not to laugh here, somehow.

"And you go to Cornersville Trace High?"

"For a few more weeks. Graduation is coming up."

"Would you be leaving us for college at the end of the summer?"

"I'll probably just go to community college or junior college for a couple of years," I said. "So I wouldn't have to quit."

Brad gave me a thoughtful look. "That's probably smart, in this economy," he said. "Not that I wouldn't hire you if you were going to college, but I wouldn't love it if you left us in three or four months."

He read over the application again, while making noises like *choo choo choo choo choo* under his breath, which I guess he thought made him look very busy.

"Now, if we hire you, you'll have a lot of responsibility," he said. "We value our guests here, and we always want them to have a positive experience."

Everyone calls customers "guests" now. Stan and I preferred to call them "idiots."

But I smiled and nodded.

"So, Leon," Brad said, "do you think you can handle the responsibility of a job here?"

"I'm sure I can," I said.

"I know you were asking for a server job, but would you be okay with starting out in the dish pit? We like to start people at the bottom here."

I shrugged. "I guess," I said.

"Well then," he said, "we're actively and aggressively hiring right now, so all I'll need you to do is fill out your W-2, sign the contract, and take the personality test, then we'll get you started on the training program."

"Personality test?"

"It's nothing serious, just something we have all our new hires do. I don't love it, personally, but it's company-wide policy. We'll have to let you go if it turns out that you're a psychopath or you fail the drug test, but I'm sure you'll be fine." He winked, then held up a large packet and handed it to me. "Just fill in all these answers, and let me know when you're done."

He set me up at an empty table, and I was soon joined by another potential new hire: a scruffy guy who looked to be a couple of years older than me and didn't seem capable of reading silently to himself. He whispered the questions and talked to himself as he worked his way through his packet.

The packet was labeled *Spumoni Restaurant Concepts, Inc. Personality Assessment Survey*. It was full of multiple-choice questions about what I thought about employee theft, snitching on employees who break the rules, and of course, leadership skills.

What a crock of shit.

An awful lot of the questions repeated themselves. One yes-or-no asked, "Have you tried illegal drugs?" Then, a couple of pages later, there was a multiple-choice question that asked, "Which of these drugs have you tried? Check all that apply."

I suppose I could see the logic behind the whole thing—it was a good way to weed out the complete dumbasses. Anyone who took a test like this and said that they'd tried heroin, thought employee theft was "acceptable in most cases," and thought that honesty was "not very important" or "not at all important" was probably too dumb to hire. It'd be like getting stoned on the way to a drug test.

I finished in ten minutes, then waited a few minutes for the other guy to finish.

"Pretty stupid, huh?" I asked.

He shrugged. "I've seen worse, man."

The two of us brought our tests over to Brad, and he put them into a manila envelope.

"Don't worry," he said. "This thing is really just for insurance reasons. We'll have to fire you if we get the results back and they say you're a psychopath, though."

He'd already made that joke, but I let it slide.

"That's tough but fair," I said. He pulled a couple of contracts out of a file drawer and handed them to us.

According to the contract I'd be making a buck more per hour than I did at the Cave. At part-time that came to about twenty more bucks a week, minus the extra money I'd spend on gas for the longer commute. Not exactly big bucks.

"All right," said Brad. "Now we can get you guys started on the training videos."

He led us back to the office and loaded up a couple of videos that I guess were supposed to be our initiation into the West Egg family.

The first was basically propaganda about why unions were evil. The way they made it look, the United Food and Commercial Workers Union was actually a sleeper cell for al-Qaeda, and union dues paid for drug cartels to have families lined up against the wall and shot. The whole thing reminded me of one of the antidrug videos they'd shown in health class.

I looked over at the other guy midway through it.

"Man," I said. "They sure as hell don't want us joining a union."

"I've seen that same video about a million times," he said with a yawn.

"Worked a lot of name-tag jobs?"

"Yeah."

I'd once known a guy who called himself a McHobo. He bummed from job to job, never took a promotion, never stayed anywhere long. Never anywhere longer than six months. He said that to specialize was to settle, and settling into a retail and restaurant job was the same thing as dying.

I'd settled into the Cave, for sure. I think the guy would have approved of that place, but as I sat back in the chair watching the video, I told myself that I shouldn't be settling anywhere. It was time to move on. Paige was right. And I didn't have to stay at West Egg forever. Just a few months, until I found something better.

The next video was about the dress and appearance code. The West Egg was a classy restaurant, the kind of place where people came to get engaged or celebrate retirements or whatever, and as the video said about six times, they weren't *selling food*, they were *creating memories.* And no one wanted any memories of unkempt employees. I didn't remember any event from my past where my memories were tarnished because a guy had a stain on his shirt, but that was just me. I lived my life in a world of stains.

Now and then as we sat there watching the videos, the various assistant managers, buyers, chefs, and other people who made the machine that was the West Egg Steakhouse run smoothly came in and out of the office. Some of them ignored us, and others introduced themselves. Brad came in to check on us right during the part about facial hair regulations and got a goofy look on his face as he looked down at the scruffy guy.

"You might wanna pay attention to that part," he said.

"Even if I'm just in the dish pit?" the guy asked.

Brad opened up one of the drawers underneath the computer monitor and pulled out a disposable razor that probably should have been disposed of a long time ago.

"This is what I make my people use if they come in looking like you do," he said. "The store razor."

"That doesn't look very sanitary," I said.

"And that's how we make sure no one shows up with an appearance violation," Brad said with a turdish smirk. "Goes for you, too. You might not need it yet, though."

"I shave," I said.

"Keep at it." He laughed.

He put the razor away and started rifling through some paperwork from the desk, muttering something about how many people were asking for weekend nights off around prom season.

This whole place was starting to piss me off. What was the point of all this, anyway? The money wasn't that much better.

I thought about the servers at Casa Bravo. The people here were probably no different. Having them for coworkers instead of Stan and Dustin probably wouldn't exactly help me shape up and live my life on the straight and narrow.

Maybe Lando Calrissian made more money administrating a gas

mine on Cloud City in *The Empire Strikes Back* than he did when he was smuggling spices in his space pirate days with Han Solo, and I'm sure it was more respectable and all, but do you think he was happier? Do you think he found it more fulfilling? Hell no. And it didn't keep him out of trouble, either.

This deal kept getting worse all the time.

Paige would be mad if I didn't take the job, but she'd also probably be mad if I *did* take it and couldn't get the night of her debutante ball off.

When the door opened again and another manager or somebody came in, I looked out and caught a glance at some of the people in button-down shirts who were sliding in for an early dinner. Slick sons of bitches who reminded me of Avery the Asshole from the suit shop, all ready to eat a steak, chug a few beers, and harass a waitress after a long day of laying people off.

My eyelid began to twitch.

No money was worth this.

"You know what?" I said. "Fuck this shit."

I gathered up my paperwork and shoved it at Brad.

"You're leaving?" he asked.

"Yeah." I said. "And in case you didn't get the joke on my application, 'nards' means 'balls.'"

The soon-to-be-less-scruffy guy chuckled, so I felt like I was leaving on a high note when I walked out the door. I marched into my car and drove to the Ice Cave. Home.

In the back room Stan was going over something on the computer with George, the owner, and both of them were so wrapped up that they didn't notice me coming in at all. Dustin was scratching his crotch as he sat on a barrel. Jenny was cuddling very casually with Jake on the couch, as she sometimes did, and Edie was leaning in enough that she could be said to be halfway cuddling with both of them as she typed something on her phone. True Norwegian Black Metal was on the stereo. It smelled like candy and BO and the walk-in freezer was humming.

Jake was saying that his Uncle Travis believed that all a man needs is a six-pack of beer, a decent chair, and a remote control. That was it.

"TV is evil," said Comrade Edie.

"You don't need a TV," said Jake. "The remote control is just so you can hit people over the head with it if they try to get you off the chair."

"That's the life," said Stan. "A beer to drink, a chair to sit on, and a remote control to smite your enemies."

These were my people. It felt good to be home.

If I wanted a better-paying job, I could wait a few years take a gig at Big Jake's High-Class House of Ass.

24. LEGEND

Things felt a bit rocky with Paige for the first week of school after spring break. She didn't seem to understand that places like the West Egg just weren't for me.

Meanwhile, in the aftermath of the Nontoxic Club debacle, we picked up a stray at the Cave. For the rest of spring break, and every day after school the week after, one of the girls from Autumn's group, Natasha, came in by herself every afternoon. She had been the only one besides Autumn who ate her whole cookie; while the others giggled and shrieked, she had mostly just sat there, not really saying anything. But I guess she fell in love with the seamy underbelly of suburbia that day.

She had been dressed like all the other girls before, but now she was showing up in black blouses and a lot of mascara, like she was trying to go goth using only things she already had in her wardrobe. We didn't let her into the back room, obviously, and we watched what we talked about when she was around, but it was kind of charming to see her going from prep to freak, in her way. I guess she found that she felt more at home among the weirdos in black than she did in "girl world." She'd found her place in the universe.

The fact that her place in the universe was a joint like the Ice Cave was sort of bad luck for her, but sometimes your place in the world is enough just because it's *yours*. That's what I decided when I walked out of the West Egg. It may have been better than the Cave, but it would never be *mine.*

Just because something is classier than something else doesn't make it automatically better. Take my parents, for one. All the times they could have been at the West Egg, they were staying home, dressing like hillbillies, and making fun of meals like creamed cow brains on toast and dips where the main ingredient was crumbled Cheetos. They chose fun over class, and there's something to be said for that.

The weekend before the debutante ball, they decided to do another food disaster night, and Paige came to eat with us again. This time I persuaded my parents *not* to do Lester and Wanda, or to do the meal "in character" at all, but they still insisted that we at least dress according to the cookbook, which in this case meant dressing up like we worked in an early 1960s advertising office.

"The important thing," my mom said, "is that you have to wear your suit."

"Yeah," said Dad. "If you think we're going to let you get away with not wearing it in front of us now and then, you've got another thing coming, kid."

The cookbook of the night was *Cooking to Reel Him In*, a weird little volume from 1962 that featured a cartoonish drawing of a mermaid with pointy, nippleless bare breasts on the cover. She was holding a fishing line and reeling in a guy dressed as an executive. I took a picture of it and sent it to Paige as soon as I saw it.

"Oh, God," she texted back. "Do you think they're trying to tell us they know we have sex?"

"Why would they use a mermaid to tell us that?" I replied. "Mermaids can't do anything. No parts below the belly button."

I didn't tell her that my parents *always* used to give me thinly veiled warnings about the dangers of drugs, casual sex, and online fandom communities and shit during food disasters; I guess they thought that hearing that sort of stuff from Lester and Wanda or whomever made it seem less traumatic. So the topless mermaid might *have* been a subtle message from them, for all I knew. Maybe they'd picked a mermaid with really pointy boobs as a way of warning me that I could poke my eye out.

Paige spent the rest of the afternoon while I was at work texting me ideas of *exactly* what she could do with me as a mermaid, and did such a good job of convincing me that I was tempted to pick her up early so we could spend some time in the nook.

With my suit on and hair combed in the early sixties "duck's ass" style, I could have passed for a junior ad exec, or maybe even a wannabe member of the Rat Pack from the days before any of them had gone to "Stan's place." I looked in the mirror and tried to be smooth, early sixties style.

"Hey there, doll face," I said. "Dynamite gams. Get 'em into the kitchen or it's ring-a-ding-ding."

I felt like a complete asshole, but I couldn't help but wonder if Paige would actually *like* it if I talked like that. She loved those romance books where the guys act like controlling dicks, and girls in her circle certainly didn't seem to mind dating douche bags. Douchey guys never did seem to hurt for company.

Paige liked the suit, in any case. When I picked her up, she was wearing a more modest version of the sort of dress she'd been wearing on Valentine's Day, and she gave me a look like she wanted to eat me alive as soon as she opened the door.

"You should wear that *much* more often," she said.

"Where *could* I wear it?" I asked.

"School."

"No one wears a suit to school except teachers."

"Trust me," she said. "If you had been dressing like *that* all year, I would have had a *lot* more competition than just a girl who lives four thousand miles away."

"The fact that it's black doesn't intimidate you?" I asked. "The salesman said girls are afraid of men in black."

"Not me."

And she moved her hand across my chest and sort of purred, which I'd never heard her do before. As we drove to my house, she showed me just how unafraid she really was. I tried to return the favor as well as I could while driving, but pretty soon I had to insist that we stop fooling around, before I ended up at home with a conspicuous hard-on. I spent the last block or two of the drive forcing myself to think about unsexy things like Stan's underpants, the razor from the West Egg, and Mrs. Smollet.

My parents' outfits were actual period getups that Dad had found in some vintage store out in Valley Junction, and while they cooked, they were talking to each other like they worked in a midcentury ad agency. Mom was pretending to be a secretary who wanted a coffee break every five minutes and dreamed of marrying an exec and moving to Long Island. Dad kept calling her "sweet cheeks" and generally harassing her, which just made her giggle. Paige and I sat at the table, and she seemed to be enjoying the show, while I wished I could just disappear. I did not need to see my parents pinching each other's butts.

"You guys said you'd just be yourselves tonight," I said. "You promised."

"We said we'd be ourselves when we *ate*," said Dad. "Didn't say anything about when we were cooking."

Paige leaned over to me. "It's adorable," she said. "They're role-playing!"

"Don't even say it," I whispered.

I'd already figured out that Mom and Dad weren't really going to food disaster conventions when they went away for the weekend, but I'd never really connected the dots to notice the general kinkiness behind their hobby.

"So, what are you two office drones cooking up?" I called out, if only to change the subject.

"Turkey Marco Polo," said Mom. "Turkey, broccoli, and Gilbert's supreme sauce. Only without any actual Gilbert's products, since they went belly-up years ago."

She passed us over the cookbook, which featured the logo for Gilbert's Condiments right on the rock the mermaid was sitting on. This meant that it was one of those cookbooks that wasn't so much a collection of recipes as an ad for Gilbert's Condiments. Every recipe called for ungodly amounts of some Gilbert's product or another;

the "supreme sauce" used three different Gilbert's sauces mixed together. The turkey and broccoli part sounded okay, but when slathered in the sauce, I wasn't sure. The grainy black-and-white picture made it look like a mass of engine oil and boogers.

Mom and Dad had substituted store-brand condiments for the Gilbert's, of course. Around the stove the two of them were still carrying on like they'd just snuck out of a production of *How to Succeed in Business Without Really Trying*. Dad was making lewd advances and Mom was giggling and saying, "Oh, Mr. Harris, you're such a card!"

"Seriously, you guys," I said. "I'm gonna need therapy over here."

"If you squares want us to knock it off, come finish the cooking for us and we'll sit down," said Dad.

"Gladly."

We switched places, and they sat down and just talked about real estate and accounting, like normal parents, while Paige and I picked up the cooking. There wasn't much left to do besides stir at that point.

The sauce, to my utter surprise, actually smelled fantastic. This appeared to be one of those rare food disasters that was a whole lot better than it looked. I turned up the heat and leaned over to stir it while Paige worked on one of the side dishes, and for a minute we were just cooking together, and it was kind of awesome. Not counting sex, we hadn't had a project to collaborate on since the Slushee hunt. I'd been feeling like I was in the doghouse since the whole thing with her sister, but things seemed okay now, and any resentment or animosity seemed to disappear in the steam that rose above the stove. When we were just about finished, Paige leaned in to me.

"This is fun," she said. "Thanks for having me."

"Of course," I said.

"I thought the food disaster thing was kind of weird the first time, but I think I get it now. My parents never have fun together like that."

"Not in front of you, anyway."

She socked me in the shoulder, and we got back to cooking.

True to their word, Mom and Dad didn't pretend to be 1960s office employees at the table. Instead of pretending to be a secretary who enjoyed sexual harassment, Mom talked about real estate horror stories, and Paige and I told customer horror stories, and we all laughed and had a good time.

When we were all finished, Dad suggested we all go someplace for dessert.

"I wouldn't mind going into the Ice Cave dressed like this," I said. "Just to see the looks on everyone's faces."

"Please not there," said Paige.

"Well, not Penguin Foot Creamery, either," I said.

"We're all dressed up," said Dad. "Why don't we go to the West Egg Steakhouse or something?"

Everyone else seemed to think this was a great idea, and I couldn't exactly object. I'd *just* been picking on Dad for not going to more places like the West Egg a couple of weeks before, and I guess that in doing so I'd basically dared him to start going there more. I could only hope that no one there would recognize me from a few days before. I hadn't been totally up-front with Paige about what had gone on there, and my parents didn't know I was applying for new jobs at all.

With the suit on, and a mission to keep from being recognized, I could easily imagine myself as James Bond as we walked into the West Egg. I almost wanted to try out some of Bond's old single entendres on Paige, but it wasn't the sort of thing I dared to do in front of my parents.

We sat at a table near the bar, surrounded by a bunch of overgrown business school bozos, and just kept chatting, but I zoned out while I looked around. I recognized the formerly scruffy guy when he came out of the kitchen for a second, and he caught my eye. Bad news.

A few minutes later, when a waiter brought out our desserts, he grinned at me.

"We've been passing your application around in the kitchen all week," he said.

"What application?" I asked.

"Aren't you the guy who cussed Brad out the other day?"

"Who's Brad?" I asked.

"The manager. Some guy sent in this funny job application, and Brad somehow didn't notice it was a joke and offered the guy a gig. I hear the guy threw the application in his face, cussed him out, and ran off. One of the guys in the dish pit said it was you."

I was swelling with pride on the inside—my antics seemed to have made me a legend among the staff. But I couldn't take credit for it. Not here. Not in front of Paige or my parents.

"Must have been someone else," I said.

My parents didn't suspect a thing, as far as I could tell, since they didn't even know I was sending applications around. But Paige started to look ill and basically dropped out of the conversation for most of dessert, and I felt that gnawing feeling back in my guts, knowing that a fight was probably coming as soon as we were alone.

But she still looked ill when we were in my car later. When I started to drive in the direction of the nook, she just shook her head and pointed me in the general direction of Oak Meadow Mills.

"Okay," I admitted. "I went in for an interview there and walked out. It wasn't quite like that guy was saying, though."

"Huh," she said, looking out the window and not at me, so I couldn't see how serious the look on her face was.

"It didn't pay much more than the Cave, and I doubt they would have let me take the night of the debutante ball off."

She nodded weakly, and I asked if she was mad.

She took a deep breath, then, instead of actually answering, she asked me what was in the "supreme sauce" from the Turkey Marco Polo.

"I just stirred it, but I think it was three sauces, a bit of white wine, and some half-and-half. Maybe some other seasonings."

"I think I might have gotten food poisoning," she said. "I started feeling sick at the West Egg and now I feel like shit."

A minute later I dropped her off, and before I'd even found my way out of Oak Meadow Mills, she texted that she was puking, and that my parents and I had probably better watch out. She wouldn't have been the first person to get sick after a food disaster. It was one of the many side effects of the hobby.

I felt fine, though. Especially now that I knew she had started to seem sick because she *was* sick, not because she'd figured out that I'd made a bit of a scene at the West Egg. I felt better than I had in a while, if anything. I felt like she'd found out the truth about what had happened and hadn't wanted to argue about it, and that was enough to make me want to break into song, Dustin Eddlebeck–style.

Instead of going right home I swung by the Ice Cave, just for the sheer novelty of showing up in a suit. George and Stan were so wrapped up in one of their conversations over paperwork that they barely seemed to notice me, except to encourage me to join in the contest Dustin and Jake were having in the back. I found them deeply engaged in a battle over who could fit the most gummy worms in his mouth. Jake had a clear biological advantage, being roughly twice Dustin's size, but Dustin put up a respectable fight.

When Dustin started to throw up, I thought it was just because of all the candy he'd crammed down his gullet.

But it turned out it wasn't the gummy worms for him, and it wasn't food poisoning for Paige. They were simply among the first people in town to come down with the Montreal Flu, which was roaring in from Canada to the midwestern states.

It would leave the school looking like a ghost town the next week.

25. BARF

I know you aren't supposed to go around judging other people's cultures, but there are some traditions that people really ought to rethink. Like, take that thing in the Middle East where they celebrate special occasions by firing semiautomatic rifles in the air. That's just asking for trouble. Sometimes you can get away with keeping dumb things going just because they're an ancient tradition, but obviously that custom isn't *that* old. It's not like people in ancient times had assault weapons.

Another is the thing where everyone takes communion out of the same cup in Catholic churches. At my grandparents' church, the one my family went to now and then, they pass out little individual cups, but the time I went to a service at Dustin's cathedral (which is also Stan's, at least on paper, though he never actually goes), everyone went to the front and took a turn drinking out of one big goblet. They wiped it down between drinkers, but still. When a virus is going around, you'd think they'd at least tell everyone to bring a straw or something.

But they don't. Or, even if they normally do, as of Sunday morning, no one seemed to realize that the Montreal Flu had hit Des Moines, so they didn't take any extra precautions. I can't help but think that even though Dustin probably didn't single-handedly spread the virus around by taking communion the morning after he was puking at the Ice Cave, he couldn't have helped much.

On Monday there were a lot of empty chairs at school, including Paige's. During second period two people got up to go to the bathroom and never came back. Three more did the same thing halfway through third. By the end of the day it was like the rapture had come and half the people in school had disappeared.

The Montreal Flu wasn't exactly the Black Death; it was just one of those bugs that messes you up for a few days and that's it, unless you already have a heart condition or something. It made its way to me on Thursday, the day Paige went back to school, and for two days I was barely able to lift my hand to answer all the texts from her. Even when she sent me naughty texts asking if Nurse Paige needed to give me a very thorough examination, I didn't have the energy to respond. All I had the strength to do was throw up.

On Sunday night, when we finally both felt better, we headed straight for the nook behind Earthways to celebrate. We barely spoke at all until after we finished, when we were curled up in the backseat with her on my lap, her hair spilling onto my shoulders and my hand reaching underneath her butt and coming to rest between her legs. With half the town still sick, no one else was waiting for a turn behind us, so we could just lie there and enjoy the sweaty afterglow.

"So, the yearbook looked really good," she said.

"You saw it?" I asked.

She turned her head towards me. "We got the proofs in," she said. "I texted you about it."

"It might have gotten lost in the shuffle when I was sick," I said. "Sorry."

"They looked great. You did a good job on the layout."

I smiled. It wasn't every day that someone told me I did a good job on anything. I was usually willing to settle for just not being told I'd been a letdown.

That was how it was with the sex, still. Paige seemed to be having a good time when we did it, and she wasn't actively complaining, but I wasn't entirely sure I was doing a particularly great job. I couldn't quite figure out exactly what she wanted, what she really liked. And I hadn't told her all the things *I* wanted to try, because I was afraid she'd decide I was a sick bastard.

But she hadn't complained, and I always made a point of getting her off before we went all the way. I didn't think she was faking. I stood by my work, even if there was probably room for improvement.

"By the way," she said, "I might have gotten you a new job."

"Huh?" I asked.

"The country club needed caddies for Memorial Day weekend," she said. "And I signed you up. If you do a good job, they might bring you on full-time for the summer."

"What the hell do I know about golf?" I asked.

"You don't need to know anything," she said. "All you really have to do is carry the golf clubs around."

"Don't people ask caddies for advice on which club to use and stuff?"

"Not the ones who just work at the country club," she said. "That's, like, what pro caddies do. I think."

"I don't know if I want to spend my summer sweating my ass off with a bunch of country club bozos. I've never been on a golf course in my life. Unless you count the time in eighth grade when Dustin and I snuck into one at midnight to mess around and pee on stuff."

She rolled a bit so she was looking up at me without craning her neck. This put her in a position that twisted my wrist, the one that was hooked underneath between her legs, into a painful position.

"You're going to make a lot more money in tips alone than you do at that stupid ice cream place," she said.

"But I'd hate it," I told her. "I *like* working at the Cave."

"You don't *work* there," she said. "You just hang out there. You said yourself you need to find someplace better."

"And I tried to. But the only place that called me in for an interview was that awful steak place."

"Being a caddie is at least honest work, and you'll get to meet a lot of important people. Maybe one of them will give you a job you like better someday. It's all about connections."

"Just what I always wanted," I said. "A career in the exciting field of affirmative masculinity."

"Huh?"

"A yes-man."

In one little sigh she managed to convey all the information that I normally got from one of those "you have so much potential" speeches. I always hated that speech, but there was something surreal about getting it in sigh form from a girl who had my forearm wedged between her butt cheeks like a hot dog in a bun. Now she readjusted herself so that my arm was still in the same place, but my hand wasn't touching her anywhere, and she leaned back into me. It stopped feeling like we were cuddling. Instead, I just felt her weight on me. It was hard to breathe.

"Want to go to Hurricane's or something?" I asked.

"You can't *afford* to go to Hurricane's," she said.

"What the hell is your problem tonight?" I asked. "I thought we were done with all this fighting."

She shrugged. "Sorry," she said. "I know I'm kind of picking fights, but while I was sick and lying in bed, I just kept thinking about you, and it was awesome, except then I'd imagine what you'd be like when you're thirty or something if you don't shape up."

"I'm wearing a polo shirt right now, aren't I?" I asked. "And I have a suit."

"It's a start," she said. "But you've got a long way to go. And it's going to be hard work."

She sighed again and lay there quietly for a minute.

Love is getting a lecture from someone who could fart right on your bare arm at any second.

After I dropped Paige at home, I went to the Cave and sat in the back room with Jason Keyes and Amber Hexam, a couple of the local goths. When I checked my e-mail on my phone, I saw that Paige was sending me links about debutante balls. It was getting to be clear that it was a much bigger deal to her than she'd let on before.

I told Amber and Jason about it, and they laughed whenever I said "balls." As one does. It's like with the Kum and Go. If I ever stop laughing when people say "balls," I'll know my heart is dead.

26. BALLS

The day of the debutante ball I got a six-dollar haircut (which I swear was just as good as one from the place Paige wanted me to go would have been), shaved, cleaned out my car, and put on my suit. When I arrived at Paige's house, she was wearing the gown she'd bought a month before, but hadn't let me see yet. It was silver, and flowing, and sparkled in the light of her foyer. Her hair was done up and curls dangled gracefully in front of her face.

She looked so good that she literally took my breath away for a minute.

I just stared at her for a second, then choked out a word. "Hi."

"Hi, you," she said. She gave me a quick kiss that sort of stuck to my lips, on account of the lipstick, when she pulled away. Then she smiled again.

"You look fantastic," I said.

Her mom appeared over her shoulder.

"Well, look at you!" she said. "Someone here cleans up nice."

"Thanks," I said.

Autumn appeared behind both of them.

"You dried your forehead," she said.

"Autumn!" said her mom. "That's not nice."

"What?" she asked. "He has a really greasy forehead most of the time."

"Autumn!" her mom said again.

Paige didn't say a thing through all of this, other than a quick "We'll meet you guys there." She just looked at me and my dry forehead and smiled.

I escorted Paige to my car, the same way I'd be escorting her down the walkway, and for the whole drive there we just talked and joked and laughed, like we used to on Slushee hunts. We hadn't argued much since the weekend before. Things were getting back to normal, and I hoped a night at a ball would clear up any lingering resentment she might be nursing. Such was the power of a well-cut suit.

The ball was at this classy banquet hall in the Ruan building, one of the three or four biggest skyscrapers in Des Moines. I'd never been inside of it, and I was pretty surprised at how swanky it was. All the banquets and receptions I'd been to before were in places that just looked like bingo parlors with tablecloths. This looked almost like a ballroom from a Disney movie, everything crystal and glitter and mahogany. They sat Paige and me at a big round table with a few people that I'd never met before but that Paige knew from other Harvester Club events that she'd been dragged to over the years.

The fancy decor made me hope that the food would be pretty fancy too, but it turned out that it wasn't that great. It was Cornish hens, which are like miniature chickens, stuffed with herbs and smothered in butter. I got the idea they'd probably been in cold storage while three generations of chickens lived and died. And they're a pain in the ass to eat; you really have to go picking and picking to get any meat off the damned things after you get the breasts out of the way, and half of the butter ends up on the table. Or on your tie. They look a lot classier than they are.

The conversation was light—I wouldn't have dreamed of bringing up poop, but it was pretty hard to resist the urge to talk in a fake British accent about playing badminton and rogering chambermaids. Honestly, doing anything else felt faintly ridiculous. After all, most of the conversation among the guys seemed to be about how much everyone's suit cost. The guy across from me paid so much for his that I wanted to ask him if it was woven from hairs plucked from the queen's butt, but I didn't.

We were just about done eating when Leslie came over, dressed in a long red dress.

"Oh my God, Paige," she said. "Did you get Mr. Perkins's e-mail?"

"I haven't checked my mail in a while," Paige said. "What's up?"

"The yearbooks came in, and when he was looking through it he noticed that one of the poems has a hidden Satanic message in it."

I did my best to remain calm while Paige gave me a look that would have killed most mere mortals.

"Who wrote it?" she asked, without looking away from me.

"It was anonymous," said Leslie. "And no one's sure who even accepted it. It's a lousy poem to start with."

"Which poem is it?" I asked.

"Some stupid thing about 'Sing a Song of Cornersville Trace,'" she said. "Do you remember laying it out?"

"Vaguely," I said. "I remember thinking it really sucked."

"But you didn't notice it was an acrostic for SATAN RULES?"

"Well, no," I said. "I didn't really read through them; I just took the ones from the box, typed them in, and laid them out."

"I can't believe you didn't notice it," said Leslie.

"It got past the proof page check too, didn't it?" I asked.

"Everyone had the flu that week," Leslie said. "So they couldn't check it carefully. We're having an emergency meeting after school on Monday to decide whether to send them back and print up another run or what."

"How much would that cost?" I asked.

"Thousands," said Paige, whose expression had not changed.

"So why bother?" I asked. "If you don't make a big deal out it, no one's even going to notice."

"People will notice," said Leslie.

"Well, you have Christian poems in there sometimes," I said.

"So what?"

"So don't you have to give Satanists the same right to express themselves as you give to the Christians?"

"Satanism's not a real religion," said Leslie. "It's all, like, sacrificing babies."

"Not really," I said. "I mean, I'm not one myself or anything, but my boss says it's really just Ayn Rand's philosophy with a flair for the dramatic attached to it."

Leslie looked off to the ballroom area, then back at me. "It's not like we have a Satanic community in the school," she said. "You can't just claim freedom of religion on this."

Before I could say anything, a woman with hair like you normally only see on the Christian Big Hair channel came and tapped the girls on the shoulder, and they excused themselves to go get ready to be debuted or whatever it is they call it, leaving me alone with three guys in expensive suits who were all just sort of staring at me.

"Gentlemen," I said, "if you'll excuse, I've got some work to do."

I immediately pulled out my phone and started sending out text messages about what was happening with the yearbook. With a little effort we could have a regular Satanic rally at school on Monday; I imagined a whole herd of guys in devil horns crashing the yearbook meeting. I knew that ritual sacrifice wasn't really a part of the Satanism that Stan espoused, but I thought maybe we could make an exception for Mrs. Smollet.

Stan, of course, offered to help any way he could. Everyone I texted said they'd be glad to help.

I didn't expect it to *work*—my schemes pretty much never did—but maybe we could at least make the point that freedom of religion means freedom of *all* religions. Even the weird ones that some bald dude made up in the 1960s by copying Ayn Rand and H. P. Lovecraft, the ones students made up themselves, the ones based on long-disproven science, and the ones where you just pretend you worship the assistant manager down at the ice cream parlor.

This was *exactly* the kind of stuff we used to pull back in the gifted pool. Hell, after Anna started doing it, lots of girls in the gifted pool started wearing devil horns to freak Smollet out. It was time to break out the old horns for one last hurrah.

I was still sending out texts when some old guy in a suit went onto the stage and made a little speech about the Harvester Club's commitment to the community and youth development and shit. After him, the big-haired woman, whose name looked like it was probably Althea or Hildegarde, came out and gave a pep talk about moral character, and the role of manners and grace in society. Then she struck up the band, stepped to the side, and began to introduce the debutantes.

One by one, the big-haired woman called out the girls' names, and the girls came onto the stage in gowns that probably cost more than my car. I probably would have felt dizzy and out of place, but knowing that I was plotting a sort of rebellion kept me grounded. My phone was buzzing in my pocket with texts and messages from people I'd contacted about the poem. I didn't dare pull it out to check it, and I turned it off completely before they could announce Paige, of course, but it was nice to know that things were off the ground already.

When Paige was introduced, I took the stage, held her hands, and walked her down the runway and onto the dance floor while people clapped. Paige's parents waved at me from their table, and Autumn stuck out her tongue and wiggled it more than was probably strictly necessary. Paige smiled and kissed me on the cheek and I had to admit that it felt pretty awesome.

"I love you," I said, as we reached the dance floor and began slow dancing around.

"I love you, too," she said. "But *please* tell me you didn't put that poem into the yearbook."

"I put *all* of the poems into the yearbook," I said.

"Then tell me you didn't personally plot for *that* one to be in there."

I didn't want to lie, so I just didn't say anything. "Can we just dance?" I asked. "We can worry about this later."

She kissed me on the cheek, then sort of looked off into space without saying anything.

"I puked again this morning," she whispered. "I've puked a few times this week."

"It's probably just nerves," I said. "Or the residual effects of the flu."

"I don't think I ever actually had the flu," she said. "I think I'm just pregnant."

27. BEDTIME

You know how, when you're a kid and you have a babysitter coming for the night, and you plan on having a good time and staying up later than you normally get to? On those nights there's nothing worse than hearing the sound of the babysitter's boyfriend knocking on the door. The minute that guy shows up, you *know* you're going to bed *right* on time. The bottom drops out of all your plans, and your senses kind of get distorted while reality realigns itself in your head.

Hearing your girlfriend say the word "pregnant" is kind of like that, only on a much, much grander scale. All of the plans you've been making for your life suddenly seem totally irrelevant. Everything about the future suddenly looks totally different. You can actually feel the brain cells bouncing around, rebuilding all your images of yourself at thirty, of how you fit into the world, and all of that, even if you didn't think you even *had* any grander plans for the future other than just staying up later and eating a butt load of gummy worms. Which pretty much *had* been my plan, both when I was a kid getting babysat, and now that I was a teenager getting ready to graduate high school.

Pregnant.

The word felt like it hung in the air behind my ear and followed behind me like a mosquito while we slowly danced through the room.

The center of gravity shifted in my body, and the sounds and sights of the ball around me became a total blur, but somehow I kept on dancing.

We moved slowly, rocking back and forth and holding each other tight, and in the static that the ball became, after a while all I was aware of was the feel of Paige's cheek touching mine. It was wet and slimy and I was probably getting her makeup on me. By the time the song ended, I felt like we'd been dancing in silence for hours. In reality it couldn't have been more than sixty seconds.

When the music changed, my head emerged from its fog enough that I could talk, though not necessarily enough that I could say anything intelligent. The first thing out of my mouth was, per my usual habit, probably the single dumbest thing I could have said.

"We always used condoms," I said. "*You're* the one who always wanted me not to."

"Do *not* throw that in my face," she said. "And even *with* one, this stuff can happen. I'm late."

"Has that happened to you before?" I asked.

"No."

"Did you take a test or anything?"

"No. I'm kind of afraid to."

I took a deep breath. I didn't blame her. I never looked up my grades online. It was better to just wait and not know for *sure* that I was screwed.

"What else can it be?" she asked. "I'm never late."

For a loaded minute we just went back to dancing. Her face was frozen into a smile that didn't match her eyes at all. Her eyes and lips were so out of harmony that I had to look away. My vision cleared up enough to see that her parents were beaming with pride on the sidelines of the dance floor.

"What do you want to do about it?" I asked.

"Have it," she said. "I don't believe in abortion, and I could never give it up for adoption. So I really, really need you to grow up in a hurry."

I held her close and kept on dancing. The music seemed louder and louder, and my vision was going in and out of being blurry. I worried that I'd puke myself. But I held it together. What else could I do?

"I'll do everything I can," I said. "I'll take the caddie job. I'll learn everything there is to know about golf and be the best caddie in the club by the Fourth of July. I'll work there *and* at a steak place or something."

"And you're going to college," she said. "So you can get a decent job that pays enough to take care of a baby. It probably won't be a job you *like*, but you'll just have to deal with that."

"Yeah," I said. "Yeah."

"I haven't told anyone else yet," she said. "I'm not going to until, like, the last minute before I start to show. That won't happen until I'm at least out of high school, but I need you to start being a grown-up right this second."

"I am," I said. "I already am. My SATs are in the morning."

"Then kick some ass. You're smart. You're *so* smart. I *know* you can do it."

She hugged me tight, and we made it through the rest of the debutante ball. I mingled as well as I could, and didn't mention poop once. If I had, it would have just made me think of diapers, anyway.

I had never changed a diaper in my life.

I had never held a baby, that I recalled.

I didn't know anything about them, except that you don't go around pushing on the soft spot or dropping them on their heads, and that you probably shouldn't let them get a job in a restaurant when they're sixteen, because the kitchen and the smoking areas aren't safe environments for anyone under the age of forty. It would be like letting a kid join a biker gang. Back when bikers were tough guys.

But when reality was done lining itself back up in my brain, at least enough that I could think a bit, the first thing that wasn't baby-related to come to mind was the Satanic poem in the year-book, and the text messages I'd sent.

I still wanted to fight.

If Christian kids had a right to pray privately in school (and they do—anyone who says prayer just plain isn't allowed is full of shit), then we had a right to worship Satan, too. Fighting for the rights of Satanists to express themselves in a high school yearbook may not have been *the* worthiest cause in the world, but if I didn't stand up for this, *that* would make me more of a bum than any amount of covering up stains in my car with duct tape ever did.

If I was going to be a dad, I was going to have to grow a pair of nards. I was going to have to stop living like a bum and be a man.

And a man stands up.

We spent the rest of the night dancing and mingling, but not really saying anything to each other, let alone to anyone else. Just a lot of "Thank you," "It's beautiful, isn't it?" and "Have you seen the view from these windows? You can see half the state." On the car ride home I told Paige she looked gorgeous, and how she'd taken my breath away when I first saw her in the gown, and she smiled a bit but didn't really reply.

And when she was in her house, and I was back in my car, I turned my phone back on and saw that I had about fifty messages about the Satanic poem.

28. TESTS

One nice thing about the SAT is that it's all just multiple-choice. There were no essay questions, and no real opportunities for me to write in a sarcastic response. There was nothing I could really do but give it my best effort.

I didn't sleep for shit the night after the ball, but I showed up right on time for the test with two number two pencils, proper ID, and everything else I needed. I took every brochure about colleges and trade schools and stuff that they had set up on the table outside of the testing room except for the ones for the army. I felt like I did fine on the test; you never know for sure or anything, but there weren't all that many questions where I just had to guess. I test well. It's why they had put me in the Gifted Pool in the first place. It sure as hell wasn't my grades. There's a difference between being smart and getting good grades. Everyone with bad grades knows that.

But I can't say I was focused on the test, exactly. The idea of Paige being pregnant was on my mind the whole time, and in between sections, I was drawing pentagrams on the top corner of the desk and imagining what it would be like to have a whole bunch of Satanists marching through the halls of the school demanding a right to express their religion.

After the test Stan met me at Earthways, where he used a credit card to buy up every pentagram necklace and button they had in the store. They sold them for pagans, not Satanists (pagans never get sick of telling people that it's not the same thing), but they'd work just fine for our purposes.

I hadn't done anything more than send out a handful of texts when I first heard about the poem and the meeting, but while my phone was off, things had apparently snowballed. I'd never really imagined having more than a handful of people actually get involved, but from what Stan was saying, we could probably expect a small army on Monday morning. There were even a couple of local metal bands that offered to play a benefit show if we needed it—like, if the school should find out that Dustin wrote the thing and take action against him, and we needed to raise up a legal defense fund. I didn't think it would go that far, but it was nice to know that the resources were there.

Operation Satanic Youth Gone Wild was off the ground.

It was about midway through my shift on Sunday afternoon that Jenny came in. She helped herself to a pentagram from the box of supplies we'd set up on a table by the ice cream cake freezer, then leaned over the counter.

"I just talked to Anna on the phone," she said.

"Yeah?"

She nodded.

I could handle talking about Anna a bit. The whole idea of going out with her ever again just seemed absurd now. That sort of thing just wasn't going to be a part of my life anymore.

"What was she up to?" I asked.

"She said she was in the process of breaking up with some idiot."

"Yeah?"

A month or so before, hearing that Anna was dating someone else would have felt like someone twisting a knife around inside of my kidneys, and then I would have felt like an even bigger asshole than ever for feeling bad about her seeing other people when I was too. But now it just gave me a sort of numb sensation, like finding out a swing set you really liked at your old elementary school had been torn down. It was sad in a way, but didn't affect me much, really.

"Didn't you say she was always actually trying really hard to impress me back in the day?" I asked.

"Yeah," said Jenny. "She wasn't as . . . worldly . . . as she made herself out to be. Didn't she tell you she sat in on nude figure-drawing classes at the college where her dad taught?"

"Uh-huh."

"She totally made that up."

"Huh." I said. "See, I've imagined her as this artsy genius girl, and I guess that she really wasn't. I always thought she was pretty awesome, but it was all probably just in my head this whole time."

"No, fucker," said Jenny. "She wasn't perfect, but you somehow saw her as the kind of person she *wanted* to be already. And she saw you kind of the same way. She saw stuff in you that most people didn't."

"Maybe."

"Definitely. Can I have a free milk shake for my words of ancient Chinese wisdom?"

"You're Japanese."

She giggled. "But 'Chinese wisdom' sounds more like it'd get me a milk shake."

"And you're, what, third generation Iowan?"

"Just give me a milk shake."

I made her a one—the proper kind that required ice cream, milk, and a blender—and thought for a minute about what she'd said about Anna seeing me as the kind of person I *could* be, not as an eighth-grade dork, which is what I was.

Paige saw what kind of person I *could* be too. She just saw a different possible version of me than Anna had, I guess. A more responsible version—the kind who had a job with a 401K and wore shirts with collars on them. And what she saw was the person I was going to *have* to be now. Becoming that person was going to be a much bigger test than the SAT. The SAT just seemed like a game in comparison. A formality. Nothing.

I didn't go into the back room once during my entire shift.

But all through the day the groundwork for a Satanic rally was being laid around me. Edie and Jill, her girlfriend, came in with a boxload of T-shirts they'd ironed Satanic phrases onto. PROUD AMERICAN SATANIST, RELIGION IS THE OPIATE OF THE MASSES, I SOLD MY SOUL FOR ROCKY ROAD, stuff like that. Stan put them in the back room with a sign saying they were free to anyone who promised to wear them to school Monday. I didn't think we'd get many takers, but when I got off work and went to get my jacket from my locker, I saw that half the shirts were gone. The idea that we might actually get a pretty good rally going, maybe even a regular student riot, made me feel proud.

The feeling I got from working on the rally was the one thing that made me think that I could handle the whole thing with the baby. That I could rise to the occasion if I had to.

Mostly.

On the other hand, I knew that raising a person, and paying for it, was a whole hell of a lot harder than talking kids into wearing funny T-shirts to school.

After work I bought Paige a pregnancy test at Kum and Go (which, of course, I thought was a hilarious thing to do) before our scheduled outing to Hurricane's. She saw it on my dashboard when she got in the car.

"You better not have bought that anyplace where people might know who you are."

"It was at a Kum and Go."

"They have pregnancy tests *there*?"

I shrugged. "Surely you can see how people would mentally link pregnancy to a place with a name like that."

She socked me in the arm, but she smiled a bit as she looked at the box.

"Those Kum and Go guys *know* us. Whoever sold it to you is going to know about it."

"I was almost sure it was going to be that one guy who looks like a pirate when I went in. It wasn't anyone I recognized, though."

"They all probably know each other. If my parents find out because a gas station clerk congratulates them, I'll never talk to you again."

It should have occurred to me that even if they knew *us*, they didn't know who Paige's parents were. But at that moment it felt like one more thing to get all paranoid about.

We sat there in silence, staring at the blue box on the dashboard like it was a gun that one of us was going to have to fire at the other sooner or later.

And it had to be Paige. She was the one who had to pee on the thing. That gnawing feeling in my guts was strong enough to dissolve a couple of my internal organs now; I could only imagine what she was feeling. And she wasn't used to feeling like she was in huge trouble, like I was.

"You want to take it now?" I asked.

"Hell no. Not in my house."

"You want to take it at Hurricane's?" I asked.

She shook her head emphatically. "I am *not* going to be sitting around Hurricane's holding something I peed on."

"Well, you throw it away, don't you?"

She shrugged. I had to admit it seemed like it would be weird to throw something that monumentally important away, but you don't go around keeping stuff that's got pee on it, do you? I wondered if my mom took a pregnancy test when I was first conceived, and if she still had it sitting in a scrapbook someplace. She *would*. I was lucky it wasn't framed on the living room wall, knowing my parents.

"Ice Cave?" I asked. "Then you could put it in a plastic bag or something, at least."

"Under no circumstances am I pulling my pants down in the Ice Cave."

"I meant in the bathroom. I wasn't, like, thinking you'd pop a squat on the couch."

"Same answer applies."

"Where, then?" I asked. "Some bushes?"

She shrugged. "I don't really want to know yet. I want to hang on to the uncertainty for a bit longer."

"Fair enough. I don't think I could bring myself to pee under this kind of pressure, if it was the guy who did it."

"Nope."

We drove along the rest of the way without really saying anything, then ended up just sitting in the Hurricane's parking lot, staring at the box. I should have at least put it in the glove compartment.

"My parents have extra rooms," she said. "I guess the baby will live with them while I'm in school."

"It could stay with *my* parents too," I said.

Paige looked off into the distance for a minute, then said, "It'll live at my house."

I didn't fight with her.

We went a few more seconds not talking, while I tried to get my head around all of this stuff. Every few minutes I'd think of something else that hadn't occurred to me before, like that I was stuck with Paige's family now, if her dad didn't use a butcher's knife to end my life prematurely. Neither of us was talking about getting married (though I wouldn't be surprised if her parents were still the sort who thought *that* was the right thing to do in this situation), but no matter what happened with us, I'd be seeing her parents and Autumn at birthday parties, school events, and all sorts of shit like that for the rest of my life.

I was going to get a decent job. I wasn't just going to let Paige's parents pay for everything. I wasn't going to be beholden to them. Just taking a job at their country club was bad enough.

And I was going to have to tell my parents too. I'd have to tell them everything. About how I hadn't really made any plans for after graduation yet, and about just how far I'd let myself sink. I'd done a great job of keeping up a charade for the last few years, but that was going to have to end.

I could just imagine my mom responding by saying, "Well, I hope you kept the pregnancy test, because we're going to start scrapbooking right now."

After she killed me, of course.

Even though, now that I thought about it, she was only four or five years older than I was now when she had me. She was out of college by then, though, so there's that.

"Maybe my mom can help me get a real estate license," I said. "There's good money in real estate."

"You'd be a *great* Realtor."

I don't think I'd ever felt more grown-up in my life than I did in that moment. The moment when the idea of being a great Realtor seemed like my fondest hope.

If realty didn't work out, I could probably move to some other city and get a job in the insurance business. I didn't know shit about insurance, but I imagined that in most towns I could just walk into an insurance office, tell them I was from Des Moines, the insurance capital of the world, and be put on payroll right away, no questions asked.

And all through the time we talked about this my phone kept

on buzzing with texts. I didn't check them or anything, but Paige noticed.

"You're popular tonight," she said.

"Kind of a big night in the Ice Cave," I said. "Word about that dumb poem in the yearbook got around, and a bunch of people are going to fight to keep it in. Edie and Jill even made T-shirts."

Paige looked over at me.

"You can't be serious."

"Sounds like there might be a miniature riot."

"Just tell me you're not a part of it."

I didn't say anything for a second, and she started to groan.

"Call it off," she said. "Get on your phone right now, and call it off."

"Look," I said. "All I did was send a few text messages saying what was happening, and then things kind of snowballed. It mostly happened during the test and the dance, when my phone was off. It's too late to stop it."

"But at least tell me you're not going to be a part of it. You're going to come to the meeting with me, and we're going to say that the yearbook can't go out as is."

"No," I said. "I'm for the poem. And I'm going to help."

"Are you seriously telling me you're planning to lead a riot to fight for the rights of devil worshippers?"

"This isn't about Satanism, it's about freedom of religion," I said. "Kids wear shirts with stuff about Jesus on them all the time. You can't just be for freedom of your *own* religion."

"If this is really going to be a riot, it could end up on the news. I don't want the baby to be, like, twelve and looking his parents up online and finding out that one of them was part of a rally of Satanists."

"Look," I said. "When the baby comes, I'll go to church with you every Sunday if you want. I'm going to be the best damned father that baby can have. But if I'm going to be a dad, that means I've got to be a man, and a man stands up."

I gave *her* a steely gaze for the first time in our relationship, and she gave me one back, then sighed.

"Fine," she said. "Do whatever you want. I don't even care. But I'm going to be arguing to have the books recalled at the meeting."

"Great," I said. "Do what you think is right. We don't have to agree on everything."

"We should," she said.

"But we can't," I said. "No couple agrees on everything all the time."

She nodded a bit, then sighed, then looked back at the pregnancy test for a minute before putting it in the glove compartment, so if anyone who was going to Hurricane's walked by and looked in the windshield, they wouldn't see it. We just kind of stared out at Cedar Avenue for a few minutes before Paige said, "Teddy bears."

"I still have a bunch of them in the attic," I said. "I solemnly swear, this kid will never want for teddy bears."

"No," she said. "I'm playing free-form Dead Celebrities. Teddy bears."

"Oh," I said. "Log cabins."

"Raincoats."

"Candelabras."

"Cheese sticks."

"Souvenir-hunting Viennese undertakers."

She paused a bit after that one before saying, "Uh . . . Leslie's pantsuits."

"*The Woman Pissing* by Picasso."

"Headlights."

"Un Chien Andalou."

"Wooden fences."

"Thomas Edison."

"Licorice."

"Wackford's Coffee."

"That nasty body spray Keith wears too much of."

We never did go into Hurricane's. Other people from Paige's crowd walked right past the car and didn't even see us, and Paige turned off her phone so she wouldn't get texts asking where she was. The two of us just sat there in the front seat, playing free-form Dead Celebrities until neither of us could think of anything at all to say.

29. BLOOD

We were lucky this wasn't caucus season, the time when all the presidential hopefuls swarm on Iowa and bombard us with ads about what's wrong with America and how they're going to fix it (usually the problem is "we've strayed from the course," and the solution is to hug a cute kid on television and talk about "values"). We get so many political commercials for so many candidates that people go on vacation just to get away from them.

If that was all going on now, having a "Satan Rules" poem in a yearbook could have turned into a regular nationwide political issue, if it was a slow news week otherwise. Every candidate would have to make a statement about it. And not even the most liberal guy in town was likely to come out in favor of the poem. No one's going to get elected as the "pro-Satanism" candidate.

And I can only imagine what some of those guys would have thought if they had come into Cornersville Trace High School that Monday, the day of Operation Satanic Youth Gone Wild. People in the shirts were everywhere, particularly in front of the school, where a bunch of people in devil horns were drumming up support for our cause.

Even Stan was helping out. When I got to the school campus, he was standing just outside of school grounds with the box of T-shirts, passing them out to anyone bold enough to wear them. Dustin was distributing pentagrams. I was enlisted to hand out pamphlets about Satanism that Stan had printed up (or possibly just had in stock at all times). A couple of guys were loudly singing that Mountain Goats song about the death metal band, the one that goes "Hail Satan," over and over at the end. People were throwing horns in the air everywhere I looked. It gave me a warm, fuzzy feeling.

It's a good thing the guy who shows up now and then to stand right off campus and pass out free Bibles wasn't there that day. That would have been awkward.

I flipped through the pamphlet, which explained that Satanism isn't *really* about worshipping the devil; it's about ego, intellect, and moral objectivism. From what I read it all boiled down to one of those "as long as I'm okay, screw the rest of you" philosophies.

Some if it was at least halfway sensible, really, but I think I liked worshipping Stan a lot better than actual Satanism. Still, Satanists were people too, and as far as I was concerned, they had the same rights as everybody else.

We were working our way through our supplies, glad-handing and encouraging people like we were lower-tier presidential candidates doing a meet and greet at a pancake breakfast, when Leslie came up to me, looking pissed.

"What in the fuck are you doing?" she asked.

"I'm standing up," I said.

"You're convincing kids to worship the devil?"

"Nah," I said. "This pamphlet just sort of explains their side. It's mostly crap, really, but you've got to let them say their thing, right?"

She ripped the one I was holding out my hand and tore it up.

"You could at least read it first," I said.

"I don't have to," she said.

"See you at the meeting, then."

Most of the yearbook committee seemed to be on Leslie's side, but not necessarily all of them. Catherine showed up a few minutes later, slipped an I SOLD MY SOUL FOR ROCKY ROAD T-shirt over the white one she'd been wearing, and started clapping her hands and going "Woooo" to draw people over to us, not unlike the way cheerleaders advertised roadside car washes. It worked. When someone came up who wasn't, like, one of *us*, she was able to speak in their language. She was like a Satanic liaison to the prep community.

By the time we all got to class the word was out that there would be a meeting in the yearbook room after school to stand up for the rights of Satanists to have their message in any school yearbook that also let the Christians have their say. By then there was at least one "Satanist" in just about every classroom. I saw some of the pamphlets ripped up and tossed on the floor of the hallway, but that was no worse than what kids did to the free Bibles that people passed out now and then.

None of the teachers really seemed to take much notice of what was going on, except for Mrs. Mandlebaum, my English teacher. She called me up to her desk while everyone else was filling out a worksheet about *The Canterbury Tales*.

"I understand you're one of the ringleaders of this whole Satan thing," she said.

"I'm not really a Satanist," I said, "but I believe in freedom of religion."

"This is not a religion," she said. "It's *anti*religion."

"That's a *kind* of religion," I said. "Have any of them hurt anybody today?"

She glared at me, but admitted they hadn't.

"Have they been acting up in class?"

She shook her head.

"Well, there you are, then," I said. "There's no rule in the handbook about what religion you can be."

And I went back to my seat.

Maybe it was just my imagination, but I actually thought that the kids who were wearing the devil shirts, the pentagrams, and the horns were better behaved than they usually were. A lot of them were back-row hooligans and smart-asses who spent most of their time in class mouthing off and throwing paper around. Today they were pretty calm. Maybe they were taking one of the Eleven Satanic Rules, the one that said "When in another's lair, show him respect," to heart. The big-haired woman who gave the talk about manners and grace at the debutante ball would have found a lot to agree with in the Satanic Rules.

I didn't see Paige much during the day, except for once when we passed in the hall. She blew her hair upwards, then gave me kind of a half smile and a shrug, and I gave her one back.

Then, when the yearbook meeting came, the tribes assembled. Plenty of people had offered to come back the poem up, and probably an equal number were so offended that they decided to come help argue for a reprint.

The whole yearbook staff was present, of course, with Leslie and Paige representing the anti-Satan side, along with Mr. Perkins, Mrs. Smollet (of course), and a couple of other teachers. We were up against a lot. They had all the people with any actual power.

But the room was filled to overflowing with kids wearing pentagrams, Satanic T-shirts, and devil horns.

"All right," I said. "Here we are. We've come to argue against reprinting."

"To be honest," said Mr. Perkins. "the decision has already been made, but I'll let you make your speech, Leon. Why do you think we should still let this yearbook go out as is?"

"As you can see," I said, "we have a number of people who might be Satanists in the school. If you can put poems in like that Jesus one that was in the yearbook from last year, why not a Satanic one?"

"I don't think the person responsible for the poem thought they were representing a religion," said Leslie. "They were just trying to cause trouble, and they must have somehow slipped it into the pile of poems to be laid out, because I *know* we never approved it."

Paige looked at me, as though she knew exactly what had happened, which she probably did. She didn't say anything, though.

"I agree," said Mrs. Smollet. "It would be one thing if someone would even take responsibility for it."

"That's not how Satanic messages work," I said. "Hiding messages is a sort of Satanic tradition."

"So is hiding your identity, apparently," said Mrs. Smollet.

"Then *I'm* a Satanist, and *I* wrote it," I said.

Then Jenny stood up and said *she* was a Satanist and *she* wrote it.

And pretty soon half the room was taking credit for it. They were all chuckling, so it wasn't so dramatic that I could really compare it to people saying "I am Spartacus" or anything. But good feelings swelled inside of me. Mrs. Smollet looked like she was going to be sick.

Mr. Perkins sighed. "Okay," he said. "If you're all done, I'll tell you what we're doing. It would be *way* too expensive to recall and reprint the yearbook on short notice, but I still don't think we can put it out as is. We're going to go through every copy and put a sticker over the poem."

"Why not just put a sticker over the second line so the acrostic says 'Stan Rules'?" I asked.

"Because Stan doesn't rule," said Paige.

This was the first thing she'd said to me the whole day.

"Let's be totally blunt," said Mr. Perkins. "The poem is lousy anyway, and if you changed one line, that would wreck the rhyme scheme and make it even worse. No one approved it, anyway. So we're just going to cover it up and forget about it. Everyone on yearbook, please grab some stickers from the pile on the desk, and let's get to work. Meeting adjourned."

Mrs. Smollet gave me an "I win" kind of smile from the back of the room. I wondered if maybe she could *tell* that Paige was pregnant and was already plotting out ways to get the placenta for her next batch of eternal youth potion.

Either way I didn't care much. We hadn't exactly won, but it was close enough for me if they didn't recall the whole thing and no one got suspended. Any fool could just unpeel the sticker if they felt like it and have themselves a Satanist-friendly yearbook. The message was still there if you looked close enough. It would just be more hidden than ever, which is how Satanic messages are supposed to be, anyway. Maybe it was even better like this, in a way.

I didn't stay to help with the stickers. As far as I was concerned, my duties with the yearbook committee were finished. I followed the group of people in devil horns out into the hall. Paige followed me, and we hung around back behind the crowd a bit.

"Well," she said, "are you proud of yourself?"

"Kind of," I said.

"You tried, at least," she said. "I guess I can respect that. But I am really, really mad at you for this. I might have to yell later."

"I understand," I said. "I was just thinking about how, if I'm going to be an adult, I have to stop sitting on my ass and stand up for myself every now and then. You know what I mean?"

When she didn't answer, I noticed that she had stopped walking a few steps ago, and I turned back towards her. She had a look on her face that was kind of a mix of shock and fear, like she'd just seen Mrs. Smollet naked or something.

"You okay?" I asked.

"I have to go to the bathroom," she said. "Now."

"Puking?"

She shook her head and ran. I ran after her and stood outside the girls' room for a couple of minutes until she yelled for me to come inside.

"It's a girls' room," I said. "I'm not allowed."

"There's no one else in here. Just come in."

I stepped inside and she was standing in front of an open stall, buttoning her jeans.

"Well," she said, "I'm not pregnant."

"Seriously?"

"I just got my period," she said. "I guess something just screwed up my cycle. Maybe it *was* the flu. Or food poisoning."

"Oh, thank God," I said.

I started to hug her, but she held up her hands and stopped me.

"Listen," she said. "I didn't stab you for organizing a Satanist rally, but I have some thinking to do about us."

"What's wrong?"

"The last few days I've had to picture living my whole life with you, and it scared the hell out of me. Because you're *not* the perfect guy for me. What you did today just proved it."

"Nobody's perfect."

"No, but I want the man I spend my life with to come closer. He should be imperfect in ways that complement the way *I'm* imperfect. And I don't know if you do. Even if one of my dad's friends gave you a job, you'd probably show up with your hair dyed green."

"My dad had green hair for a while," I said. "What's wrong with that?"

She shrugged. "Nothing, I guess. But it's just not . . . the kind of person who's right for me. Plus, we're graduating, there's going to be other guys and other girls at college. . . ." She let out a sort of rueful chuckle, then said, "Not to mention that I think there's a pretty good chance I'll end up going to Hell when I die if I stick with you."

We just stood there for a second, then we both sat down on the tile floor with our backs to the wall, near the sinks. We stared at the stalls and toilets and didn't say anything for a few minutes.

"Sometimes I feel like I really love you," she went on. "We have so much fun sometimes. But sometimes . . . sometimes I just don't know."

I nodded.

In quieter moments I'd sometimes wondered if she really loved me, or if she was just going through the motions of being in love. And I wondered the same thing about myself and how I felt about her. I cared about her, and I liked being with her, but I never felt like my whole soul was on fire when I was with her. I'd just told myself that wasn't really what love feels like in real life.

I didn't say this out loud, though. I just stared at the toilets.

"I've been single for exactly twenty-seven days since sixth grade," she said. "I don't know. Maybe I just . . . I don't know."

For a long time we both just sat there and felt like shit together. When she got up and walked out of the bathroom without saying anything, I felt a strange mix of relief and shock. I kept sitting there for quite a bit; it wasn't until Leslie came into the bathroom and I had to awkwardly creep out that it really hit me that I had basically been dumped. Not officially, but tentatively.

I was embarrassed, shocked, crushed, and sort of relieved (about the baby part, at least) all at once. In a weird way it even kind of sucked that she wasn't pregnant after all. I'd spent enough time trying to look at the positive side of things that a part of me was almost looking forward to being a dad. I was just starting to think I'd be okay at it. This was a loss, in a way.

Going back to a life where all I'd need was a couch to sit on, a six-pack to drink, and a remote control to smite my enemies didn't totally feel like something to celebrate.

I went to my car and drove to the Cave, where Stan was sitting on the counter, as though he was waiting for me.

"Don't look so down, man," he said. "You didn't really think the school would pass out a yearbook with a Satanic message in it, did you?"

I shrugged. "It's not that," I said. "The whole thing was actually sort of awesome, and no one got expelled or anything, so we sort of won. But Paige sort of dumped me after the meeeting."

Stan hopped off the counter, stood upright, and nodded.

"Let's go to the back," he said.

We went to the back and he mixed me up a drink—one of his hot toddies or whatever you call them, and I melted into the couch and recounted the whole story of how Paige thought she was pregnant, but now that she knew she wasn't, she was probably going to take the chance to avoid any further risk of being stuck with me for life.

I let the drink just sit there in my hand, untouched. The way it was glowing was weirdly hypnotic, and I was focusing on it while I talked, like it was a crystal ball. I wanted something to focus on more than I wanted a drink.

Stan listened and nodded in the right places while I told the story, but at the end, he was smiling.

Then, when I finished, the son of a bitch laughed a long, slow, evil laugh.

"What are you laughing at?" I asked.

"It all happened because everyone got sick with the Montreal Flu. That's why the poem got overlooked when the proofs came in."

"Right."

"And I assume Paige found out she wasn't pregnant because she got her period, right?"

"Uh-huh." I hadn't been that specific when I told the story, but how else do you find out right after school?

"And I suppose it happened while you guys were in the hallway, outside the yearbook room?"

"Yeah."

"So it's just like I've been telling you," Stan said. "There came a great plague, and the blood of the unbeliever flowed in the high school hallway."

I groaned, then I stood up, dropped my drink on the cement floor, grabbed a handful of Reese's Pieces out of the barrel, and threw them at Stan.

"Fuck you!" I said. "Fuck you, fuck you, fuck you!"

"What the fuck?" he asked, still grinning like a villain who'd just finished testing his doomsday device.

"Fuck you!"

I threw a few more handfuls of mix-ins at him, then threw a stack of plastic cups in his general direction as I made my way out of the break room. In the front a bunch of people from the rally were just coming in. I threw a handful of napkins around, and they fluttered to the ground like snow. I guess people thought I was throwing them like confetti, because there was actual cheering. Cheering.

Stan followed me as I stormed along.

"Did you ever finish *Moby-Dick*?" he asked.

"Christ!" I said. "We stopped listening after we found the Slushee, but I know how it ends. The whale kills everybody."

"That's the lesson," he said. "If you try to fight fate, you end up getting eaten by a big fucking whale. Go finish listening to it. Now.

Go. Don't show your face back here until you've listened to the end of it. Drive clear the Hell to Mexico if you have to."

"Go to Hell," I said.

But I decided to do what he told me. I didn't want to be in the Cave right then. I didn't want to be anywhere I'd ever been with Paige. Not even in the same city. I was going to drive as far away as I could.

I walked out the door just as Jenny was coming in. She tried to talk to me, but I walked right past like I didn't see her, got into my car, and headed for the interstate with the audiobook playing on the speakers.

30. THE WHALE

I drove and drove and drove and drove, as though something was chasing me. Like some underachieving supervillain had announced his plans to blow up Des Moines and I wanted to be as far away from the fallout as I could when the bomb went off. I drove past the suburbs and into farm country, the rolling green hills of central Iowa. There were no traces of snow left. The corn had started to grow.

I tried, off and on, to pay attention to what Ishmael was saying about the ragtag band of scruffy misfits, the half-crazy sailors, going off to get killed, but mostly I hit pause and thought of Paige and everything else. I was probably never going to kiss her again. Never feel her skin against mine.

I missed the way her hair smelled already. All of a sudden the fact that I'd never smell that same aroma again without thinking of her hit me almost as hard as the pregnancy scare had.

I was pulling in for gas at a town that happened to be named Atlantic, like the ocean where the sailors were sailing, when she sent a text saying, "Call me." I knew what that meant, of course. I didn't call her back right away. I got back in the car and kept heading west.

I half suspected that she'd at least want me to still go to prom with her, because it was too much trouble to find someone else, and skipping prom just did not fit into her view of the way things ought to be.

I wasn't sure what I'd tell her.

I was almost to Nebraska, almost two hours from home, when I got to the part in the audiobook where Captain Ahab finally takes his shot at Moby Dick. Naturally, before he throws the harpoon, he goes into a monologue. That's pretty much how people function in that fucking book—whenever something happens to someone, something in their head goes, "Hey, you'd better make a big speech!"

If I ever look up the book in print, I'll bet the speech Ahab makes before he throws his harpoon goes on for a whole damned page. As usual, I couldn't imagine how Ishmael could have remembered the whole thing, except for the fact that it *was* a real beast of a speech. "Towards thee I roll, thou all-destroying but unconquering whale," he says. "To the last I grapple with thee, from hell's heart I stab at thee, for hate's sake I spit my last breath at thee. Sink all coffins and all hearses to one common pool!"

Damn.

He was wrong about the unconquering part though, because as soon as he finishes up the monologue, the fucker throws his harpoon, catches himself on the line, and gets yanked out of the boat. If I was picturing it right, he was tied up to the whale and dragged along to his doom. I thought maybe his corpse would be attached to Moby Dick forever, but then I figured that pretty soon his body would rot away enough that even if he was wrapped up really tight, he'd slip out of the ropes and sink down to the bottom of the ocean.

Or maybe old Moby would notice a body being dragged along and eat it. Maybe trying to get the dead guy on the end of the rope into his mouth would be like playing one of those little games where you try to get a ball on some string into a cup. Ahab couldn't kill the whale, but maybe he'd at least frustrate him a little.

But then I played it back and got the impression that he wasn't tied to the line at the end of the harpoon at all. He just drowned, and Moby Dick probably took no notice of him at all.

I was crossing the big green bridge over the river that takes you out of Iowa and into Nebraska a few minutes later when the whale sinks the ship and everybody dies except Ishmael.

And the great shroud of the sea rolled on as it rolled five thousand years ago.

That's the last thing Ishmael says before the epilogue.

I still say he was already long dead by then and spent the whole last half of the book as a ghost. Hell, in the epilogue, he says that the sharks swam by him as though they had padlocks on their mouths until another ship came up to save him. You don't get *that* lucky.

But according to him another ship picked him up, and that was the end.

I didn't learn a single damned lesson about myself from the whole thing.

And Ishmael, in a rare show of keeping his big yap shut, doesn't explain what anyone *should* have learned from the whole fucking thing, either.

I had finished the whole book, and I was broken, beaten, and adrift in unfamiliar territory. Tired, lonely, and just about broke.

And in Omaha, no less.

I pulled a map up on my phone and found the nearest Captain Jack's. After I finished my hush puppies, I called Paige and let her break up with me officially.

She was right that I wasn't perfect for her, of course. She wasn't perfect for me, either.

But it still sucked.

I loved Paige. I was pretty sure of that. I was ready to go into real estate for her. I would have let her eat my hush puppies if she wanted them.

But I hadn't gotten that dizzy feeling very often, the one I got when Anna and I kissed in the snow, when I was with her. Do you just not get that when you're an adult? Everyone always says that when you're a teenager, your highs are higher and your lows are lower. I was still a teenager, but I could see the end in sight. I was only a couple of weeks away from graduating. I'd be twenty in a year and a half.

I didn't feel devastated. Mostly just numb.

As I drove away, my parents tried to call a few times, and I eventually just turned my phone off. There was a good chance Paige would still be texting me a million times, probably trying to explain in minute detail what had gone wrong between us, and I just didn't need to see it. It was over.

When I rolled back into Iowa, the sky was dark with midnight blue clouds, and such trees as there were among the cornfields and hog farms were blowing around like they were banging their heads to a Motörhead song. One cloud off in the distance looked like it was forming into a funnel.

I turned on the radio and found that there were tornado warnings all across western Iowa. This, I thought, was going to be how it ended for me. At the end of *Moby-Dick,* the whale head-butts the ship, then spins around it and creates a whirlpool that sinks the whole thing. It only made sense that I would die in a sort of whirlpool myself. That a tornado would crush my bones and suck me up into the sky, a broken corpse, then spit my body back out into a cornfield someplace. Or into the parking lot of the Ice Cave, if it was a tornado with a sense of the poetic. You always hear stories about tornadoes blowing pianos a hundred miles and setting them down in perfect condition, almost like they had minds of their own. Maybe a tornado would be my great white whale.

But, like Ishmael, I survived. Even my car didn't collapse and die. It stalled out every time I came to a complete stop, but it always came back to life with a roar of messianic glory.

No tornado ever actually appeared, and no whale ate me.

In fact, when I got back to the Ice Cave at ten o'clock, I took the antique Willy the Whale ice cream cake out of the freezer and decided that I would eat the whole thing right then and there, just to show the universe that whales don't eat me, I eat *them*.

I didn't make it past the first bite; it tasted like it hadn't been safe to eat in a good three or four years, and I spit it out on the floor. If I'd eaten it, I really *would* have quite likely been killed by a whale.

But it didn't kill me.

Instead, I hauled it outside and tossed it onto the pavement out back to die. To help it along, I poured a couple of buckets of hot water over it and watched it dissolve into a goop at my feet. The water melted the ice cream down to nothing a lot faster than I would have expected; in seconds there was nothing left but sludge rolling down the pavement, with fresh raindrops splattering in the puddles it formed.

Towards thee I roll, thou all-destroying but unconquering whale.

Melt, melt, and let your chocolaty innards roll down the drain between Earthways and the Ice Cave, into the Des Moines River and onwards to the great shroud of the sea.

31. FLAVORS

It turned out I wasn't such an idiot after all; a couple of weeks after Paige and I ended things, during which I mostly just moped around and worked as many hours as I could get, I got my SAT scores back, and I don't mind saying that I kicked some ass. I could take my pick of junior colleges, community colleges, and trade schools, even with my fair-to-middling GPA.

Around the same time, Stan announced that he was now part owner of the Ice Cave, a position that didn't seem like it should give him a much larger income, but somehow did. He bought a nice car, by Ice Cave standards, and started talking about getting his own place and everything. Maybe he'd gotten George to cut him into whatever money he was using the Cave to launder. Maybe he was using his unholy powers to help George pick winning horses down at the track. I never asked.

I could imagine that one day soon we'd find the entrance to his basement locked, and if we knocked on the front door, some old lady would come to the door and say she'd never heard of anyone named Stan, and she'd been living in the house with her husband, Van, ever since they retired ten years ago. She'd be lonely and bored enough that she'd take us in to see the basement, and it would be full of doilies and crafts and the kind of old-people shit you see taking up space on the tables at crappy garage sales. We'd never see or hear from Stan again.

And if I went back for another white grape Slushee, there'd be an H&R Block or something where the gas station in Waukee used to be.

By the end of May everything that came before seemed to have happened a million years ago. School was wrapping up and I was getting money from all my parents' friends and all my relatives in the mail for graduation.

Prom came and went. I half expected Paige would still want me to take her, but she never asked. I heard she was going with some guy she knew from the Harvester Club or something. I missed her sometimes, but it didn't feel like a knife in my back to imagine her with someone else. I wished her the best.

For my part I'd talked to Brianna a bit, and we'd even flirted enough that I thought she'd probably say yes if I asked her to prom, but one fancy ball a year was more than enough for me, and it certainly didn't seem like her scene, especially for a first date. So I happily volunteered to work the counter on prom night, and spent my evening doing something productive, instead. With no customers to distract me I spent the whole night mixing different ice creams together to invent new flavors. Jake had apparently given up on starting a strip club, and now he was talking about starting up a food truck, so I figured that maybe if I invented some amazing new ice cream, I could get in on it with him. I mixed strawberry with bubble gum, rocky road with peach, and a bunch of other stuff, trying to make an exciting new combination that would be greater than the sum of its parts.

None of them were all that good, really. But it occurred to me that they were no worse than most food disasters, which made me think that maybe I could suggest that we start up a food truck specializing in those. You never can tell what hipsters will buy. I could imagine them lining up for Turkey Marco Polo. Or bowls of Nards. Hipsters would love to buy bowls of Nards.

On the night before graduation I was alone in the store again. There was a storm going on outside, a classic midwestern crasher that reminded me of the night when Paige and I first went to the nook. To pass the time I mixed orange sorbet with Superman ice cream in the blender as the satellite radio played a bunch of the same Billy Joel songs that had been playing in Captain Jack's on Valentine's Day. Between songs it was quiet enough in the store to hear the walk-in freezer in the back room humming its familiar refrain in harmony with the distant thunder.

Then, at around nine o'clock, cars began to pull into the parking lot. One by one the car doors opened, and a handful of people ran through the rain.

It was a few people from the usual crowd. Couples, mostly. Jenny and Jake. Dustin and Catherine. Edie and Jill. They gathered in the parking lot, in the rain, and then came in, led by Stan.

"Hey, guys," I said.

They all crowded towards the counter, and I became aware of

the fact that they weren't there to hang out in the back. They'd come to see me. And they were smiling.

Stan made his way through to the counter and grinned at me as the lightning crashed in the window behind him. He was wearing a suit. A nice one. It was probably of the "so expensive it must have been woven from hairs from the queen's butt" variety.

"Your time has come, minion," he said. "I've come for your soul. Pay up."

"You brought all these people with you to ask for my soul?" I asked. "And dressed up?"

"You don't go around taking people's souls in a T-shirt. You want some gravity for a ceremony like this. And some witnesses."

"I never said I'd give it to you," I said. "Unless you're finally ready to pay, now that you're apparently so flush with cash."

He just kept grinning, and I noticed that Jenny was trying really, really hard not to crack up behind him.

"I think I've earned it," he said. "Remind us all of how you felt on Valentine's Day, after you heard that Anna might be moving back."

I didn't answer, so he answered for me. "You felt like a loser. You didn't want her to see you like that."

I wiped down the counter again and avoided everyone's gaze. It's embarrassing to have people call you a loser to your face.

"Am I right?" Stan asked.

"Something like that, I guess," I said. "Seems like a million years ago now. I don't remember."

Stan turned back to the crowd. "He was freaked out. His car was a mess, he hadn't eaten a vegetable in ages, he probably only bathed once a week, he wasn't sure he was graduating, and hadn't stirred up any shit at school in years. Mrs. Smollet thought he had matured."

People laughed and said "Ooooh" and "For shame" in funny accents.

Then he turned back to face me, spinning on his heel like he was Michael Jackson or something, and laughing like Vincent Price.

"What the fuck is this?" I asked. "Can't I just mail in a form about ownership of my soul if I want to turn it over?"

He ignored me and kept up his monologue.

"You're graduating tomorrow," he said. "Your car barely smells, you've killed the SAT, you're probably going to college, and you led a band of Satanists on a campaign to promote their first amendment rights. You probably got over some performance anxiety issues in bed, too, if I'm not mistaken. And it's *all* because I made you listen to *Moby-Dick*."

Jenny started to giggle uncontrollably, and I hoped she wasn't giggling about the performance anxiety stuff.

But as the thunder crashed and the rain poured ever harder against the glass windows at the front of the store, it occurred to me that he was right. In addition to all the stuff he pointed out, I'd freaked the hell out of Mrs. Smollet more than once, not to mention a couple of other teachers. I'd become a legend among the staff at a fancy restaurant, and any number of other things. I may not have accomplished too much, but I wasn't just sitting on my ass anymore. I wasn't quite as disgusting a human being as I'd been a few months before.

Now that I thought about it, I didn't even feel that old, gnawing, hungry feeling of dread in my gut anymore. I hadn't since the day I drove to Omaha and back.

I felt like myself again. The version of myself that I liked.

I was saved.

And it really was all because I'd listened to *Moby-Dick,* if you looked at it from a certain angle.

The son of a bitch really had done it.

Stan jumped up onto the counter and faced the crowd.

"There came a great plague, and the hallway flowed with the blood of the unbeliever," he said. "And I believe in the resurrection of Leon."

People cheered and laughed and shouted, "Hail Satan," and Stan turned back to me, looking down from above with a shit-eating grin. I almost expected his eyes to start glowing red. My face already was.

"Yeah, yeah," I said. "You guys want any ice cream, or what?"

"No," said Stan. "I told you. The soul. I earned it."

With everyone staring, I couldn't argue much. He was right. He'd earned my soul.

One of them, anyway.

I stepped over to the cash register, printed up a blank receipt, and wrote LEON'S OLD SOUL FROM HIGH SCHOOL on it with the pen that sat beside the credit card reader.

I made a point of putting "*old* soul."

Anyone who thinks you only get one soul has never known what it feels like to be fourteen years old and kiss Anna Brandenburg in a snowstorm beneath the streetlight outside of Sip coffee. That's not just acupressure. It's the feeling of getting a new soul.

I'd let that soul, the one I got in that snowstorm, go to waste after Anna moved. It was a beautiful thing once, but now it was just a heavy burden that I'd been lugging around for too long. Being with

Paige had helped me get enough of the rust off that I could pry it loose, and now Stan was welcome to whatever was left of it. I was glad to be rid of it, and I was sure he could find something creative to do with it. Even if he wasn't the actual devil, he had to at least be some sort of trickster spirit.

"Good-bye, high school version of my soul," I said as I handed the receipt over. "From Hell's heart, I stab at thee."

Stan folded it up and put it in the pocket on the inside of his suit with all due pomp.

"You know what would have happened if Anna *had* come back, and I hadn't resurrected your ass?" he asked. "You would have fucked it up. Big-time."

"Probably."

"You didn't know shit about women or relationships or anything," he said. "You do now."

I nodded. "I've learned a bit about how you have to play things backwards to get the hidden messages."

His grin got wider and wider as he kept talking.

"Of course, if she *did* come back you'd probably find out she wasn't really all that great, and it was all in your head. Or that she grew up and wasn't as cool as she used to be. Or that she was just faking it and had you fooled the whole time."

"Maybe."

"Or maybe you'd realize that all of her talk about being artsy and worldly was about as genuine as me telling that girl about carbonated milk."

"I guess. And her name's Brianna."

I tried to keep wiping the counter down, but I felt like everyone was just staring at me. They were. I noticed that, when he was grinning a particularly wide grin, Stan appeared to have more teeth than most people. That had to be an optical illusion.

"But, then again," he went on, "you might also end up moving to England to raise a bunch of babies with her. A bunch of little British twits named after jazz greats who spell color with a *U* and get free glasses from the National Health Service. Shit."

"Right," I said.

"You're not a freshman anymore. Moving to England isn't completely out of the question."

I finally put down the rag I was using on the counter and just looked up.

"So, what do you think, in your infernal wisdom?" I asked. "If she came back, what would happen?"

"Sorry, asshole. You only get so many prophecies per soul. You're on your own now."

"Quit dragging it out, Stan, you fucker!" said Jenny. "Leon, just look in the parking lot."

"Huh?"

"Go," she said. "Look."

I knew right away what was probably happening, and my knees started to rattle a bit. But I made my way around the counter and stood against the soaking wet window, so I could see that there was one car, Jenny's, with a light on inside of it. Through the splattering rain on the windshield, I could make out the silhouette of someone who hadn't come inside. Someone with long hair.

"Oh, God," I said.

Jenny came to stand next to me. In her reflection in the window

I could see she was smiling so big she would probably be sore in the morning. "We've been planning this all month," she said. "She's just here for a couple of days, but her dad's meeting got scheduled for this weekend, and she wanted to see us all graduate. Surprise!"

"Is she coming in, or what?"

"No," said Jenny. "We're kidnapping you, and we're all going to go to Cafe di Scala. Now."

"I have to work," I said.

"I'll handle the counter the rest of the night," said Stan. "Go get some closure."

I turned around and faced everyone, but couldn't think of anything to say. I didn't say anything stupid, though, so I guess I was coming out ahead of my usual average.

"Aw," said Catherine. "He's nervous!"

"No, I'm not," I said. "I'm fine."

I was at least a little nervous, not having prepared for this at all. But I wasn't terrified or disgusted with myself or any of the things I would have been feeling if she'd shown up a few months before.

I stood there for a second, staring at her silhouette like I was seeing some mythical creature, like a unicorn or a leprechaun, still too in shock to move.

"Go on," said Stan. "Or I'll drive you to Chicago and personally feed your ass to a whale at the aquarium."

Jenny and Edie each took one of my wrists and dragged me through the stinging rain towards Jenny's car. I didn't put up a struggle, but my head was spinning in every direction at once and there was a puddle deep enough that the water got into my shoes.

When we made it to the car, I stood there like an idiot in the rain, looking at the window for a few seconds before I found the sense to open the door.

"Get in, dumbass!" said Jenny as she ran to her own door. I climbed in and sat there.

And there she was, smiling in the seat next to me.

Anna Brandenburg.

She was older now. She looked like an adult. Her hair was chestnut brown, not blond anymore, and in a totally different style.

"Hey," she said. "Surprise."

"Hey," I said. "How've you been?"

"Up and down," she said. "But I'm feeling better lately."

"Yeah," I said. "Yeah."

Jenny was laughing like a hyena as Jake joined her in the front seat. "We totally fucking got you, Leon!" she said. "You had no idea, did you?"

I shook my head out and tried to look back at the Cave, but it was just a blurry blob of lights through the rain and mist now. The other couples were going back to their cars. Edie patted the windows as she passed us.

Anna dug in her purse and pulled out a pair of devil horns.

"I heard about the rally a few weeks ago," she said as she put them on. "Nicely done."

The rain and the thunder kept coming down, and Seventieth Street seemed almost like a river, washing away all that came before it as we talked about this and that and what we'd been up to and what we were planning to do next. We joked about old times and regaled Jake, who we hadn't known back then, with tales of Gifted Pool glory.

Anna wasn't the same Anna I remembered. She was the real one, not the version of her that had lived in my head for three years. I almost felt like I was meeting her for the first time. Maybe nothing I could do with her now would make me feel like I was getting a new soul again. Maybe we'd just have a fun weekend and never see each other again, and we'd just shake hands before she left. Maybe even if we kissed at the same streetlight it wouldn't feel the same.

But, then again, maybe it would.

Just as hard as the snow fell on that night years before, the rain fell now, and as we rode up the slowly flooding road towards the interstate, past Anna's old neighborhood and the last pay phone in town, I felt more like I was finally saying good-bye to an old friend than rekindling an old flame. But it still felt good just to be laughing with her again. I didn't need her to kiss a new soul into me. I'd get one somehow.

It was the first night in years that I felt as though I deserved to have one at all.